VOYAGE TO THE RED PLANET

Other Avon Books by
Terry Bisson

FIRE ON THE MOUNTAIN

VOYAGE TO THE RED PLANET

TERRY BISSON

AVON BOOKS ◆ NEW YORK

Lyrics from "The Promised Land" by Chuck Berry. Copyright © 1964 by Arc Music Corporation. Reprinted by permission. All rights reserved.

Lyrics from "Speedoo" by Esther Navarro. Copyright © 1955 by Windswept Pacific Entertainment Co. d/b/a Longitude Music Co., renewed 1983. Reprinted by permission of Longitude Music Co. All rights reserved.

AVON BOOKS
A division of
The Hearst Corporation
1350 Avenue of the Americas
New York, New York 10019

Copyright © 1990 by Terry Bisson
Cover art by Vincent DiFate
Published by arrangement with the author
Library of Congress Catalog Card Number: 89-14279
ISBN: 0-380-75574-2

Published in hardcover by William Morrow and Company, Inc; for information address Avon Books.

First Avon Books Printing: September 1991

AVON TRADEMARK REG. U.S. PAT. OFF. AND IN OTHER COUNTRIES, MARCA REGISTRADA, HECHO EN U.S.A.

Printed in the U.S.A.

RA   10   9   8   7   6   5   4   3   2   1

For my parents,
MAX AND MARTHA,
who taught us kids to fly

Thanks to David Ansen, Meg Blackstone, Kim Stanley Robinson and Charles Sheffield, who helped the author avoid many errors and grotesqueries. Those that remain in the book are the ones he just couldn't resist.

BOOK ONE

Gravity is the enemy
of every boy.
—BRADBURY

1

As HUGE AS IT WAS lonely, it looked like a great folded umbrella, with three cylinders as long as football fields clustered alongside the forward end of a mile-long plastic beam; not yet darkened with the dust that slowly darkens the universe, it gleamed in the light of the snowcapped planet below. On the forward, and only, spherical module (the bridge) was a painting of a woman with high-button shoes and an umbrella. In the manner of the NASA projects of the time, the painting had cost $114,750.36 even though it was only standard Chevy van-grade airbrush work. Unlike most orbiting objects, the ship was absolutely stationary, gyro-locked so it would neither roll nor pitch nor yaw nor turn. It toiled not, neither did it spin. Its fans were silent, its shafts were dark, its batteries were cold and its 115,867.12 miles of wiring waited for orders. It swept the heavens perfectly aligned, because if it turned, its refractive index would change and it might be seen by one of Earth's inquisitive astronomers, and only 618 people on the planet knew of its existence. And they had all been sworn to secrecy.

1,235.3 miles below, one of the 618 was feeding his dogs when he heard the unmistakable, unexpected sound of a car coming up the hill. He didn't bother to look up. There was only one speed a car could go on the rutted dirt road, and only one spot on the road where it could be seen from the house. At precisely the right moment he set down his bag of

13

Hunter's Horn Premium Hound Chow, straightened up and looked down the hill. Bass's eyes as well as his timing had outlasted his career, and in the 1.7 seconds it took for the car to cross the bare patch a quarter of a mile away, he saw that it was a Jeep la Ville 4wd limo. An unusual car for the western Kentucky hills. Bass dusted the dog food off his hands and headed toward his house trailer. Like all truly solitary people, he loved company.

"They don't bite," Bass said from the porch. "You can get out of the car."

The driver, a young man in snappy new livery, got out and opened the back door of the limo. Nobody got out. After a moment, Bass realized he was expected to get in.

"Phone call for you," the driver said.

Bass stuck his head in. The back of the limo was cool and dark; it smelled of leather and electronics. There was a bar and a camera-monitor combo circuited into a cellular phone. On the nine-inch screen, a man sat behind a desk in front of a big window. "Rocket Man Bass," he said, rising, with a wide smile and narrow eyes like a preacher.

It wasn't a question, it was a statement.

"They don't exactly call me that around Allen County," Bass said. "That was twenty-five years ago. What's this, is *People* magazine doing their where-are-they-now issue?"

"My name's Markson. I was told you never come into town, and since you don't have a phone—"

"He hired me to drive all the way from Nashville," the driver said proudly. He was kneeling to rough up the dogs. Bass could see he knew hounds.

"Well, here you are. More or less. What do you want? I'm better paid not to talk about the space program," Bass said, "than you could ever pay me to talk about it."

"Don't want to just talk about it," Markson said. "Talk won't get me to Mars."

"Mars?"

"Mars. The red planet Mars."

"Will that phone thing move?" Bass asked the driver. "You can follow me if you want to. I got to feed these hounds."

Carrying the monitor/cam/speaker/mike unit in one hand, and a cigarette in the other, the driver followed Bass up the concrete block steps and into the trailer. While Bass filled a milk jug with water, the driver panned around the interior: one wall of books, one wall of guns. On Markson's desk three thousand miles away, the monitor showed a chuffing kerosene-powered refrigerator ("Ain't smelled that smell since I was a kid," the driver said) with a snapshot of Earthrise over the Moon's horizon taped to the door. The kitchenette table was neatly divided between a plastic "Kentucky Lake, Fisherman's Heaven" placemat and an ancient, yellowed Apple IIe. Skillfully operating the screen door with their noses, dogs walked in and out at will.

"What'd you say your name was?" Bass asked the video unit.

"Markson."

"You with the government?"

Markson laughed. "You of all people ought to know better than that. No government in the world could afford such a venture as I propose—not since the Grand Depression. No, I represent something quite different. An industry that has the vision to undertake such a voyage. The ability to make it happen. And the money to finance it—"

Definitely preacher material, Bass decided. "I got to water the hounds out back," he said. "You can come along if you like."

"Movies!" said Markson's image to Bass's departing back.

The driver followed Bass around the house, trying to keep his red, gold, green and black Acme boots out of the mud. Hoping to get a response out of Bass, Markson was using his

most potent incantations: "Cinema. Motion pictures. Hollywood."

"Mars is a long way off, I seem to recall."

"As you know, the space station you used to fly out of is
still used regularly; it's in fact the only working vestige of the
NASA space program—"

"Turned over to the National Parks Department twelve
years ago," Bass said. "Then sold along with Wildlife Management to Disney-Gerber, along with the other national
parks. Then unloaded on—"

"Do I detect a trace of bitterness?" said Markson. "No
wonder, it was your life's work! At any rate, my company,
Pellucidar Pictures, a wholly owned subsidiary of Greyhound-
Thermos, is booked for Nixon Orbital Park in exactly five
weeks"—he pressed a button on his watch—"four days and
eleven hours."

"What does that have to do with Mars? And what does
that have to do with me? If you booked the station, you booked
the shuttle."

"The shuttle's been sold off, haven't you heard? We're
taking our own shuttle up and we want you to fly it. For
starters."

At the side of the barn they stopped in front of a stainless
steel hulk in the weeds.

"Well, I'll be damned," said the driver.

"I pulled it up here with a tractor," Bass said. "I crank it
up once a month just to keep the rings free. They're the only
things on the whole car that can rust."

"Very interesting," Markson said as the driver kicked a
tire. "But a DeLorean won't take you back into space."

"Maybe not. But a shuttle won't take you to Mars, either.
Even if you could find some damn fool to fly it."

"We're talking with one other flight officer, an old friend
of yours. Do you remember a Natasha Kirov?"

Bass's eyes narrowed. "Since when did it become your
business what I remember and what I don't? Now look,
mister—"

Sensing that his time was running out, Markson played his trump. "The Mars ship is already built, even if only you and a few hundred others know about it."

Bass bent down and looked directly into the monitor/cam's glowing eye. "What the hell are you talking about?"

"I'm talking about the *Mary Poppins*."

2

"MADAME KIROV," the waiter said rather than asked. The blond woman in the yellow jumpsuit nodded and the waiter put the brass-inlaid mock Regency phone monitor down on the glass-topped table and retreated.

"Captain Kirov," said a tiny voice in English. "Please forgive the intrusion." Natasha Kirov bent over and looked down. On the three-inch screen there was a man sitting at a desk. His face was smaller than a pencil eraser but his desk was huge, the size of a matchbox. Through the window, on a hillside in back of him, a giant sign spelled HOL YWOOD with one "L" missing.

"Who are you and what do you want?" asked Kirov, never one for beating around what the Americans called the bush.

"Does the name *Mary Poppins* mean anything to you?"

Kirov didn't miss a beat. "You have perhaps confused me with Julie Andrews?"

"Can we speak directly? As you know, the Soviet-American Mars voyage . . ."

"That's ancient history. The project was dropped twenty years ago, when the Grand Depression hit. No one has ever been to Mars, and I suspect no one ever will."

"The project was canceled, yes." The man dropped his voice dramatically as his image grew in the screen to the size of a walnut. "But not, as we both know, before the ship was built. Do you mind if I smoke?"

Kirov shook her head slowly while her caller lit a cigar.

"As only a few hundred people in the entire world know,

18

it's in a secret holding orbit right now—mothballed, they say, but abandoned, as you and I know, because there will never be a joint US-Soviet project now, and neither country will allow the other to use it."

"Science fantasy, Mr. uh—"

"Markson. And my colleagues and I think not. We know, to be precise, that the *Mary Poppins* is in orbit 1,988 kilometers above you at this very moment. In addition to being hidden behind the nuclear waste belt, where no one ever goes, it is protected by a special null-reflective foil that makes a six-billion-dollar spacecraft bigger than the *Queen Elizabeth* look like a small hole in the ozone layer. We know that it is stocked with food and water that after twenty years will still be usable, even tasty."

"Even if such a phildickian fantasy were true," said Kirov, "it could have nothing to do with me. That was twenty years ago, and according to your own figures that would make me sixteen at the time."

"Twenty-one," Markson corrected, and for the first time Kirov blushed. "We know that there were three twenty-one-year-old trainees on that project. One of them later went mad; one was killed in a traffic accident; the third, the only woman and the most promising of all, they say, married a doctor after the program was shut down, taught at the University in Leningrad, separated three years ago, and . . ."

"Divorced," Kirov said.

"This hypothetical person is now flying Tupolevs into Antarctica for Sikorsky-Reebok, and currently vacationing in Salvador, Brazil, during layover. Lunching at the beautiful Axe Bahia overlooking the bay."

Kirov didn't say anything.

"Wearing a yellow jumpsuit. The one person in the world with the ability, and now the opportunity, to take the *Mary Poppins* to Mars."

Natasha Alyosha Katerina Ivanovna Kirov carefully folded her napkin and got up from the table. As always when she was angry, she spoke English with a Texas accent. "Of all the goddamned nerve!" she said. "That you and your colleagues, whoever the hell they are, think that I would even consider working for the Americans."

"Please, please, please. Sit down," Markson said. "Be assured. After the Grand Depression, no government on Earth could take on such a project, even if they were to admit its existence. However, there is an industry that has the vision to finance such a voyage. The resources to make it happen. And the ability to go ahead with it."

"Go to Mars to make a movie?"

"Exactly! Everyone on the planet would want to see it. The romance and fascination with space flight hasn't died. Even before allowing for licensing and royalties, our P&Ls show that an investment of less than fifty million would bring a guaranteed return of—"

"Supposing there were such a spacecraft," Kirov interrupted. "Even supposing it were still operational. Even supposing I could operate it. The trip to Mars is eighteen months each way. No crew could be sustained physically or mentally for that long. Certainly not a bunch of movie stars, grips and hairdressers."

"Suppose, however, that that problem, also, were being solved," Markson said smoothly. The telltale on the monitor glowed, alerting Kirov that he was pulling her in for a close-up. "Does the name 'Ursula' mean anything to you?"

3

Did you ever wonder what would happen if you could extend your career and delay growing older—if you could strategically space your public appearances? Career Spacing is the confidential, medically proven life extension program that can enhance, prolong and creatively expand your active career. Used in strictest confidence by athletes, artists, entertainers, many of the top film and television artists in the USA and around the world. Consultation by referral only.

Dr. S. C. Jeffries liked to read his own brochure while he was waiting to screen new patients. It put him in a persuasive frame of mind, essential for an innovative and costly business. Then he liked to read his client referral files. It put him in a cautious frame of mind, essential for a semilegal (at best) business. The client he was about to see had been referred to him by one of the most familiar names in America—a man who most people had no idea hibernated nine months out of every year, chewing his old paw like a bear in a cave, carefully husbanding his remaining years for the Oscars and the big awards shows every January and February. A man who knew everyone in Hollywood...

The nurse buzzed. Jeffries buzzed back and watched the door. The nurse ushered in a middle-aged white man in a chamois sport coat over a designer T-shirt and ruffsilk jeans.

"Mr. Markson," Jeffries said.

"Dr. Jeffries. Thank you for seeing me."

"No problem," Jeffries said. He had checked all the man's

references, not just the primary ones. Markson was a second-line producer who moved from studio to studio making monster potboilers. So what did he want? Since producers had to work year-round, they never used Career Spacing.

"I need your help in a most confidential matter."

Jeffries relaxed. "That's my stock-in-trade. Shoot."

"I am currently employed, as you must know, since I am sure you checked me out thoroughly, with Pellucidar Pictures, the American film subsidiary of Greyhound-Thermos. We are in early preproduction on a very unique picture, of which I am Producer. We are going to shoot a movie on Mars."

"About Mars?"

"*On* Mars. The mysterious red planet Mars. A major motion picture. The first. We have the ship and we are in the process of assembling the crew. I will be hiring a director and casting later this week. Mars is, however, a thirty-six-month trip, eighteen or so each way, and the long periods in space will be difficult under the best of conditions, especially for untrained personnel. Which is where you come in. We need you to screen our people to make sure they can tolerate hibernation, and then—"

"Career Spacing in space? Are you crazy? It's never been tried—"

"But it has. Dr. Jeffries, I happen to know that the hibernation trigger technology your company uses was originally developed while you were assigned to the Navy's orbital station. Do you mind if I smoke?"

"I sure as hell do."

"In fact," Markson continued, lighting his cigar, "there were those in the government who knew that the research was for the joint US-CCCP Mars Mission. When the project was canned, the records were sealed—PROJECT URSULA, TOP SECRET, CODE BLACK. Soon afterward the Second Medical Officer on the project, a some say brilliant and all say ambitious young Howard University Naval ROTC M.D., suddenly resigned his commission and dropped out of sight."

"Mr. Markson," Jeffries said, rising, "this is highly improper. I must ask you to—"

"Or, shall we say, went into private practice. A very lucrative private practice, as it turned out. He set up in Beverly Hills, where discretion is a way of life, and his shadowy enterprise has netted close to between two point one and two point four million a year for six years now, a tidy sum since you—excuse me, he—pays no royalties on the HT serum. Which, of course, doesn't officially exist."

"Bullshit." Jeffries sat back down.

"Is it, doctor? I was working for Twenty-first Century–Fox, which was a subsidiary of Beatrice-Texaco when they acquired the US Navy. As an executive with access to personnel records, I've known about this little operation for some time."

Jeffries sighed and held out his hands. "What is it you want? You want me to shoot up your Movie Stars with HT? It's not that simple."

"I know it's not. That's why I want you to go with them."

Jeffries was so shocked that he smiled, but he didn't blink. "Surely you jest."

"Why not? You are an experienced Navy man with over six months in orbital space. You are a medical doctor, perhaps the only one in the world with a working knowledge of the Ursula HT, which we need for the voyage. Plus you're licensed to practice here in Beverly Hills, which we need under Guild regs."

"But you're talking about Mars, not orbital space. And you're looking at S. C. Jeffries, not Magellan. I'm interested in making money, not history."

"Perfect. Then let's talk money. We are prepared to compensate you for your services for the next thirty-six months at double your usual rate. Which would come out to twelve million dollars for thirty-six months."

"In the bank for my heirs? I don't have any, thanks." Jeffries stood up again and held out his hand in Hollywood's curious gesture of rejection. "Look, I've been in space. I'd rather make my money here in Beverly Hills where I don't have to squeeze my dinner out of a tube or drink recycled urine. Now, if you'll excuse me . . ."

"You won't be making your money in Beverly Hills if Beatrice-Texaco finds out about their serum. You will be making twenty-seven cents an hour in federal prison."

For the first time, Jeffries blinked. "Are you trying to blackmail me?"

For the first time, Markson smiled

4

LOUIS GLAMOUR WAS ON the Trump-Hearst Freeway, stopping for a light, when he got Markson's call.

Not a traffic light—there are none on the T&H—but a late afternoon light. A cloud and ocean light. There is a long turn coming down from the Santa Monica Mountains, where the Pacific is seen for the first time, morris blue on a pearl-overcast day; and this was just such a day, with that shadowless world-enhancing sky-rounding illumination that a cinematographer hates to see wasted on mere fleeting reality. As soon as Glamour saw it he cut sharply over into the middle lanes, toward the right shoulder.

There was a squealing of brakes and one minor wreck, which of course was not Glamour's problem. He had the right-of-way, since he had punched in for Executive Class. The slower, Business Class lanes had honking rights, but if they hit him, it was their fault. He cut over two more lanes into Freeway Class, and even though honking was illegal here, the clamor continued. The rear-wheel drive replicas so popular in LA lately, some with "steering wheels," had loud horns. Glamour would have given them the finger but since he was a midget, driving with hand controls only, he didn't have a free hand. He had slowed to eighty by the time he moved into the Roadway Class lanes, running a couple of "crips" with altered FI chips into a lane of motorcycles enjoying the weekly amnesty day from the helmet laws. There was no more honking here, since the plebe lanes (Roadway and Local Class) had audio jammers, so for the first time Glamour heard the dash phone ringing.

If the vid had come up first, he might not have answered. But Markson was using a pay phone, and the still from his card came up slowly.

"Remember me?"

"How could I forget?" Glamour said as he pulled to a stop on the shoulder. Markson specialized in low-budget patched-together films in horrendous locations. The last time Glamour had worked for him, he had spent six weeks in the Sundarab and had almost been carried away by mosquitoes. (It had been worth it for the green translucent light, but there was no reason to let Markson know that.)

"Markson, you know you can't afford me!" Glamour said, leaning over the backseat and putting together his camera. "Besides, I'm busy right now." He hung up the phone.

The light had swelled over the ocean and now was breaking in waves against the shore. Behind, there were the hills, glimmering as if newmade, every dry canyon and burned-out house etched against a china-blue sky. Even the ancient gap-toothed HOL LYWOOD sign looked alive and renewed. Glamour slid a power disk into his camera and got ready to shoot. Book the image now and find a use for it later, that was his philosophy.

"Have you ever heard of a *Demogorgon*?" Markson asked.

"You're still there? I hung up on you."

"I'm working for Pellucidar now, and I can afford a hang-up bypass. You didn't answer my question. Have you ever heard of a *Demogorgon*?"

"Of course," said Glamour. "Who hasn't?" The *Demogorgon* was a hand-held digital video-image synthesizer that had just been developed in England. Like all modern video synthesizers, it could store and reshape light and scenery, but the *Demogorgon* went one step further. It was capable of digitizing, storing, editing, reshaping and even reconstructing a living actor's image; thus it threatened to make actors obsolete. "But I've never used one. The Guild is strictly against the *Demogorgon*, and I'm Guild, remember? There's a law against filming with it, a worldwide ban."

"Worldwide, exactly," said Markson. "But it might interest you to know that I have obtained a Guild waiver to use the *Demogorgon*—for a very special film."

Glamour had never even seen, much less held, a *Demogorgon*; it would be interesting to see what it could actually do. But there was no point letting Markson know that. "I charge a very special fee for very special films," he said. "Besides, I'm already working."

Markson laughed. "You're a poor liar, Glamour. You're between jobs or you wouldn't be out cruising around like a teenager. What I have is what you might call steady work, since it pays for three years."

"Three years? I thought the *Demogorgon* speeded things up. What kind of picture takes three years to make?"

"It's a location picture. With lots of travel time."

5

THERE IS A PECULIAR INTIMACY between certain kinds of comrades—soldiers, prisoners, fliers—who never say the words "good-bye" or "hello"; who, when it's time to leave, just turn on one heel and are suddenly gone; who, on meeting even after long separations, merely pick up a conversation as if the years between had never been: as if to signify their affection with an embrace, a handshake, or even a greeting, would by embodying, diminish it; as if remarking the years of separation would somehow grant them power and risk weakening the unspoken connection that defied them; as if spacetime, once acknowledged, might engulf them all.

So it was that Bass didn't even look around when he heard Natasha Kirov's voice, even though he had been waiting for her all morning.

"What're you doing, Bass?" she asked. "Buying scrap iron?" She pronounced it *arn*, like all the Russian cosmonauts who had learned English in Texas.

"The McAuliffe Maneuver." Bass was checking the O-rings on the tank, feeling through the inspection hole with a Popsicle stick to see if the rubber had been brittled by too many coolings and heatings. Though the Landfill Island government (a wholly owned subsidiary of the US government) had passed on the ship when it was sold, Bass always considered it best to err on the side of caution.

"Where'd they get this hot rod?" Kirov asked, clambering up onto the power scaffold with him. The name of the ship, written in florid script along the root of the tail, was *Old Moulmein Pagoda*.

Bass pointed to a row of spacecraft, light planes, and even a few ancient 707s and DC-3s lined up in the bone-white Caribbean sun. Painted on the cracked concrete, to be read from the air, was:

"U" HAVE TO LAND TO BUY

OUR PRICES "R" SO LOW

LANDFILL MOTORS

"Plenty of used stuff here," he said. "This baby's a Korean *Columbia* clone, last flag, Singapore. Two engines are re-furbed Rocketdynes and this one is new." He lowered the scaffold four feet and looked up. "It's the one that worries me. Hold this spectra light for me, will you"—he grinned at Kirov—"Captain?"

Kirov hadn't seen Bass for nineteen years, though she had thought of him often. Their affair had lasted less than two months, but the friendship that followed had carried them well into the training for the Mars voyage before it had been canceled. When Bass moved his head from side to side, squinting, looking for the telltale black sparkle that would betray cracks in the web of cooling pipes that covered the engine, she saw the web of cracks that covered his cheeks. He claimed to be sixteen years older than she was, and age was the only thing men didn't lie about. He'd be fifty-seven.

"So?" she said.

Bass shrugged that Bass shrug. "Good as new."

Kirov let that enigmatic statement go and said, "Let's check out the bridge."

Together they rode the tiny open elevator up to 119 feet. Kirov leaned back against the railing; she took off her blue NASA flight cap and let the dry hot white Carib wind scratch her inch-long hair and swing her two long yellow braids. As the cage rattled upward, Landfill Island spread around them. One of the first of the corporate sovereignty nations, it had been built up to order from the shallow ocean floor. The smell that was cloying on the ground was a pleasant sweet tang up here. The edible (almost) island attracted vast quantities of fish, and though there were no yachts in the harbor there were plenty of fishing craft—overshadowed by two huge factory ships, fish processors from Japan. To the north, a junkyard of light planes, commercial discontinueds and recovered spacecraft lay bleaching in the sun like artifacts of coral and aluminum. The equipment at Landfill Motors to the south and at Midori's Aerospace Parts to the north looked, to Bass, disturbingly interchangeable.

"Heard you got married," he said.

"Heard you were raising dogs."

"Hounds. I wouldn't fool with dogs. Sold them all to make this trip."

"You're getting old, Bass," Kirov said as, at the top, the rusted orange mesh cage groaned, clicked, moaned to a stop. It was the highest of compliments. The years in space carried their own clock in the bone

From the deck the island was visible all the way around: a low sandy bank north of Haiti and south of the Bahamas, covered with scrub. Landfill Island had been the major spaceport of the Caribbean before the Grand Depression; but now that people rarely went into space the low, two-story high, two-block-long town of Port Orbital looked like the ghost town it was.

Two other *Columbia*-class ships, an *Ariane* with a Geminisized one-man repair capsule, and one *Soyuz*-class shuttle were parked on the runway in varied states of disrepair. The US Park Service shuttle, before it was sold, had gone up from Canaveral, which was owned by Heinz-Krupp. Only a few independents still flew from Landfill, mostly servicing communications satellites

Inside the open hatch, a ladder led up to the flight deck. It was filthy. There was gum under the seats and a Furry Freak Brothers sticker on the instrument panel. The inner panel of the emergency door was streaked with graffiti in Tagalog. Without asking, Bass sat down in the pilot's barca. Kirov was commander of the voyage, but he would be flying all the small craft. She would fly only the *Mary Poppins* herself.

"Think this thing'll fly?"

This was Bass's standard joke. Or was it a joke? He had once worked for a major airline until he had asked the question during takeoff roll with the cabin speakers on.

"I don't see why not," Kirov said, knocking on the forward control panel. Bass had just meant the shuttle, but she was already thinking of the whole voyage. "The hardware's all in place. Twenty years older but what's twenty years? This ship is junk, but the *Mary P*. . . . I'll bet even the food is still good! Half the hardware is already at Mars. The lander is in Phobos orbit, the fuel processors are on the surface and have been since the turn of the century. It seems to play. What do you think?"

"Let me tell you a story," Bass said. "I bought a Pontiac once. Back when I was rocket shipping."

Kirov turned and walked back out to the orange steel elevator deck. She remembered Bass's stories as long-winded, and it was too hot to listen to one inside the cramped flight deck.

"It was a sixty-nine GTO a woman had bought for her son as a welcome home present from Vietnam. Only he never made it. The car showed up in the inventory of her estate thirty years later with only ninety-six point four miles on it. I was made out of money at the time—this was right after the Moon solo caper when I was selling endorsements. I remember going to pick it up. It was in a horse barn out on this fancy estate. The vinyl top was rotted but I had expected that. I had brought a new battery with me, and an air tank; the tires were down. I checked the oil and water—"

"You didn't want to change the oil after it had been sitting all those years?" Kirov asked.

"Oil's already a million years old in the can," Bass said. "I turned the key and it started right up," he said. "There was a little squealing from the mice nesting in the flywheel cover, but that was all. It drove smooth as silk all the way into town—six or eight miles. Then at a stoplight this kid in a pickup . . ."

The elevator whined and clicked. The cage appeared. They stepped back just as it stopped and a red-haired, red-bearded, three-foot seven-inch midget in a $1,700 butter-leather jacket stepped off.

"Looks like a duck taking a shit," Kirov said.

Bass wondered if she was as vulgar in Russian as in English. "Guess it takes a lot of stuff to make a movie," he said.

They were watching Glamour unload his equipment from the chartered Conair, a little twin-engine flying boxcar. The plane squatted down hydraulically, first one leg and then the other, so that Glamour could drive straight onto it with a forklift. Kirov had never seen a midget drive a forklift before. He stood on the seat and operated the foot pedals from a black panel fitted over the wheel. There were four identical boxes, each as large as a coffin, marked *Demogorgon* 7120. Other boxes contained, according to their markings, lights, reflectors, generators, welding tools, tape decks, wardrobe cases, a unisex chemical toilet and two cases of insect repellent.

"Insect repellent?" Bass asked.

"What's wrong with that?"

"No bugs on Mars."

Glamour shrugged and set everything but the four camera boxes at the side of the airstrip. "I won't need most of this stuff with the *Demogorgon* anyway. The studio fitted me out through an outfitter in the Valley," he said. "Probably told him we were going to the Amazon."

"That makes sense; the fact that we're going to Mars is

still top secret," Kirov said. "Hush-hush until the press conference Monday."

"Monday we'll be in high orbit," Bass said, relieved. He hated press conferences.

"That's where the press conference is going to be held," Kirov said. "The first press conference in space in twenty years."

The De Havilland Comet was the first commercial jet, a 471-knot craft with four Rolls-Royce engines. Two Comets had come apart in midair, terminating the aircraft's commercial viability, and one of the leftovers had ended up on Landfill, at the end of the airstrip, where it had been peeled open and turned into the Comet Diner.

"Oil is already a million years old in the can," Bass said in answer to Glamour's question. They were sitting at the end of the counter, by the big window, waiting for the Hollywood doctor and the Movie Stars. Since loading the *Demogorgon* on the *Old Moulmein Pagoda*, they had drunk three rounds of Red Stripe and watched six incoming flights (two Lear jets, one commercial STOL, and three out-island DC-3s), mostly half-filled with mechanics, used rocket-ship brokers and seafood buyers. There were plenty of middle-thirtyish Black men (Markson's description of Jeffries), but none with doctor bags, and no Movie Stars whatsoever.

"So then you crank her up," Glamour prompted.

"She runs smooth as silk until I get to a stoplight, and this kid in a pickup is pointing under the car," Bass said. "Jesus, I wish they would get here. It's ten o'clock already."

"If they don't get here by tomorrow, we leave without them," Kirov said.

"So then you get out," Glamour prompted.

"I get out and look under the car. She's pumping oil out the front and the back, and water through the water pump, and transmission fluid out the front and rear seals."

Bass paused; he looked at Glamour, as if waiting for a response

"That's it? I don't get it," said Glamour.

Kirov stepped to the door. Overhead the stars gleamed in their splendid, meaningless array. Once you had been in space, they never looked right from Earth.

Down the runway a replica Ford Trimotor was landing, its turbines almost silent in the night. Maybe this is them, Kirov thought.

"The point is, the mechanical parts were perfect but the seals were dried out all through the engine. It's not just miles but time that wears out a car. I had to have the whole thing torn down and new seals put in from front to back. It cost me thirty-six hundred dollars."

"I still don't get it," insisted Glamour.

No one got out of the Trimotor except the pilot, who took a leak and got back in. The cockpit light went out, as if he had bedded down for the night.

"I think he's trying to tell us that we're going to drip oil across the solar system," Kirov said, turning and signaling the waiter. "Check, please! Gentlemen, let's hang it up and go to bed. We leave at nine A.M. with or without the Hollywood doctor or the Movie Stars. They can come up later with the press conference."

Bass raised his bottle of club soda. "One last toast. To the *Mary Poppins.*"

Glamour raised his Red Stripe. "To the first film on Mars."

Kirov clinked her Diet Coke. "To the first trip to Mars."

Glamour set his bottle down carefully so that it didn't clink.

"Wait wait wait wait wait," he said. He looked at Bass and then at Kirov as if seeing them both for the first time. "First trip to Mars? You mean, you guys have never been there before?"

"START CABIN LEAK CHECK."

"Roger."

"Arm OMS engines."

"Roger."

"Open cabin vents," said Bass, for this was his flight: second-in-command on the voyage, he was pilot for the first leg on the *Columbia*-class *Old Moulmein Pagoda*.

"Roger," said Kirov, for she was faithful to the vernacular of flight that had been passed down from the barnstormers and their Jennys, through the Southern-fratboy lingo of NASA, to the Soviet crew that had exchange-trained in secret at Houston.

"*Pagoda*, this is Control," came a singsong Bahamian accent. "Crew access arm retract beginning. Please affirm."

"Okay," said Bass.

"*Pagoda*, this is Control. Your side hatch is dis-secure on visual. Please affirm."

"Okay," said Bass. Then, back over his shoulder to Glamour: "Hey, Scotty, would you pull that door shut?"

"*Pagoda*, this is Control. You may initiate APU prestart procedure."

"Okay."

"You are on internal power," said Kirov. "And please say 'roger' instead of 'okay.'"

"Aye-aye, Cap'n." Bass ran through the checklist, amazed at how easily it all came back to him. The rocket felt like a racehorse straining under his seat; its flanks trembling with pent-up excitement.

"Main engine gimbaling check."

"Hydraulic check."

"Roger," said Kirov. "Main engines gimbaling check completed."

"Ten," said Bass.

"Nine."

"Eight."

"We have Go," he said, reaching for the override.

"*Pagoda*, this is Control," said the Bahamian voice. "You have an abort."

"What?"

"You have a scrub, a stay-home, a no-go. Confirm. Kill your APUs."

Bass killed his APUs. "What's going on? Do you see a leak?"

"Negatory. This is not an equipment failure, it's a command override."

"Then to hell with it," Bass said, reaching for the APU switch to resume the countdown, but Kirov stopped him, her hand touching the back of his with the gentle but firm touch of command.

"Control, this is Captain Kirov, what's the problem?"

"Captain, you have a passenger here on the tarmac. A Brother with a big black bag."

"Start cabin leak check."

"Roger."

"Arm OMS engines."

"Roger"

"Open cabin vents . . ."

While Bass redid the countdown, Kirov did a visual of the flight deck. Their new passenger was securely stowed beside Glamour in the row of seats just below the flight deck. His big black doctor's bag, which he had refused to stow, was on his lap. Was it her imagination or was it squirming? Or was he just nervous?

"Eight."

Or was *she* just nervous? This was her first trip into space in almost twenty years.

"Six "

"Five."

"Four . ..."

"We have SSE ignition."

"SSE ignition."

"We have SBR ignition."

"SBR ignition."

"We have liftoff."

"Have liftoff."

Kirov closed her eyes for a long delicious moment and let the sound wash over her. It was like long thunder, like a waterfall of fire, like the booming of a glacier, like a hundred Colorados; like mountains that had learned to sing, and learned to fly, and flew straight up. Like a rocket taking off.

"Engine specs look good," Kirov read.

"Look good," Bass repeated.

"Ten feet per second. Twelve. Twenty."

"Twenty."

The *Old Moulmein Pagoda* shook the Earth, rattled, rose. Bass felt the launch press him back deep into his seat as his weight increased to two gs, then three, then almost four. Tame compared to the new parabolic roller coasters, but still a thrill. Beside him he saw Kirov with her lips pulled back over her teeth in that wide, forced, terrified, ecstatic, blissful and familiar spaceman grin.

"Air speed 7,294."

"Check."

"8,225."

"... 225."

Bass trimmed the burn and reached behind the console, pulled out a pack of Red Man chewing tobacco, and picked out a good wad. He only chewed when he was flying, and he was flying.

"Elevation 110,325."

"110, check."

*Columbia*s were supposed to have a life span of three hundred launches, but what about clones? Kirov wondered. Better or worse? How many times had this old tin can ridden the elevator of fire? Probably five hundred. How many more before it came apart in the air?

"Speed 9,725."

"Check."

"Ten and up. How's our pitch?"

"Okay," Bass said. Fighting the increased gs, he reached behind the console for another chaw of Red Man. In the rearview mirror he caught a glimpse of Glamour squashed in his seat, looking angry. The doctor's face showed only boredom and no terror. Bass wondered how long it had been since he had been in the Navy.

"Pitch down two."

"Check."

"Yaw check."

"Check."

Glamour gritted his teeth as the roaring grew to a howl and seven million pounds of thrust flattened him into the cheap composite of his seat. The oversized (even for full-sized people) barca made Glamour feel even smaller than usual, and the thrust slamming the seat into his backside made him feel even more insulted by gravity. It went on, past discomfort, past terror, to indignity: the certainty that he would disappear altogether and be found by the ship cleaners, Louis Glamour, ASC, jammed between the cushions like a lost billfold.

* * *

"We have rollover."

"Have rollover."

"Critical burn, throttle back to sixty-five."

"Back to sixty-five."

Dr. S. C. Jeffries jiggled the bag on his lap gently until it stopped squirming. Then he relaxed and stared at the curved wall, wishing it were a window. He had been to the orbital station twice when the Navy had run half of it as the Farragut Space Medicine Center. Now, as then, he found Earth separation dull: a brute force exercise as unexciting as a one-car drag race.

"We have ET separation."

"Have ET."

"ET phone home," Bass and Glamour said at the same time.

The ship leaped ahead in one final lunge for orbit. Then there it was: the sudden silence and weightlessness together as if sound had weight and silence, wings. Zero g was familiar to Kirov, Bass and Jeffries, but as strange to Glamour as light to a newborn babe. Feeling his heart turn a loop inside his breast, Glamour gulped, then grinned. Then took his heart for another loop for fun.

"Mission time thirty-three."

"Thirty-three."

Kirov was just savoring the almost forgotten feeling of weightlessness when there was a familiar, unwelcome, not totally unexpected sound.

"It's Glamour," Bass said.

"I know," said Kirov. "I can smell the oysters." Kirov looked back at Jeffries, pointed at the wall slot that held the cudbuster, and said, "You're on duty, Bones. You have a sick passenger."

"Got it," said Jeffries; then muttered, "Please don't call me Bones."

Glamour looked surprised rather than sick: he was staring at his own puke which was spinning in a small globe, gray with swirls of blue and cream, like a model of Neptune.

Jeffries took the cudbuster out of its wall slot and tried it; it was dead. He shook it. The globe was drifting toward the wall, where Jeffries knew from his Navy experience, it would shatter into droplets and spread around the room.

Glamour reached for the cudbuster and swiftly opened it, pulling the batteries out. He cracked them together and touched his tongue to the ends. That did it: Jeffries threw up himself, neatly, the Navy way. Then he turned away while Glamour vacuumed up both drifting vomit globes.

Kirov turned back to the controls, where Bass was locking in for the approach to the orbital station. This Hollywood doctor didn't look too swift to her. But she would deal with him later.

"OME's charged."

"Charged," Bass repeated.

They were in medium Earth orbit: floating in space, but still tied to the familiar dock of the Earth. Kirov was amazed at how easily the routines came back. She signed orbital insertion complete, and Bass checked the engine specs while they both watched the blue agate Earth, like a new and more interesting sky replacing the old one, drift "overhead." There were the still smoldering Amazon plains, a brown sear touched with new green in one corner. To the east, the sun shone brilliantly off a Scotland-sized oil slick that spun lazily, like a gleaming Sargasso, in the South Atlantic. Clouds puffed eastward across the Sahara like sheep.

"We have visual," said Bass.

"Have visual."

Pitch and yaw corrected, they sailed at 15,588 mph toward the flashing speck that had just come over the horizon.

"How's the situation back there?" Kirov asked.

Jeffries pulled himself forward to her barca and spoke in a whisper. "I don't like it. Something's wrong with this guy."

Behind them both, illuminated by the blue Earthlight, Glamour's eyes were shining; his teeth were gleaming through his bright red beard. His arms were folded across his chest. Bass looked at him and recognized his expression immediately.

It was ecstasy.

7

NIXON STATION WAS BOTH bigger and smaller than Jeffries remembered. He had been here as part of the Farragut Space Medicine Center Team, before the Navy had been acquired by Beatrice-Texaco, and the station he remembered was boy-awesome: a spinning chrome and plastic wheel with a quarter-mile-long tube through the middle; a complex as big as a mall, one third military-scientific, and the other two thirds divided among gambling concessionaires, each vying to outdo the others in luxury, plant life and the interior architectural style known as Texas Hotel. The wheel was, since the Trump Sky Palace disaster, dark, still and no longer spinning. The casinos had all gone home, driven to ground by the negative publicity of an eighteen-month shower of shooting stars, each, at least in the popular imagination, a grinning space-bloated gambler.

The *Old Moulmein Pagoda* approached from darkside through a mismatched and seemingly random collection of fuel tanks, parts nets, experimental lab cells and hab tanks tied together with poly lines like rubber bands. The entire station complex was a mile long, and most of it was dark. At the far end, distinguished by a blinking light, were the tied-together tin cans of McAuliffe Orbiting Lodge, their destination.

According to Park Service rules, the ship had to be docked by a Ranger, but over the years the reg had been modified into a talkdown.

"Johnson?" Bass asked when he heard the smokey's voice "Leroy Johnson? Houston, 19—?"

"Bass? Is that you? I'll be damned. Don't bang up my station docking that scrap iron."

Bass trimmed the ship with the OMEs so it glided in between the scarred bumpers with a minimum of fuss. "Your station?"

"I'm station chief here."

"You're dowxxxzzzxxx," said a computer-generated voice over the cabin speaker. "Welcome to Nixon Staxxzzxxzzxxzx."

Jeffries unstrapped, and floated down from the flight deck to the air lock, with Kirov right behind. Glamour unstrapped but stayed by his seat. Bass listened to the muffled clunks as the air locks sealed, then to the hissing as the two craft equalized pressures, both at .8 Earth atmosphere. He wasn't in any hurry to leave the *Old Moulmein Pagoda*. "Cash or crexxzzxxzz?" the computer voice asked. Bass punched in the credit code Markson had given him; in a moment he heard the low rumble of LOX boiling into the lines.

He heard a sigh of pleasure and turned around. "You're still here?" he asked the red-bearded midget floating upside down over his barca.

"Ever take acid?" Glamour asked.

The good old days were over, Kirov could see. When she had been with NASA, on exchange, the equipment had been second-rate and new; now it was second-rate and old. The interior of Nixon Station's McAuliffe Orbital Lodge was as cheerless and dank as the steerage of an oil tanker—which in a way it was, being made out of discarded external fuel tanks welded together. The pumps whined, the filters howled, the air was smelly and the walls were slick with cold moisture, so that the entire effort of zero-g maneuvering was to stay away from them.

She followed Jeffries through the passage from the air lock into a large cylindrical room. Two tourists, overweight American white folks in their sixties, were parked on the Velcro lounger in front of a curved crystal window with a supertaped

crack running across it, looking out at the panorama of the
Earth sweeping below them. At the bar on a Velcro stool "sat"
a young woman, no more than a teenager, with dirty blond
hair; she was wrapped in two sweaters and shivering. EARTH-
LIGHT LOUNGE, the sign behind the bar said: *All drinks
$45 no Canadian money, s'il vous plait.* "It's the honor sys-
tem," the teenager said. "But let me mix them. I'm trying to
learn."

"A Stoly, please," Kirov said. She wouldn't be flying until
day after tomorrow, when they were scheduled to go up to
the *Mary Poppins.* Might as well enjoy this little break.

"Oh, are you Commander Kirkov? There's a phone call
for you."

"*Captain,* and it's *Kirov.*"

"I'll have the same," said Jeffries.

"We don't have actual Russian vodka," the teenager said.
"How about Illinois? The phone's over there by the door."

When Glamour was sixteen, working in Hollywood as a
location extra for his uncle's Gaelic Little People, Ltd., a
friend had slipped him a tab of sunshine at Coyote Farms'
backlot. The world had taken on its proper dimensionality:
they spent the afternoon climbing a tree, admiring the inter-
action of bark and light and time. Now the third and fourth
dimensions were there again, without the tree. Plus, there
was something special about this blue Earth-reflected light
that rang through the flight deck, filtered through seas of air!
And with his compact size Glamour seemed to be having less
trouble than even the old salts in maneuvering.

"That's pretty good," Bass said. "But don't make all those
little swimming motions. You're not a goldfish. That's better."
He had never seen anyone take to zero g so easily.

A head poked into the cabin: a grizzled almost-old man,
Bass's age, in the archaic forest green of the National Park
Service.

"Johnson," Bass said. "You old space dog. Meet Louis
Glamour, ASC. I thought you had retired."

"Next year. This is my last tour. Glad to meet you, Lou. Is he okay? When NASA was sold to Chase-Gillette, they trimmed everybody with the old medical plan. I went to work for Disney-Gerber, out of Canaveral, until they caught me trying to get the union going again. I sold satellite time shares for five years before I got this berth. Come on in and I'll buy you a drink. Only one pump is working and this thing'll take forever to refuel. What the hell are you guys doing up here?"

"It's top secret," said Bass, "so don't tell anybody, but we're going to Mars."

The call for Kirov was Markson, from Beverly Hills. At first Kirov thought the vertical hold was skewed, then she saw it was the worried look on his face.

"We've got a problem," he said. "How quickly can you get up to the Mars ship itself?"

"The *Mary Poppins?* A couple of days. We don't have any figures, any trajectories. The *Old Moulmein Pagoda* isn't re-fueled or fitted with interorbitals yet—" But Kirov was eager to see the ship she had trained on and wasn't particularly eager to spend any more time than necessary on the smelly, cold station. "Unless we could persuade Johnson to let us use the Park Service pickup—"

"Perfect! You and Bass must get up there as soon as possible to secure the ship—"

"What's going on?"

"Somehow, word has gotten out about our project. There is a rumor that Disney-Gerber is preparing to make a move on it. They may even try and claim the ship. They could make their move at the UN tomorrow, or even—"

"The UN?"

"It's still functioning, though you don't hear about it every day. Meets the second Tuesday of every month. Disney-Gerber has corporate observer status, and since they are over thirty-three and a third percent Russian capital, our lawyers are afraid they might make a move on the ship under joint ownership statutes. We can't take any chances. Let Jeffries stay at the station and handle the press when they come up on the regular shuttle from Canaveral tomorrow afternoon. The main thing is for you and Bass to be in physical possession of the *Mary Poppins* as soon as possible. Can you fly this Park Service flivver or whatever they call it?"

"There it is again!" said Mr. Gentry. He showed his daughter where he was born every time it came around, like a favorite horse on a carousel. He pointed to a dark spot in the serrated desert of the New Dust Bowl, where the Iowa River used to run.

"We had to ride a yellow bus to school every day," he said. "Rain or shine."

Mrs. Gentry groaned. She saw it six times a day. She and her husband and daughter had spent four days looking down at the Earth as people used to gaze down into the Grand Canyon before it was made into a lake. The view from space was awesome, grand, and finally, boring; an afternoon of looking at it would have been long enough. The station was cold, and there was nothing to do except watch the world turn below. You couldn't go outside. There were no other tourists and the place traveled but never arrived anywhere. It wasn't like a cruise ship where you could get off and shop. Even the novelty of weighing nothing soon wore off; it just made it hard to get around, and a chore to go to the bathroom, except of course for the men, as usual.

At least now there were some new people: a woman from Texas, and a nice colored man. And now this older fellow—mature was the word—and a midget.

Obviously show business people.

"Do you folks come here often?" Jeffries asked.

Mr. Gentry shook his head. "Our daughter won this trip in a magazine contest. A week's vacation. It's over tomorrow and we can go home."

"First prize was Bermuda," the daughter said. "It was cloudy there for two days, and then sunshine, sunshine, sunshine. I know because we can see it from here six times a day. The contest was for the weirdest name."

"What was it?"

"*Seventeen.*"

"I mean the weirdest name."

"Greetings Brother Buffalo. That's my full name. But my friends call me Greetings."

"Indian?"

"Hippie," said Mrs. Gentry. "She's named after her grandmother. See those mountains just to the north of those clouds that look like marching soldiers? Anyway, they look like marching soldiers to me. My mother was the last baby born in a commune there called The Red Rockers."

"The first, Mother, not the last," Greetings said. "They were trying to call the buffalo back," she explained to Jeffries.

"Whatever. Bermuda would have been better," said Mrs. Gentry. "It's cold and damp here all the time. I don't see the point in space at all. They never clean this place. Don't use that toilet there. And don't use the officers' lounge. What did you folks win?"

"You mean what did we lose," said Jeffries.

"It's top secret," said Kirov, hanging up the phone. "But we're on our way to Mars."

"In the first place, can't just *anybody* fly to the Silkwood belt," Johnson said to Kirov and Bass. They were at the end of the bar. "It's only an hour and a half away, but it's off limits without a UN certification. In the second place . . ."

"There was no desert there at all," said Glamour.

"That's right. The entire continent of Antarctica was covered with ice," said Bass.

"What'll they think of next," said Mrs. Gentry.

"I like it even though it doesn't work," said Greetings.

"What doesn't work?" said Jeffries.

"My name. The buffalo never came back."

* * *

"In the second place," said Johnson, "the Park Service pickup is a little old benzine-powered job that is tricky as hell to fly. We hardly ever use it because it likes to spin and it hasn't been cleaned out in a month. . . ."

"Isn't that the phone?" said Bass.

"Jeffries," said Kirov, "will you get it this time?"

"Kirov?" It was Markson again.

"She's, uh"—Kirov was shaking her head and waving her hands—"consulting with Ranger Johnson, the station chief," Jeffries said.

"Then Bass."

"He's consulting with them." Bass was shaking his head.

"Then Jeffries."

"Speaking, dammit."

"Good. You're just the man I wanted to talk to. Tell the others to get up to the ship right away. The other shoe just dropped."

"What do you mean, the other shoe just dropped?"

"It's an old expression. Can you catch the seven o'clock news?"

On an inner station like Nixon Park there are six sunsets and sunrises every "day," but in accordance with tradition the clocks are set on Houston Time and the bar collects Texas sales tax. At 7:00 P.M. (HT) the forty-eight-inch Samsung over the bar comes on so people can catch the evening news.

"*Wall Street rallied late yesterday—*" the announcers said in unison, "*with word of a big deal.*" Then the left anchor went into her solo: "*With the news that Disney-Gerber has agreed to purchase the financially troubled Parks Department from Kawasaki-Philip Morris.*" The right anchor picked up the beat smoothly: "*The deal, which will be finalized tomorrow, includes the money-losing Nixon Orbital Park and dried-up Yellowstone, as well as the superprofitable Yosemite and Smokey Mountain Natural Amusement Areas.*"

"I thought the government owned the parks," Mrs. Gentry

said. "Isn't that why they're called national parks?"

"Honey, that would be socialism," Mr. Gentry explained.

"*. . . one of the largest single purchases since the government agencies were sold off to private enterprise in the latter part of the last century to service the deficit,*" the center anchor closed.

"It's confusing to us old folks," Ranger Johnson said, coming over with Kirov and Bass to hear the news. "Because many of them, like Parks Department or Welfare, are still called by their old names. Though most of them, like Everyday Eagle, have changed their names."

"Used to be the Post Office," Glamour said.

"*In other news today,*" the trio continued in chorus, "*the President left her winter White House in Puerto Rico to begin . . .*"

"And in the third place?" asked Bass.

"In the third place," said Johnson, "since I'm working for Disney-Gerber again, and they'll fire me as soon as they check the blacklist, I'll fly you up there myself. I've always wanted to see this Mars ship anyway."

8

THE UN-AEC WASTE ORBIT was Earth's high-orbit spacefill—a ten-mile-long silvery arc of radioactive water ice, contaminated candy wrappers, Poland and Pennsylvania hogs (puffed up to twice normal size), protective clothing, hairpieces, tissues, contaminated waste canisters, truck tires and septic tanks. All the radioactive wastes from sixteen nations had been dumped here for thirty years, before the Antarctic had been environmentally okayed; and now the zone was off limits without a special permit, since any dislocation of the articles could conceivably cause an eventual rain of radioactive debris on the Earth below.

The Silkwood belt, or Twenty-five-Hundred-Mile Island, some wits called it.

It was this arc of junk that had hidden the *Mary Poppins* for twenty years.

The Park Service pickup was a small interorbital with two benzine engines, only one gimbaled. The interior was the size of a mid-twentieth–century Volkswagen bus filled with tools, cables, dirty clothes and squeezed hamburger tubes. "My predecessor was supposed to clean this," Johnson apologized, "but—"

"It's okay," Kirov said. "I know how it is."

The air locks unsealed with a sigh, and while Johnson drove, she and Bass watched Nixon Station dwindle behind them like a cheap piece of tossed-away jewelry. Then the bright specks were gobbled by the terminator, and they were in space: not deep space but deeper than the low orbit of the station.

Ahead, since they were still in Earth's shadow, only darkness showed; the clouds were luminescent below as they sailed around the dark side of the planet. In less than twenty minutes they reached high orbit.

The Silkwood belt was most clearly visible from its edge, where it appeared as a silver arc against the dark terminator ahead. Then it darkened against the planet's brightness as it hove into view and passed five miles below, a gray cloud against the bright blue seas of the planet.

And what was hidden above it came into view.

"Holy Mary, Mother of Armstrong, Aldrin and Collins," Johnson said. It was the *Mary Poppins*. Millions of people had read about it. Thousands had seen "artist's renderings" in *Popular Science* and *Aviation Week and Space Technology* twenty years before; but most of them, all but 618, had believed when the project was canceled that it had never been built.

"It's gorgeous," Johnson breathed as it grew in the forward screen of the pickup. Bass, looking on, agreed. The Mars ship was 1,712.5 meters, over a mile long. In the front, three cigarette-shaped cylinders, the habitat modules, were folded back along the spine in the approximation of an umbrella that had given the ship her name. Ahead of and behind the cylinders were two globes, the bridge and the rear (or "South") observatory, actually a hemisphere. Then the long, slightly curved girders soared back almost a mile to a coolie-hat shield, a hundred meters in diameter, facing front. Behind the shield, the engine itself—a combustion chamber, with a reactor tube and two small expansion tanks of expellant—was no larger than a car. Less than half a ton of water, superheated and expelled at a high fraction of the speed of light by the Daewoo reactor, would provide the delta V to take the *Mary Poppins* to Mars.

They passed under the ship, between it and the Silkwood belt. Pasted to the Earth-facing side of the *Mary Poppins* were white and silver strips of light-scattering foil—the camouflage that had blended it in with the arc of junk a half mile below. It had worked for twenty years.

At 150 meters they were close enough to make out the painting of Mary Poppins near the bridge, still familiar, even after twenty years.

"Welcome home," said Bass.

"You lucky dogs," Johnson said. "Where do we dock?"

"Huh?" Kirov said, lost in her own thoughts. "Oh, don't dock. Just mag on and I'll EVA over."

As Kirov locked out of the pickup, the air in which she had been swimming turned to snow and then to nothing in an instant, disappearing with an almost audible sigh, and she was in space for the first time in twenty years. Space with its booming silences, space with its familiar blue-white Earth for a sky. Unlike Bass, who had been around the Moon, she had never been deeper. The program had closed down before she had been able to do all the things she had trained to do. Bass was right behind her; he paid out her line and she pushed off for the twenty yards across to the *Mary Poppins*. She hit perfectly, boots first, neither fast nor slow; grabbed the sissy bar by the air lock, and plugged in the make-ready electrical cable she was carrying. Four prong male; four prong female: so far so good. The ready light came on beside the air lock. She turned to signal Bass across but he was already beside her.

WhooSH Haah

Their radios were on, so each heard the other breathing; but neither wanted to talk.

Bass waited for Kirov to get ahead of him again at the outside air-lock door: this was her ship and it would be her command. When she nodded he touched the panel with his glove and the door slid open; just like the supermarket—a little slow. He followed her in, she shut the door behind them, and they were in a small, closed space the size of a phone booth and a half; this was not the main air lock but one of the three auxiliaries on the outer hab modules. Kirov pressed the panel on the inside air-lock door but nothing happened. They were locked in. Bass felt a flash of panic and quickly, expertly, turned it off in his mind just as one would flick off a light. While Kirov pressed the panel again, Bass put his helmet to the wall; he could hear solenoids click, but no motors groaned. There wasn't enough juice coming through.

"It's okay," Kirov said, her voice startlingly loud in Bass's earcom. "There's a wheel."

Locking her bootsoles into triangular holders, Kirov tugged on the inside air-lock wheel. It snowed again, and this time the snow stayed in the air around them, flakes the size of quarters dancing in their helmet lights. Kirov opened the door and slipped through in one motion. Bass followed, leaving the inner air-lock door open behind him.

They were in the long hall of a ghost house, dust and snow dancing madly in their headlight beams. Cases and coils, strange shapes of colorless cardboard lurked in the darkness on every side. Kirov found the control bud and hit a switch but nothing happened. The ship was still dead. The cable they had brought only carried across enough power for the outer lock door; the rest was soaking into the batteries after their twenty-year sleep.

"We're going to have to jump-start her," Bass said.

Kirov nodded and Bass clicked on the three-way so that Johnson could hear back at the pickup. "Patch in a fuel cell and port me out another cable," he said.

"Go back and help him," Kirov said. "I'll call you from the bridge."

"Are you sure?"

But Kirov was already gone, through the round door, up the long hall, toward the top of the cylinder where it attached to the spine of the ship, toward the blue glow of the Earthlit Hab #1 and rec room.

* * *

WhooSH Haah
WhooSH Haah
WhooSH Haah

Kirov checked the dicktracy on her wrist, then with a quick, decisive motion, unlocked her helmet and pulled it off. The air was bitter, sour, cold. But it was air.

Clipping her helmet to her pack, pulling her red knit hat down to keep her ears warm, she went on up the darkened corridor. As a child she had gone with her father every spring to open the dacha in the woods north near Krasnoje Selo, and the smell was familiar: the pleasant stink of damp wood and long winters. In the exercise room the Nautilus machines were covered with Siberian kudzu, which had flourished when the ship was abandoned. The corridors were choked with vines, and the walls were scummy with mold. As she moved up the cylinder toward the central spine of the ship, she opened each door slowly, deliberately, as if expecting to see mice or snakes.

Hygiene.

Rec.

Research.

Kirov knew them all. Unlike the utilitarian NASA tubs, the *Mary Poppins* was designed for long-range, deep-space travel: NASA made U-boats, this was a *Normandie*. It had been built to accommodate a crew of sixty-six for a three-year round-trip voyage without hibernation; and since mass was not critical with the nuclear drive, the ship was equipped with wood-paneled rooms, carpeting, plants, paintings and real books, windows and mirrors. On the far side of the sun, it would be important to be surrounded by Earth things, things with fingerprints and smells. The kudzu was for the spirit; so was the wood trim in the corridors, the real books in the library, the Astrakhan rugs in the lounge.

In the library a crystal lens window opened to the stars. They looked much farther away from here than from the Earth's surface. Microfilm and cassettes filled wall slots between the wooden shelves, filled with real bound books. Kirov pulled off her glove and picked out one of the cassettes from the shelf. WORLD'S ALL-TIME FIFTY GREATEST ROCK N ROLL HITS OF THE UNIVERSE, the label said in Russian. When she had been in training on the *Mary Poppins*, Natasha had brought aboard her bootleg tapes. When she had left, she hadn't taken them with her. The music of America's 1950s, and her own Moscow youth almost half a century later, it seemed appropriate only to heaven.

She warmed the tape under her shirt and popped it into the deck but nothing happened; still no juice. She left it there.

In no hurry to get to the bridge, she cruised from room to room, cutting back the kudzu and wiping the worst of the mold off the walls. Luckily, it had only formed on the walls that received direct Earthlight, looking almost as if it were the pale green reverse of shadows.

The ship was cold and it stank and she loved it.

"Just got a call from Jeffries at the station," Bass said, calling from the pickup. "He's on the phone with Markson, who says the studio wants us to leave for Mars tomorrow."

"Good," said Kirov. "No press conference."

"He wants to have the press conference here, on the *Mary Poppins*."

"What? That's impossible."

"Can we go three-way?" Jeffries said. "Markson, I'm patching you in—"

"Kirov, the press is already on the way!" said Markson. "I've rented a special shuttle for them."

"This is absurd," said Kirov. "The ship has to be cleaned and restocked, we have to calculate delta V, the engine has to be checked and fueled, and what about the Movie Stars?"

"They're coming up with the press at noon. Leave all that to me. The problem is, if we don't leave in a hurry we may not leave at all. Since Disney-Gerber bought the national parks, they are trying to claim the *Mary Poppins* as part of Nixon Station's improvements under an old Bureau of Land Management fencing law."

"I thought Pellucidar had already claimed the ship," put in Bass.

"That's under sea salvage law. Depends on where the ship is at any given moment. Meanwhile, the Russians are calling a UN special session at eight A.M., claiming they own the ship."

"And they're right," said Kirov. "We do."

"Yeah, but they're just fronting for Disney-Gerber," said Markson. "Look, do you guys want to get tied up in red tape for six months, or do you want to go to Mars? Officially, I can't even be saying this but—"

"What about the equipment and supplies?" Kirov asked.

"We could bring them up on the *Pagoda*," Johnson said. "Hell, I'd be proud to help screw Disney-Gerber."

"Go ahead, then," Kirov said. "Meanwhile, I'll check out the ship and try to clean up enough for the press."

"I don't know," said Bass. "I don't like leaving you up here all alone."

"What do you mean, *you* don't know! *I'm* the Captain, Bass."

"Aye-aye, sir."

The silence was deafening. The peace was exhilarating. Kirov moved on up the hab cylinder and into the axis stalk of the ship. She was saving the bridge for last. In the mirrors of the Stalin Lounge she saw a woman alone and at peace for perhaps the last time for three years: blond, with china-blue eyes, hair more white than yellow, pale muscular arms. As Russian as the ship. As ready to be off.

She heard what she thought was a voice and turned up her earcom, but there was nothing. Bass and Johnson had gone to bring up the *Pagoda*. The sound was from inside the ship, from up ahead, toward the bridge.

It was definitely a voice. She saw a faint glow far up ahead, toward the bridge, which meant the batteries were finally saturated and the lights were coming on. The hall lights flickered and fans clattered. Then Kirov heard the voice again, louder and still familiar after twenty years:

> *Now they up and call me Speedo.*
> *but my real name*
> *is Mister Earl*

LIGHTS DOWN.

Coughs and grumbles echo in the great Tolstoy Ballroom of the *Mary Poppins*. The nervous ripping of Velcro on seat bottoms.

Music up.

Welcome to high Earth orbit, the threshold of space, and the threshold of a new era in entertainment history, an era which

"We came all the way up here to watch a video?" whispered *Christian Screen*. "Where are the Movie Stars?"

"That's them floating beside the video terminal," said *Still Rolling Stone*.

"Ssshhh!" The image of the familiar blue globe on the forty-eight-inch screen faded—

to introduce myself. I am Leonard W. Markson of Pellucidar Pictures, and I'm here to tell you about the most exciting project it has ever been my pleasure

—and was replaced by the image of a man in a distressed semisilk sport coat standing in front of a large wondawalnut desk in front of a window. Through the window, on a mountainside, a sign read: HOL YWOOD.

less than twenty-four hours, a brave band of Hollywood's Finest will leave Earth's gravitational environs for a history-

making three-year voyage, the greatest ever undertaken by humankind, and the most perilous since

"Have you seen Kirov?" asked Bass, who joined Jeffries in the forward entry of the vast, dark, almost empty Tolstoy Ballroom. "How come you're still carrying that black bag? Don't you want to put it in storage?"

"Ssshhh," said Jeffries. "You're disturbing the press conference."

"Such as it is," said Bass. "I would hardly call six people, two of them sleeping, a press conference. Where's Kirov? I need to tell her Daewoo is here."

Jeffries pointed to Kirov at the phone bank that had been installed for the press at the back of the ballroom. "She's in the back there, trying to call Beverly Hills."

new age of discovery that is about to begin, a unique age in that for the first time since the Moon landing in the last century, the eyes of everyone on Earth will be watching through the magic of film

"Thank you for using ATTT&T," the operator tape said. "If you are calling a class one number in the continental United States, please press three-three-three-eight now. If you are calling a class . . . Thank you."

so that even the announcement of this voyage is a historic event, the highest ever held and the first held in orbit in this century, representing every major news organization and network on the planet, and reaching over four hundred million

On the big screen, Markson walked toward the window and the camera followed. The warm-milk California sunshine washing through his office window washed on through the video screen, sending a dusting of digitized sunlight to corners of the windowless Tolstoy Ballroom, which had been assembled in space and had never seen daylight before.

"Pellucidar, Special Projects," the operator said on the little screen. "Mr. Markson's office. Who might I say is calling?"

to introduce our Stars, two of the boldest and most farseeing of a farseeing profession. Please give a rousing hand of

What a smile! It gave Greetings shivers just to look at Cary Fonda-Fox IV. Even though she had never seen him in a movie, his face was wonderfully familiar, his features a montage of four generations of Hollywood, evoking the shared pleasures of three hundred million Americans. Beverly Glenn was no less familiar and even more beautiful: her perfect body was a tribute to the genetic engineering the Academy made available to its hereditary members. Hearing the scattered claps in the empty ballroom, the Stars opened their eyes and waved, then dozed off again . .

undertaking we are here to celebrate today is more than a physical voyage through space. It is in its own way a voyage back in time, to an earlier age, an age when dreams were grander, nations were bolder, and movies were

"Can you spell that, please?"

"K-I-R-O-V. K as in candy," said Kirov, who had learned spelling as well as conversation in Texas.

"And where might I tell him you're calling from?"

"Tell him I'm calling from outer space and he'd better get his ass on the phone."

"Thank you. Please hold."

On a deep-space vessel, a legacy from another age—an age with vaster resources and grander dreams—these voyagers will cross to the other side of the sun, where waits an untrodden planet that has beckoned humankind for a million

* * *

"I've been looking all over for you," said Bass to Kirov. "Daewoo is here. They say they need a release for any damage to the Earth's atmosphere or the Van Allen Belts before they can insert the nuclear core in the engine."

"So sign it!" Kirov said, covering the phone receiver with her palm. "Fake a name."

"I already did," said Bass, who had signed it Abbie Hoffman. "Meanwhile, there's this guy from *National Geographic* on the bridge and he won't leave until he talks to you "

"Tell him he has to deal with you. Can't you see I'm on the phone? Is all the equipment off the *Old Moulmein Pagoda*? And tell Jeffries to stow that bag; he looks stupid carrying it around. Did you get through to Mission Design?"

"Okay. I can. It is. I did. He says it's scientific instruments and he has to hang on to it until after delta V. And Mission Design's phone is disconnected."

"Disconnected? Impossible. Go on back to the bridge and keep trying. I'll be there as soon as I get off the phone."

"How come you're calling from down here instead of up on the bridge?"

"The bridge phone's shunted through the Krishna-Bell satellite, which Disney-Gerber owns. I don't want to use it till we're under way. This phone's clean."

"Kirov, are you there?" Markson said.

voyage in the greatest spaceship ever built, a ship so magnificent in its size and power that if mankind were to disappear from the universe, this awesome artifact would in itself be glorious testimony to the greatness of

Markson's giant image on the forty-eight-inch screen faded into a thin, blue crescent Earth, as seen from high orbit. In the nearer darkness, a shape blocked out the horizon as it passed, spinning slowly, into the sunlight. It was a spaceship, impossibly huge, ghostly, cold. Meanwhile, Markson's live image on the small phone screen looked harassed and hurried.

"Kirov. Are you there?"

"I'm here," Kirov said. "What is this? You tell me to call and then you put me on hold. What's going on? You call this a press conference? Six people? And that's counting the kid from Nixon Station . . ."

"She bugged Johnson and he brought her along. We need bodies to fill out the video. It was too short notice to get any others. Anyway, I was told there were twelve."

"Half of them are sick. They won't leave the shuttle. And these Movie Stars, they haven't said a word."

"We had to drug them so they wouldn't throw up. They'll be okay in a day or two. Is Glamour filming the press conference?"

"No, he doesn't want to put the *Demogorgon* together until we're under way. Says it takes nine hours."

"Then what's the point!"

"That's what I'm asking you. Meanwhile, how come Bass can't get through to Mission Design?"

technology that makes this voyage possible is an exciting mix of old and new. A spaceship as vast as the Titanic, *from the past . . . and a time-compressing technique that has been a Hollywood secret now for a decade . . .*

"The *Titanic*?" said *Still Rolling Stone.*

On the big screen, the Earth and the ship were gone. An orange crescent grew larger in the screen even as it filled out into a quarter and then a half-globe. Bass, on his way to the bridge, stopped, fascinated, to watch.

"Wait up," said Glamour from the other side of the ballroom.

"That's why I was calling you," Markson said on the phone. "Mission Design's having some kind of cash flow problem. That's why their phone's been disconnected."

red planet Mars.

* * *

On the big screen, to the strains of a Strauss waltz, the ocher globe drifted closer until it became sky. Bass recognized this as a digitized enhanced sequence from the old *Viking* orbiters of the last century. On the horizon, the atmosphere, one twentieth of Earth's, was a tiered bronze haze. From space, Mars looked like the Horn of Africa or the Sinai. A world without cities or seas. Clouds as rare as mountain goats.

"Disconnected?" said Kirov.

"They were supposed to send up a technical video for the press conference, but it never came. Can you wing it? I've already patched in the intro."

"Wing it? You mean the press or the flight?"

red sands of that exotic landscape, never before traversed by the human foot, the most exciting talents in cinema will produce a film that is destined to be seen by every living individual on Earth. This film is expected to cost a little under three billion dollars, making it the most expensive motion picture in

"It's not like the ship can't handle an extra," *National Geographic* protested. "I've done my homework: the *Mary Poppins* is equipped to handle sixty people. The voyage is not weight or mass critical. The supplies are not limited. So what's the problem?"

"The problem is not the voyage," Bass said. "The problem is the landing. The lander, which is already in orbit around Mars, is *very* mass and fuel critical. The way we've calculated it there's barely room for the six of us. When we got to Mars you would be stuck in orbit for twenty-eight days while we were on the surface."

"It would be like going to the movies and staying in the lobby," offered Glamour.

"I demand to speak with the Captain."

"That's her final word on the subject," Bass said. "You're

welcome to join the rest of the press in the ballroom, where she's speaking right now. But I must ask you to leave the bridge."

"Let's go, pal," said Glamour.

all been waiting for, gentlemen, ladies, let me introduce the commander of our mission: a woman who has excited great curiosity and interest both in the west and in the east, a woman who in her own person and her career symbolizes the eternal bond of friendship between

"I'm Captain Kirov," Kirov said, switching off the big screen behind her. "Ours is what is known as a conjunction class voyage. Every two years a 'window' is available; an alignment of Earth, Mars, Venus and the sun that allows TMI with a minimum expenditure of energy. Ours opens tomorrow morning at precisely nine-oh-six A.M., Beverly Hills Time. Any questions so far? Good."

Reader's Digest leaned over to the reporter next to him and whispered, "What's TMI?"

"Trans-Mars Injection," Greetings whispered back. She had braided her almost blond hair in the back in an imitation of Kirov's and borrowed Johnson's copy of *The Spaceman's Bible.*

"Thanks. What rag you with?"

"*Seventeen.*"

"Fifteen hundred meters from here," the Captain continued, "behind a heat and radiation shield, is our primary engine, a Daewoo 440 class II, a detuned version of a nuclear thruster built for deep-space cometary probes, which generates some three hundred and fifty thousand newtons of thrust. A small reactor superheats water—ordinary table water—and expels it at almost four percent of the speed of light: with that velocity only a small amount is needed to move a mass as great as the ship we are now on. The engine will fire only four times, once to speed up and once to slow down on each leg of the trip."

Glamour glided in along the ceiling with a note from Bass on the bridge: *Hurry it up. Just got word from Johnson that an Ariane is staging up from Midlands. Thinks it's the UN*.

Kirov paused to read the note, then went on:

"It is the Daewoo engine that makes possible the size of the great ship around you. With the efficiency of nuclear power we can attain escape velocity without the crippling mass of the fuel supplies necessary for chemical-powered ships. Plus, since we know there is considerable water ice on the Martian satellites, we have only to take the expellant for the outbound trip.

"Eight months after our controlled nuclear burn, or delta V, we will transit Venus, going very close in a sort of crack-the-whip maneuver to change our trajectory and gain velocity. Four months later a braking burn will slow us sufficiently for Mars capture. We will be in a stable orbit alongside the inner moon, Phobos, where we will rendezvous with the Mars lander sent twenty years before. The previous unmanned missions, as you may know, were orbital, and used the moons of Mars to provide fuel and raw materials for the lander, the *Konstantin Tsiolkovsky*, which is also in orbit.

"There will begin the only fuel-critical portion of the trip, as with a combination of chemical and aerobraking we enter the Martian atmosphere and land on the south rim of the western end of the Valles Marineris system. There we expect to find—but we're running over our time. Are there any questions so far?"

"Is your husband a Communist?"

"What do you think of American movies?"

"When are the Movie Stars going to wake up?"

"We're not asleep," said Fonda-Fox, without opening his eyes. "Just resting."

"If there are no further questions, I will turn you over to our Chief Medical Officer, Dr. S. C. Jeffries."

"Bass, you guys better get a move on," Johnson called from the *Pagoda*. "I have a second blip coming up from Dry

Lake, California. Bet it's Disney-Gerber with a payload of lawyers."

"I heard that," said Kirov, who was just entering the bridge. "Get ready to take on passengers, Johnson. We're sending everybody back over." She punched in a rock tape and "A Whiter Shade of Pale" filled the bridge just as they crossed the terminator. Far below, Chesapeake Bay was robed in dawn mists; then the long ridges of the Appalachians, low and even, like a rug that had been kicked.

"Ain't that a sight," said Bass, wondering if this would be his last look at the South.

"There's Kentucky," Johnson said. "Ever eat a ground-hog?"

"Ate a possum once," Bass said.

"What does it taste like?"

"Possum? Tastes just like groundhog."

"The return trip will take eighteen months, during which, as on the way out, we will be in the ursa state, or hibernation," Jeffries explained as he rushed the six visitors through the second of the two wardrooms where the crew would sleep the long miles away. "This technique was developed by, uh, certain researchers who were able to isolate the HT, or hibernation trigger, from sleeping bears. The ursa state itself reduces body intake and waste to almost zero, and has been shown to counteract muscle loss and bone decalcification, which have been problems with extended periods in space. Before we go on, are there any questions?"

"Will you all sleep in the nude?"

"How come it's so cold and smelly?"

"What about solar flares?"

"Do the Stars have their own bathroom?"

"Do you expect to find life on Mars?"

"We have an automatic alarm system for solar flares," Jeffries said, "that activates a polarized water shielding by enveloping the ship in a temporary fog. And the question of life on Mars was answered, I'm sorry to say, by *Viking*, in the negative. Now down the hall here we have the library, where all the world's great literature, music and film is stored on CD. Notice the beautiful birch paneling. The carpets are from"—he checked the brochure Markson had sent up—"Astrakhan."

"Please allow me to introduce myself. I am a man of wealth and taste . . ." came over the speakers·

"And here we are at the bridge."

The long stalk that held the barcas and control consoles extended at a slight "upward" angle, like a bowsprit, from the front of the *Mary Poppins*. It was surrounded by a plexi bubble that was darkened except for a single forward panel, giving the illusion that the bridge was as enclosed as the habitat cylinders. The darkened plexi also served, in several locations, as viewscreens. "This screen shows the rear of the ship," Kirov explained. "These screens are in constant communication with Mission Design [or at least, they're supposed to be! she added to herself] and with the front office in Beverly Hills. But they will become increasingly redundant as we get farther and farther from Earth. By the time we get to Mars, it will take fifteen minutes each way for the radio waves to make the trip, making normal conversation impossible. And now, hold on—"

With the twist of a rheo she spun down the lights and luced the plexi. A gasp went up from the press as the wall seemed to disappear and they were in space itself, with nothing between themselves and the ice-on-velvet stars, or the blue, grinning Earth below and behind. The reporters all grabbed the closest part of the stalk, or one another.

Even Glamour gasped. Behind, the blue-green light seemed alive, and why not? It was tossed off clouds and wavetips, whitened on the sides of sheep and grinding glaciers, then flung back into space.

Ahead was a darkness so vast that a hundred million giant fiery suns seemed mere points of light.

Kirov turned the rheo back up and darkened the plexi. A

sigh of relief was heard; they were "inside" again.

"Farewell, ladies and gentlemen. Thank you for coming. Dr. Jeffries, as soon as he stows his bag, will take you to the air lock, where your shuttle is waiting to take you back down to Nixon Station and from there to Orange County Airport."

"You mean to John Wayne International," said *National Geographic*.

"To whatever."

10

AAA 000 GAAA

The ten-minute warning sounded far away to Kirov, as if it were sounding for someone else's departure, on some other ship. For the past two hours, since the press had been off-loaded, the atmosphere on the *Mary Poppins* had been bled down toward the one-third Earth atmosphere (five pounds per square inch) that would be maintained for the voyage. The thinner air made it hard to talk or listen to rock and roll without earphones, and made whispering impossible.

Bon Voyage, Mars Voyagers! flashed on the bridge com-screen, a message from Markson. Bass and Kirov looked at each other and winced. Didn't these Hollywood people know that farewells were bad luck?

"Good luck. See you at the Spaceman's Ball," came a familiar voice. Johnson had patched into the earcoms for the traditional spacers' nonfarewell. Kirov came back, "You got it." Both sounded the same to Bass even though Kirov was in the barca right beside his, and Johnson was on the *Old Moulmein Pagoda* 12.1 miles away, just outside the 12-mile safety limit mandated for nuclear operations.

"You got it," said Bass.

AAA 000 GAAA

"Five minutes. Prepare for delta-V positioning."

Kirov's voice had a new edge.

Johnson held up a borrowed zoom lens and watched the little wisps of gas from the OMEs as the *Mary Poppins* po-

69

sitioned herself for delta V. The ship's nuclear power plant was too large for such small maneuvers. It would ignite in 8 minutes, in a 5-g burn that would bring the *Mary Poppins* to MTI velocity in 11.5 minutes.

Mars. Johnson felt a twinge of envy, but only a twinge. It wasn't like the old days. Johnson had been a kid when Armstrong had walked on the Moon, but he remembered watching it on TV with the rest of the world. Now nobody but the magazines cared. The press pool was filming the ship's departure, but it wouldn't be on the news unless the ship blew up.

"Wish you were going?" asked *National Geographic*. The reporter was sharing the *Pagoda*'s bridge with Johnson. "My boss made me ask, but I'm glad they turned me down."

Johnson darkened the windows against the coming nuclear blast. Twelve miles away, the *Mary Poppins* was a string of lights, like a little city seen from far off on the plains.

"Do I wish I was going? Yeah, I wish I was going."

"Mission Design is on the horn," Bass said. Kirov took the call, relieved. "Well, finally," she said.

"My name's Sweeney," said a young man in front of a bank of computers. He was wearing a white drip-dry shirt with a plastic pencil holder and blue gabardine pants, NASA style. "Sorry for the delay. We've been having trouble with the phone company and—"

"Save it for later," Kirov said. "Are we Go?"

"Looks all Go from here. Got your locks?"

"Just coming in," Kirov said. There they were, lighting up on the board like fireflies: Dili Station, Darwin Bay, Arcturus, CN-861. Kirov keyed in the ship's gyros while Bass punched in the computer lock search with one hand, pulling his Red Man out of the console with the other. The appearance of Bass's chewing tobacco was as sure a sign of imminent departure as gantry ropes dropping.

"You've got Go in twelve minutes," said Sweeney.

"Check," said Kirov. "Starting countdown." If they missed

now the burn would have to wait another six hours. If they missed twice they had to wait a week. If they missed three times the trip was scrubbed. That would be disaster, Markson had warned, since Pellucidar had already booked three years of nonrefundable full-page ads in *Variety* and *People*.

The job of the Third, or Medical, Officer was to secure the personnel. Nuclear delta V was close to 8 gs, long and hard: very different from the shuttle, which at 4.6 gs was no worse than a drag racer. A dropped arm or a head rolled to one side in nuclear delta V could mean a broken arm or neck. In theory, of course: the Daewoo nuclear had never been used in manned flight.

As Jeffries strapped the Movie Stars into the second row of barcas, he wondered if anyone had checked them out for space. He had checked their blood scans to make sure they could tolerate the HT, but he had never met either of them until the press conference. Beverly Glenn had scrubbed off the makeup she had worn for the press conference. Without it, and with her long blond hair hidden under a watch cap, she looked at once more serious and less intimidating. She smiled bravely at Jeffries as he strapped her down.

Fonda-Fox had his eyes closed, looking as relaxed as a man in a dentist's chair.

Glamour's eyes were wide open.

"Earth lock complete," said Bass. "Star lock complete." The computer began the search for the two stars and two swiftly moving Earth stations. At Dili, flies buzzed crazily against a screen. At Arcturus, at the far end of the universe, hydrogen fires spat.

"Print it," said Kirov. The seventh coordinate was time, and it was counting down. Bass saw a storm darkening the Khyber Pass, so familiar from above; he had never seen it from the ground.

"You've got Go in thirty-eight seconds," said Sweeney from Mission Design.

"I'll take it."

Bass turned to Kirov with a grin, his first, she realized, all day. "Think it'll fly, Captain?"

Kirov wondered why Jeffries had his medical bag on his lap; hadn't she asked them to stow everything? He made a damn poor Third Officer.

Eighteen, seventeen, sixteen. Without her makeup, Beverly Glenn looked better, almost Russian.

"OPR," said Bass.

"OPR check," said Kirov.

Twelve, eleven, ten. Was Jeffries squirming, or was that the bag on his lap, or was it Kirov's imagination? Glamour looked like a madman. Eight, seven. Kirov grinned across at Bass. Two, one.

"You have preignition."

"You have . . ."

. . . and she was squeezing the trigger, just like in her Moscow high-school rifle club, while the computers watched the target: all girls should learn to shoot: a tiny garnet-colored target hidden behind the sun: lead it a million, no a million million, miles . . .

"You have ignition."

"You have Go."

Not long after his real father turned up, or was turned up, Jeffries's mother remarried and moved to Cincinnati. His stepfather put him into a private school with mostly white kids. After his second bloody nose he ran away, walking across the railroad bridge to Kentucky, where a Black trainman sneaked him into a boxcar heading for Atlanta where his father was in prison and his grandmother still lived. He was twelve but he looked sixteen, or the trainman would have sent him home. He fell asleep and woke up in the dark. The floor of the car was cold and the train wasn't moving. For a long, terrifying instant, he couldn't remember his old name or his new one. Then he heard what sounded like thunder, far away but coming closer. For some reason, he thought it was coming for him. He leaned out the door of the boxcar to see. Suddenly, brutally, something hit him, jerking the floor out from under him, and slamming the door into the side of his face. He fell and saw that the train was moving, taking up the slack in the unbumpered connections between the cars in a long, crashing roar. He jumped out of the car the next time it slowed down, and called his stepfather, Dr. Jeffries, who came and picked him up. He'd gone only seventy miles. He took a bath and went to bed. He stayed in school all the way through college, and beyond.

The delta V when it came was just such a roar, like thunder through the long bones of the ship. Jeffries was no more ready this time, and he felt just as betrayed and just as helpless. The booming was behind, over and around him, jerking his head to one side, kicking the black bag on his lap into his belly. It took all his strength to raise one hand. He found himself, again, struggling not to cry.

From twenty miles away all that could be seen was a sudden starburst of silver: a crystal cloud of water vapor blossoming like a white rose. A soundless light wave washed over the *Old Moulmein Pagoda* seconds later. When it faded, the white rose cloud was fading and the ship that had been inside it was gone. "See you at the Spaceman's Ball," Johnson said, saluting as he prepared his ship for reentry.

For two minutes they were heavier than any humans should ever be. Four minutes. Six minutes. Fonda-Fox weighed 865 pounds and found it hard to breathe. Beverly Glenn (560 pounds) looked down and saw that for the first time since the summer she turned twelve, she was flat-chested. Glamour, at 430 pounds, found his grin frozen on his face, his eyes locked open. The ship went dark (was this normal?). The distant roar got closer, then quit. There was no sound, just groans: all the more chilling when Fonda-Fox realized that the groans were screams mashed flat...

* * *

The weightlessness when it came this time was not like flying, but like being thrown. Glamour gritted his teeth, waiting to hit. After the violence of the acceleration, it took a minute, or even two, to believe that the zero g was not just the windup for another punch. A sigh came from Beverly Glenn, and Fonda-Fox realized that a sigh was just a weightless groan.

They were falling. They would fall for a year and a half, into Venus and back out; into the gravity well of the sun, and back out; into the desiccated red arms of Mars.

"*Mary Poppins*, this is Mission Design," said Sweeney. "I have you in the slot, that's In The Slot. Congratulations." Already his voice sounded faint, or was that Kirov's imagination?

"Do I hear cheering in the background?" she said, remembering Houston's giant communications room.

"More phone trouble," Sweeney said. "I'm calling from a bar across the street. The Lakers are up ten points."

"What's that yowling?" Kirov said, turning around.

Glamour and Fonda-Fox were both laughing. Jeffries, who had unzipped his bag, was holding up a gray and orange cat that was frantically searching with its paws for purchase in the air.

"What in the hell?" Kirov demanded. "That's your cat?"

"As Medical Officer, it's my judgment that nonhuman life is essential to the human spirit, and therefore to the success—"

"I can't believe this. That's your cat?"

"The ship's cat," Jeffries said.

"A two-pound cat. A stowaway. An insubordination. An unauthorized fucking overload," Kirov said.

"So what? We're not mass critical."

"Not here," Kirov said. "But what are you going to do with your cat when we get to Mars, and we go down? The *Tsiolkovsky* is mass critical: it's a chemical-powered lander. What about your cat then? You going to put it to sleep? Leave your little stowaway in Mars orbit for two weeks, alone?"

"Three weeks," said Bass.

Jeffries shrugged. He hadn't thought of that.

"Here, kitty, kitty, kitty," said Beverly Glenn.

"Help," said a voice from the rear of the bridge.

Bass looked at Kirov, Jeffries looked at Bass, and they all three turned and looked at their second stowaway. She had two black eyes and a split lip; she had wet her pants and was holding her elbow. "I think I broke something," she said.

"I'll be damned," said Bass. "It's the kid."

Greetings Brother Buffalo.

BOOK
TWO

Into this wild abyss,
the womb of nature
and perhaps her grave...
—MILTON

1

PELLUCIDAR PICTURES
FOR IMMEDIATE RELEASE

The red planet Mars is at this moment 60,678,098 miles from
the Earth.
       60,678,112
       60,678,124
In fact, every six seconds, the time it has taken you to read
this far, it has traveled another ninety miles on its circuit
around the sun. Our sun has nine planets, and they are all
in constant motion relative to one another, to the sun, and
with the sun, to the galaxy within which they turn as the
galaxy itself travels around a distant and unknown Galactic
Center.

    It is through this whirling maze of planetary activity that
humankind's greatest adventure is taking place: the voyage
to Mars for the making of the most ambitious, most expensive,
and most spectacular film ever made by a major Hollywood
studio.

    At this very moment, in the awesome, soundless depths of
space, the courageous Mars Voyagers are dreaming, using a
unique and hitherto little-known technology to sleep for eighteen months while their life processes slow almost to a stop:
a state heretofore known only to humankind's gruff cousin,
the bear.

    Thanks to modern HT (hibernation trigger) technology,
the Mars Voyagers' intake and elimination will drop to zero,

aging will almost cease, respiration will drop to less than 12 percent of normal. Thus not only is the boredom of the long trip avoided, but the bone and muscle deterioration feared in a long voyage at zero g is prevented, since HT is known to trigger a calcium and protein fixer that preserves the muscle tone of the bear, the King of the Forest. The HT serum is extracted from the frozen urine of the now-extinct Ursus horribilis, the legendary grizzly bear that once roamed the Rocky Mountains of the US and Canada.

Triggered by ingenious skin-patch chemical clocks, the voyagers will awaken only once during their eighteen-month voyage, in two shifts: the first shift sometime in mid-October for the Venus Transit, an interplanetary game of crack-the-whip in which a daringly close approach to the planet Venus is made in order to add velocity to the Mars ship, and at the same time alter its direction, sending it on the final leg of its historic voyage to the mysterious, beckoning . . .

BAM!

CRASH!

COMMANDER, THE ALIENS HAVE—

COME FOR SUPPER, BOYS! RATATATATATATATA!

OH MY KEERSHABLAMA FLANG!

As Bass awakened, the shots and screams receded to a barely noticeable commotion in the background of his consciousness. He was hungry. He stretched. He groaned. The delicious image of a paw overflowing with red berries drifted past his nose . . .

Paw?

Berries?

He opened his eyes. He was in a large room with curved walls, where both light and gravity were dim. He was wearing flannel pajamas and wrapped in a down sleeping bag; he was bobbing near the ceiling against the wall. Or was it a ceiling? It wore a rug. Around him, also in sleeping bags, other sleepers snored. The room was filled with a strong, musty, but not unpleasant odor. All the men had beards, and all the women long hair. A blonde in a NASA cap and a kid with her arm in a cast snored at the base of a giant plant. A dwarf—or was it a midget?—with a knit hat pulled down over his ears slept with his leg tied to a pipe, drifting out and falling back with each breath.

The NASA hat brought back memories, but Bass couldn't slow them down enough to look at them.

It was cold. That seemed right. In another room a TV droned shots and screams. Bass had to pee, but not too bad.

Curling up against the ceiling, he went back to sleep.

FOLLOW ME, BOYS! THE SPACE SCOOTER IS STILL ON—

Glamour opened one eye, shut it. Opened another. Shut it. What was that racket? He opened both eyes. Dr. Jeffries was leaning over him, poking his chest. Beside him, Bass muttered sleepily, "Who's there?"

"Morning, gentlemen," Jeffries said. He felt both their foreheads, but it was just a formality, since he had been monitoring their temperatures from the readouts on their dicktracies since he had awakened almost an hour ago.

"What's that racket?" Glamour asked.

"The snoring? That's Fonda-Fox and Beverly Glenn, our Movie Stars. They both snore. It's funny, but most Movie Stars snore. It's apparently connected with the genetic patents which—"

"Not the snoring. The shots, the screams."

"Oh, that." Jeffries pointed toward a speaker near the door. "Saturday morning cartoon sound tracks. We use them at the clinic. Studies have shown that the sound is very reassuring and anxiety-reducing, at least to Americans."

"We've been listening to that racket for six months?" Glamour muttered. He was yawning and pulling his beard, amazed at how long it was.

"Just for the past six days," Jeffries said. "It's for the light sleep transition. Here, I'll turn it off."

*   *   *

Bass headed "up" the center of the hab cylinder to where it connected with the central axis of the ship. The sleepers were bunched up against the walls. If the ship had been unfolded (the umbrella opened) before going into the slow spin necessary to stabilize temperatures, the centrifugal force toward the ends of the outflung hab cylinders would have provided a light simulation of gravity. But since they were only going to be sleeping, the Mars Voyagers had elected against it. Gravity was, as the stowaway had put it, "a drag." With the cylinders still folded along the axis, the spin provided only a fractional whisper of weight, so that the sleepers floated like butterflies amid the kudzu, drifting off the curved walls with every breath, sigh and dream.

The axis tunnel was cold. The walls were clammy and moldy, and Bass could feel the endless uncaring vacuum of space through them, sucking at his bones. The ship was as silent as a tomb. It was hard to believe they had been asleep for only six months. It seemed more like a thousand years. At the end of the central tube, far ahead, there was a light.

For an instant, Bass thought he had left the bridge lights on. Then he remembered where they were: falling into the luminescent gravity well of Venus. He found the bridge flooded with a cold ghost light unlike any light he, or any man, had ever seen before.

While Glamour joined Bass on the bridge, Jeffries separated the sleepers. Perhaps in response to the lonesomeness of space, they had drifted together into clusters and piles. They had to be separated every few months lest on awakening, like wolves, they formed cliques based on smell.

Beverly Glenn and Fonda-Fox slept curled up together like puppies. She snored delicately, the golden curls she liked to hide under a cap framing her peaches-and-cream cheeks. Their faces were almost cheek to cheek, and their features blended into a genetic cloud of memories: for Jeffries, it was like watching a montage of old movie stills, the familiar, beloved faces of fifty years all mingled together.

Beverly Glenn was supposed to have awakened this shift, along with Bass, Glamour and Jeffries, but something had gone wrong with her skin patch. Jeffries checked her pulse and temperature by hand before looking at her dicktracy: everything was okay. They would be awake for forty-eight hours, and there was plenty of time for her to wake up.

He pulled Fonda-Fox from her side and floated him over against the ceiling.

Greetings Brother Buffalo, the stowaway, and Kirov slept tangled together in the hollow of a great Siberian kudzu vine. Greetings's black eyes and fat lip were long healed, and Jeffries unclipped the cast on her arm and checked the bone with his spectra. It had already knit; he uncast and rewrapped the arm in an aloecloth, dating it to be changed in three months. As Medical Officer, he would awaken with both shifts.

Kirov looked both fierce and motherly with her cap down over her eyes and her arm around the girl's shoulder. Jeffries started to separate them, and then on second thought left them together. The kid was a special case; she could use a wolf to look after her.

"*Mary Poppins* calling Earth. *Mary Poppins* calling Earth, come on. Come on, Mission Design."

Since they were 32,231,195 miles from Earth, it would take almost three minutes for the message to reach California, and three more for the return. Bass leaned back in his barca and watched the planet ahead slowly stop rotating as the servos gradually brought the bridge into stationary alignment with it. Glamour, entering the bridge from the still rotating axis tunnel, had to grab the back of a barca to stop his own slow spin.

After twelve minutes, Bass tried the radio again, then direct-dialed Markson in Beverly Hills.

"Pellucidar Pictures," came the answer six minutes later. "Mr. Markson's office. Who might I say is calling?"

Then Markson's voice cut in: "Kirov, is that you? Cancel my lunch date, Donna, it's the Mars Voyagers! Kirov?"

"Kirov is asleep, Markson; it's me, Bass. Can you call Mission Design for me? I can't seem to get Sweeney on the radio."

"Kirov, are you there? What a great historical moment. How come they're not answering? Donna, cancel my lunch date, I say."

"You don't have one, Mr. Markson."

"Kirov, are you there?"

Markson wasn't allowing for the three-minute time delay, so it sounded like two separate conversations, then three, as Sweeney cut in on the radio: "Mission Design here. I can't talk now, though. I'll have to call you guys back at six o'clock, BHT, after I get off work."

"Kirov, are you there? Donna, did they hang up?"

"Off work? Sweeney, we need to confirm our trajectory one more time," Bass said. "We'll be making Venus Transit in a little over nine hours."

"Over," said Sweeney, signing off.

"What does he mean, off work?" said Bass.

"Kirov, are you there?" Markson said.

"Nine hours!" said Glamour.

"Huh?"

For the first time Bass noticed Glamour floating above the console, staring at the planet dead ahead. It was twice the size of the Moon from the Earth and ten times as bright; it was like the Moon through clouds except that the clouds were on it, not in front of it, and it floated in a black ink sky so deep that Glamour knew if he ever started falling he would fall forever.

"Are you okay?" Bass asked.

"Yeah, I'm okay. Nine hours! That means I have time to put the *Demogorgon* together, if you'll help me. How about it? I've got to book this image, man!"

Ahab, like Louis Glamour, had found his element in zero g. Glad to have the humans asleep for six months, he had roamed the ship's long corridors, sailing like a flying squirrel with his paws tucked up, using his claws to orient himself on the Velcro wall patches. When he wanted warmth he just fastened himself to a sleeper's back or belly and dozed peacefully. When he wanted companionship . . .

But he never wanted companionship. He was a cat. Now that half of the humans were awake again, he was irritated, although he didn't know why.

He followed one of them out of Hab #1, across the axis tunnel, and into the second of the three cylinders. The day room, bathrooms, kitchen and cat box were all in the Stalin Lounge in the lower end of Hab #2. Jeffries emptied the electrostatic cat box and opened some fresh cat food. Although there was a timed device that had fed Ahab dry food for six months, a special treat seemed in order. The way the cat was rubbing against his leg, Jeffries could tell he had been lonely and was glad to see him.

("How did you know there would be cat food and a cat box on the ship?" Greetings had asked six months before, holding the cat in one arm while Jeffries set the other, broken one

"Common sense," Jeffries had said. "The original voyage was planned for sixty-six people to be awake the whole time, with every convenience and comfort known to man. Doesn't that include a cat?")

The cupboard in the Stalin Lounge was cold and there was something Jeffries hadn't seen before: cockroaches. They seemed to adapt to zero g very well. Jeffries wondered if they even noticed.

He grabbed two boxes of cereal, some nuts and berries, and mixed up some cold milk. He knew what Glamour and Bass would be wanting. He wanted it himself

"What if Beverly Glenn doesn't wake up?" Bass said between mouthfuls of Froot Loops.

"Then I'll put on a new skin patch and wake her up with the other shift in three months," said Jeffries. "No big problem· Meanwhile, how are you guys feeling?"

"Fine," said Bass.

"Fine," said Glamour, who was anxious to start putting his camera together.

"No weird yearnings?"

"Well—"

"Normal," Jeffries said. "Have some more party mix. Don't forget, your nervous system has been on the bear path for six months now . . ."

"Earth to Mars Voyagers, this is Sweeney at Sweeney's Mission Design. We have you loud and clear. Congratulations on a smooth flight so far! Your coords and vectors are coming through straight onto disk. Meanwhile, I'm faxing through some messages from Markson and a batch of clippings, most of them I'm afraid from the local Hollywood trades. There hasn't been much interest in the voyage lately in the national press."

The video was bad, but Bass could make out a thirtyish white man in a drip-dry shirt and blue pants, standing in front of a bank of monitors.

"We're three hours from Venus Transit," Bass said. "Personnel all A-okay. How come you were so hard to reach, Sweeney? Come on."

The answer came back 5.8 minutes later.

"What happened was, I had to take a regular day job and I'm running Sweeney's at night. Figures just came up, Bass, and you're right on the money. The swing-by will bring you to within eighty kilometers of Venus, somewhat tighter than originally planned. We're looking for a forty-six-point-one-degree trajectory change, which will give us enough speed and put us on course for Mars orbit insertion. I've already sent the math through, it'll be on the disk under VT. I've got a call through to Markson. Looks like you need a haircut or is that the video? How's the weather? Where'd the other boys go, come on?"

"They're back in Hab #2 putting together the camera."

* * *

"So what's in the other boxes?" Jeffries asked. "The lights and reflectors stuff?"

"Don't need that crap with a *Demogorgon*," Glamour said as he pried the wooden cases open with a teflarbar. "It's all camera."

"But you've got twelve boxes here," Jeffries said. "I thought the *Demogorgon* was a hand-held."

"It is and it isn't," Glamour said. Assembled on Earth, the *Demogorgon* weighed 213.3 pounds. In interplanetary free fall it was, of course, weightless. "On Mars it'll weigh in at about seventy-five pounds."

"But that's more than you weigh!"

"Little folks are strong."

"Besides," Jeffries protested, "all this stuff can't possibly fit into one camera."

But it did. Each piece fit into another, like a Chinese box puzzle. Glamour began to fit pieces together and hand them to Jeffries, who would find that the piece he had been given nestled perfectly into the one he was holding, which he gave back to Glamour, who fit it into another . . . until two hours later all twelve crates of lenses, disk drives, servos, control boards, reel assemblies and refrax intregonometers had been assembled into one device the size of a suitcase, the shape of a video camera, and the approximate density of a neutron star.

While Glamour took the *Demogorgon* to the bridge, Jeffries checked the sleepers one more time. There was no point in strapping them down. Even though the ship was making an almost right-angle turn, it was following a straight line through the gravity-warped dominions of Venus. The transit would be eventless, weightless and perfectly smooth—or they would all be dead.

"Where you from in the South?" asked Bass as Jeffries arrived on the bridge with a jar of honey.

"What makes you think I'm from the South? I'm from Cincinnati. My father was from Atlanta but I hardly ever saw him. My real father, that is."

"I'm from Georgia myself but I've been living in Kentucky since they sold NASA. Few acres on a hillside near Horse Branch."

"Think you'll ever see it again?"

Bass looked at him sideways. "That's just the question I've been asking myself."

The planet forward had grown to the size of Earth from high orbit. It was a world all clouds and it filled the sky completely. The radios were off, the lights were down. Glamour was hanging near the end of the control stalk, filming nonstop the stormy, pearl-colored, world-sized bowl of clouds and lightning they were fast falling toward.

While Jeffries opened the honey.

While Bass fished through his Red Man looking for a nice piece.

2

VENUS, THE SECOND PLANET from the sun, rode the heavens moonless, mysterious, alone. It filled the forward view from the bridge, a planet of clouds like a ball of sky in space, pearlescent; two thirds, then one third, of its disk in daylight; its curving nightside illuminated by ominous flashes of lightning under the clouds. It was the closest Bass had ever been to any planet except Earth and its dead, still-attached twin, the Moon.

They were diving toward nightside.

"When do you take over the controls?" Glamour asked. It reassured him that Bass was in the pilot's barca, even if he was just sitting and dipping honey out of a jar with his fingers. Honey was one of the few everyday substances that didn't change its character in zero g.

"I don't," Bass said. "What we can do was done six months ago, with the after-burn correction. The *Mary P.* is too big for last-minute course adjustments. According to Mission Design, we're going to scrape the paint off that planet. But unless something goes wrong, I'll just sit and watch."

"And if something goes wrong?"

"I'll sit and watch that."

What could go wrong? Jeffries wondered, but knew enough not to ask. He kept his mouth shut and answered himself: *We could bump atmosphere, or an unseen debris ring. Or mascons, gravitational anomalies like on the Moon. Or something we never thought of. Or something that never thought of us. A thousand things, or nothing.*

For the next three hours, the three men sat silent, eating cold cereal out of the box and nuts and berries out of baggies, while the planet expanded in their view. Jeffries brought the cat forward but Ahab didn't like Venus; one look and he was gone, back to the Stalin Lounge.

Glamour hung near the ceiling, as if suspended by the almost imperceptible whine of the *Demogorgon*'s drive.

Bass began to snore.

During the Philippine War, Bass had flown the dead back to San Diego. They got their own separate plane, a C-141. It was not a coveted run and Bass drew it twice before he grew to like it and asked for it. The two nurses, assigned by some bureaucratic oversight, slept. The dead are as perfect patients as they are passengers, lying neatly in rows, never calling out for medication, never getting airsick, never crying out in pain and fear as the living so often do. Bass was their Charon, droning on above a bone-white sea of clouds, lighted even on a moonless night. Since those flights, he had ceased to dread his own death, associating it in his mind with the whine of the turbofans and the endless white loveliness of the insubstantial plain rolling on under him, and under it, the dark Pacific. When he awakened on the bridge of the *Mary Poppins*, he thought for a long moment that he was back in the cockpit of the C-141, seeing the star-lighted sea of clouds below. But there on the arms of his seat were an old man's hands. This was Venus, thirty years had flown, and he was ferrying the sleeping, not the dead.

"You awake?" said Jeffries. Bass nodded and found some more Red Man.

There was nothing womanly or sensual or inviting about the storm-lighted planet below. It and not Mars should have been called the planet of war. They were as close as a low Earth orbit, more airplane than spaceship in feeling, and below them the clouds glowed, illuminated from underneath by orange and purple flashes, like hidden battles.

"Is that lightning?" Glamour asked.

"Could be," Jeffries said. "Could be volcanoes, could be seas of fire."

"Could be gods quarreling," Bass said.

There was a horizon ahead now, barely curved, and something was coming at them over it, like a truck over a hill. Sunrise on Venus. As Bass gradually darkened the bridge glass, Jeffries watched the horizon separate swiftly into bands of blue, pink, mauve, green, indigo, blue again, then deep purple; then the sun rose from the horizon like a rocket and he realized for the first time how fast they were moving, three times faster than any satellite: for they were in transit, not orbit, not about to be captured—

"Look," Bass whispered, pointing: there were clouds not only "below" but "above" them now. The ship wasn't heating, so how could they be in the atmosphere, under the clouds?

"The atmosphere on Venus extends higher than Earth's," Bass said. "But it's not supposed to go this high. We're eighty klicks up, too high for—"

Jeffries and Bass both jumped as they passed through a cloud at 39,000 mph: a reddish flash, it was on them and gone. Then another. The ship's skin still wasn't heating: Bass checked, worried. The glass below them was still clear, and Glamour filmed straight down. The lightning on the dayside was orange and blue, leaping through indigo-shadowed canyons of cloud, like hidden many-colored waterfalls, glimpsed as they sped by. So close! Then gradually, then faster and faster, the clouds began dropping away. The *Mary Poppins* was leaving the planet behind.

Bass found their new star locks and faxed them to Sweeney's, then got up, stretched, spit into a vacuum hole in the console overhead. Glamour filmed him, then filmed Jeffries squeezing a liquid into three containers.

"Well, if we didn't make it, Sweeney'll let us know," said Bass.

"Drink up, gentlemen," Jeffries said.

"Is this another bear juice cocktail?"

"No, you don't need one," Jeffries said. "The one you

drank after delta V will last for another year. This is a neutra-neutralizer. It neutralizes the neutralizer that has been keeping you awake. But it'll take a half a day to work."

"There's a deck of cards in the lounge," said Bass.

"Now you're talking," Glamour said. He left the *Demogorgon*, hanging in the air, shutting down with a dying whine like a jet at the terminal. He'd seen enough new planets for a while. Killing time with five-card stud was familiar, it was comforting, it was wonderfully dull, it was the very essence of filmmaking; it was Hollywood.

It was also NASA.

It was also Navy.

3

PELLUCIDAR PICTURES
FOR IMMEDIATE RELEASE

"STAR" SHIP ON LAST LONG LEG
OF VOYAGE TO MARS

When the second group of sleepers awaken, they will find themselves on the far side of the sun, far from all humanity, past present and future—more alone than the first polar explorers or even the first men on the Moon—more alone than any humans have ever been before. And yet, they will have the unique comfort and reassurance of knowing that all of Hollywood is . . .

WINTER. The Coldest Winter Ever. There is a Terrorist Attack on Baronet Drive, but it's Okay: AmericaMan is in the Kitchen loading the Dishwasher with PowerPlus, and Greetings is totally safely rolled up in her comforter on the couch, as SheRa turns on the MicroMixer and the Terrorists wet their crummy Russian pants and we salute Old Glory and start to shoot—

"Wake up, little Suzie!"

Greetings groaned. It was not SheRa, but Space Commander Woman, the Russian. Why was this okay? Greetings couldn't sleep because the doctor was poking her wrist—

"Can't you turn that racket off?" Kirov asked, and Jeffries

reached up and slapped a switch. The shooting stopped. Kirov said: "Greetings—do you know where you are?"

"Hollywood? Mars?"

"Halfway between the two. You're on the *Mary Poppins*. You stowed away, remember?"

Jeffries asked: "How does your arm feel?"

The doctor was Black, like Dr. Huxtable. Suddenly, a Movie Star came into the room, upside down! He yawned. Greetings had never seen an upside-down Movie Star yawn before. He handed her a cup with a nipple on the top and a plastic bag of nuts and berries. Greetings was still trying to think of something to say when Space Commander Woman's dicktracy wrist radio beeped twice and she and the Movie Star were gone.

While Kirov took Fonda-Fox to the bridge, Greetings stayed behind to help Jeffries separate the sleepers. "Best to keep them stirred up," he said. Glamour and Bass had drifted together and slept butt to butt under a fern. Beverly Glenn snored delicately on a corner of the rug nearby. Zero g did miracles for breasts and hers were miraculous to start with. While Dr. Jeffries checked the Star's vital signs, Greetings gazed, transfixed, at her face as at a movie screen. In her features were hints and whispers of five generations of Movie Stars, of Lanas and Lornas and Lolas, most of whom Greetings knew only from her mother's old magazines. And male Stars, too.

Was that a little moustache on her upper lip? Probably makeup usually covered it

The kudzu had flourished and Kirov and Bass had to hack their way to the bridge with laser machetes. The bridge was cold and dark. The *Mary Poppins* was on the far side of the sun. Mars was no more than a reddish star in the port forward quadrant—still nine months away. Kirov watched Fonda-Fox staring; the distant look in his eyes worried her. The emptiness of space could suck the soul right out of the body, like decompression. Pushing past him to her control barca, she opaqued all the glass but one sector. It made the bridge seem almost cozy.

"*Mary Poppins* to Earth, come on. Second shift awake at—" Kirov read in the date and position coordinates, and added an auto-repeat. The message would take nine minutes to reach Earth and the reply another nine to return, so she squeezed a cup of coffee from her thermos and scrolled through the message bank.

KIROV FROM BASS. WELCOME TO THE FAR SIDE OF THE SUN. MISSION DESIGN'S READOUTS AFTER VE-NUS TRANSIT ALL OKAY. NUMBERS ON DISK FOR YOU TO CHECK. PLANTS LOOK A LITTLE PEAKED SO I PUT SOME 10-10-4 IN THE HUMIDIFIER CIRCUIT. SEE YOU IN TEN MONTHS.

"So that's it!" said Kirov. She instructed the ship's climate control computer to cut back the plant food while she scrolled on down:

BASS FROM MISSION DESIGN: THANKS FOR THE VE-NUS TRANSIT FILM. WE HAVE CONFIRMED THAT THOSE ARE CLOUDS AT 80 + K. AT THE SAME TIME THERE WAS NO SIGN OF FRICTION OR DRAG ON THE *MARY POPPINS*. THE BEST WE CAN FIGURE HERE IS THAT VENUS'S UPPER ATMOSPHERE IS LAYERED AND NOT CONTINUOUS.

MARS VOYAGERS FROM MARKSON: MARS VOYAGE IN ALL THE HEADLINES! CHECK FAX MACHINE!

MARS VOYAGERS FROM PRESIDENT, SCIENCE FIC-TION WRITERS OF AMERICA . . .

* * *

Kirov scrolled on past the junk mail and congratulatory messages. There was a whole file of faxed news clippings about the stowaway. She radioed Earth again, and then direct-dialed Markson's office at Pellucidar. He had discouraged this since, even though it was billed as a regular satellite call, the time lag ran up the charges. Of course, the first nine minutes, before Markson's secretary picked up the phone, were free.

"Pellucidar Pictures, Mr. Markson's office. Who might I say is calling? Hello? Hello?" She hung up.

The return signal from Sweeney came through half an hour later. "Hello, *Mary Poppins*. That you, Kirov? I guess you saw the figures from the Venus Transit, all A-okay. There's nothing really to do this wake-up but relax. I had a small midcourse correction burn plotted for you but you don't need it. Just as well since the computers here are tied up with the new Laker Stadium."

"New Laker Stadium?"

"Guess I forgot to tell you," Sweeney said, 18.4 minutes later. "Sweeney's Mission Design went belly-up. I have a new job with Stadium Computer Solutions in Santa Monica. Mostly we do crowd flow and traffic simulations for mall and parking lot designers. Don't worry, I'm still doing the Mars Voyage on my own time. Stadium has a big old Cray that can really crunch numbers and I use it during lunch hour. I'm sending the figures for the Mars orbital capture braking burn, nine months from now, so you can begin to run them through your shipboards. I've got a call in to Markson at Pellucidar and—Oh, I have call waiting, maybe that's him. Gloria, can we go three on this line?

"Gloria?"

The screen went dark. "Shit. We lost them," Kirov said.

"Look who's here, our celebrity!" said Fonda-Fox. Jeffries and Greetings glided, weightless, into the bridge. "It's a jungle out there," said Jeffries. It was Greetings who was the celebrity. Fonda-Fox scrolled through the message bank, showing her the headlines that had been faxed up:

TEEN STOWAWAY TO VISIT MYSTERY MARS FACE

STOWAWAY "SLEEPS" WITH STARS

"SHE'S MINE," BOASTS PROUDEST BOYFRIEND ON PLANET

"Boyfriend?" Greetings said. "I don't have a boyfriend. I don't think."

"I need volunteers for a brush-cutting party," said Kirov.

"I'll go," said Fonda-Fox.

"I need you on the bridge. Jeffries, how about you and the kid? But first let's have some coffee and wake up."

After the coffee was squeezed, Kirov cleared the bridge glass all around and everybody clutched the nearest seat or rail: the blackness of space came up as sudden and as fierce as a storm.

"Which one is Mars?" Fonda-Fox asked.

With the flashlight on her dicktracy, Kirov pointed out a middle-sized reddish star. Until then it had been just one in a sea of stars; but after it had been identified, Mars seemed to all of them to dominate the heavens ahead.

What boyfriend? Greetings wondered, searching through the faxes for details.

"Heartbeat, respiration, everything looks good," Jeffries said, shrugging. "I even did a dreamscan. She's fine. She just won't wake up."

"Isn't there something you can do?" Kirov demanded. "Surely the situation calls for more than a shrug."

Jeffries shrugged again. "Medicine is an uncertain business. I'm not treating it as a crisis because it isn't. Her health is fine. HT sleep is healthier than regular life."

"It may not be a medical crisis, but it's an artistic crisis," Fonda-Fox put in.

"What do you mean?" Kirov asked him.

"Well, maybe a business crisis. I mean the Guild. Without BG we don't have two Stars, which means we don't have a Guild-certifiable movie, which means we can't release nationally, which means we're not eligible for the Academy Awards, which . . ."

"Don't worry," said Jeffries. "You'll have your two Stars. Let Ms. Glenn sleep, I will awaken her when we get to Mars."

BOYFRIEND VOWS TO WAIT FOREVER

AS TEEN STOWAWAY ORBITS VENUS,

PLANET OF ROMANCE

"Orbits?" protested Kirov.

"Sssshhhh!" said Greetings.

Markson was on screen, holding up a newspaper and sitting on, not behind, his desk. "Hello, Mars Voyagers," he said. "Greetings, are you there? I have a surprise for you."

The camera panned across the room to a square-jawed teenager standing between Mr. and Mrs. Gentry. Mr. Gentry put his hand on the shoulder of the teenager and began talking nervously.

"Who's that, your boyfriend?" Kirov asked.

"I never saw him before in my life!" Greetings said. "But look, my parents! They're still together!"

"It's some Pellucidar contract player," guessed Fonda-Fox.

"It's all right, start over," said Markson on screen. "We can edit—"

"I took them up to the station hoping they would get back together," explained Greetings. "And now look!"

"Is this live?" asked Jeffries.

The boy was starting to talk. "Shut up so we can hear what he's saying," said Fonda-Fox.

But the signal went out, and what Greetings's boyfriend had to say was lost somewhere in the vacuum wilderness between Beverly Hills and the *Mary Poppins*.

"How'd you get into rock and roll?" Fonda-Fox asked Kirov. They were going through the checklist in the power center "south" of the Stalin Lounge. Even though most of the instruments could be checked from the bridge, Kirov liked to see the fuel cells and batteries herself and check them off visually.

"It was all over Russia. Chuck Berry. Elvis. Batteries, forward."

"Eighty-eight percent," Fonda-Fox said.

"Motown. The Beatles. Fuel cells, level one."

"Ninety-one percent."

"It was international currency. It was all we thought about. Boilaway."

"Less than three percent. Amazing. All the way out there in Russia. Batteries at ninety-six percent, solar, with only one cell out of a bank of a hundred and ninety-nine failed."

"Especially 'out there' in Russia. Background radiation."

"330 rads. Is that high?"

"Naw. Could be either solar storms or lingering pollution from the delta V. That's it."

Kirov was glad Fonda-Fox was on her shift. He made a better ship's officer than Jeffries, perhaps because he had played the part so many times.

"It's like *The Dating Game*," Greetings told Jeffries as they hacked at the kudzu in Hab #2. "I figured maybe if they took a vacation together, you know. They only got divorced when I was eight. And now Markson has hired this guy to be my boyfriend. What's he going to do, write me love letters? Do you think he's a Movie Star?"

"No. He's just an actor," Jeffries said. "If he was from one of the Four and Twenty Families, they would have mentioned his name."

"So that's the famous camera," said Kirov. Fonda-Fox was pointing it around the Stalin Lounge while she made tea. "Why don't you shoot a few feet while Glamour's asleep?"

"I wouldn't know where to start," Fonda-Fox said. "This is the first time I've ever seen one. The *Demogorgon*'s not a camera, technically, you know. It doesn't 'take' pictures. It digitizes and stores light, and then shapes and builds images out of it. It gets rid of the necessity for lighting control and even for reshooting, since it can store and manipulate a scene, even an actor's image, building and extrapolating from what's been done before. Once you've booked a certain amount of image, you can reconstruct an actor doing anything you want, even if the actor has never done it."

"So what's to keep you, or them, from doing away with actors altogether?"

"The Guild. Nothing but the Guild."

Kirov and Fonda-Fox found Jeffries and Greetings in the corridor. "That's enough brush cutting," Kirov said. "We're going back to sleep in a couple of hours anyway. Let's leave the others something to do. Follow me, I want to show you something."

At the end of the long axis corridor that led "south" of the Stalin Lounge, there was a small round door. It appeared to be turning. It led to a cold little clear plexi dome with a single barca in the center. The four voyagers crowded in. Straight back, the long beams soared almost a mile to the faraway rear engine shield. The observatory, like the bridge, was gyro-locked, so the whole fantastic, spidery assembly turned slowly against a still carpet of stars. It was only here that one could get an idea of how large the *Mary Poppins* was.

And how small.

"This is called the South Observatory," Kirov said. "I lived in orbit for almost a year when we were training on this ship and I used to come here when I wanted to be alone. Even on a ship this size, it's hard to find a place to be alone in space—as you all have learned by now."

Greetings pointed at the brightest star. It was blue-white, like a drop of pond water hanging in space. "There's Earth!"

Kirov shook her head. "That's Venus," she said. "We can't even see Earth from here."

At that, a long silence fell over the four of them.

* * *

After dinner, Jeffries checked the sleepers once more and passed out the neutra-neutralizer cocktails. Then he disappeared. Kirov left sign-off messages for Sweeney and Markson, then left Fonda-Fox and Greetings playing hearts in the Stalin Lounge, getting drowsy. She felt like being alone, so she headed for the South Observatory, but she found Jeffries already there, sitting with Ahab in his arms, staring out at the million cold stars.

She almost turned and left, then didn't. "What does the S. C. in your name stand for?" she asked after they had sat awhile.

"Sundiata Cinque."

"People call you Sundiata or Cinque?"

"Neither. Not in thirty years."

Kirov was held as if hypnotized by the sight of the ship's long beams spinning slowly in the void. Like a stick in a pond; no, a sea. She hung with one hand on the back of the barca for what seemed hours, even though she knew that staring into deep space was dangerous and could lead to depression.

It was Jeffries who broke the silence. "One thing you learn in space," he said, pulling off the seat and starting for the door.

"What?"

"That it's winter in the universe. That it always was and always will be."

4

PELLUCIDAR PICTURES
FOR IMMEDIATE RELEASE

With all its voyagers asleep, the great ship sails on. While here on Earth, we fall in love and rent movies and vote, protected by the friendly blue dome of our heavens from the horrifying immensity of space, the Mars Voyagers sail on through the void with their precious cargo of our most impossible dreams. All but lost in the interplanetary emptiness, the mile-long Mary Poppins is on the last leg of its historic journey, gradually slowing as it increases the distance between itself and the sun whose warmth we share with . . .

WITH ALL ITS VOYAGERS asleep but one, the great ship sailed on.

While on the Earth the sun rose on silent forests and set on howling cities; while reedy lakes whispered and shattering icefalls rang, while ships rusted on ocean floors and new grass broke through graveyard clay—the great ship sailed on.

With all its voyagers asleep but one, the great ship sailed on.

While on Mars the thin wind moaned; while red dust rose and fell and pooled like water; while heavy mists rose and fell like tides and clay buds grew, and cracked, and grew—bruise purple in the starwash light under two dim racing moons—the great ship sailed on.

Its velocity in relation to Mars was now decreasing, but

slowly. Its pitch and yaw were kept steady by the Arcturus lock. Its electrics hummed; its pumps whined; its tangled plants refreshed the aging air and its memory chips self-tested in their one-easy-lesson replication of life; its voyagers snorted and snored and dreamed. And on the bridge, the cat Ahab stared at the glowing orange spot ahead that grew a little larger every week.

Ahab had finally found something outside the ship that he liked to look upon.

5

VOYAGER PICTURES
FOR IMMEDIATE RELEASE

Having completed its journey across two hundred million miles of space, the Mary Poppins *will rendezvous with the red planet Mars at approximately 2:24 A.M., Beverly Hills Time, September 22, 20—. By this time the voyagers will have been awake for one and one-half days—the first time they have all been awake together since the beginning of the journey eighteen months ago—and will have just finished turning the ship for the braking burn that will reduce their speed and "park" the mile-long masterpiece of international brotherhood and technology neatly in Mars orbit alongside the innermost of the Martian moons, Phobos. Mysterious Phobos is . . .*

MARS WAS ABOUT the size of the Moon from the Earth, and all but eclipsed by the ship's giant engine heat shield a mile away.

Jeffries sat in the barca in the South Observatory with Ahab in his arms. He couldn't take his eyes off the planet. Venus had looked cold and warlike. It was Mars that seemed the planet of love: warm, womanly, ruddy and inviting and, hidden behind the heat shield, almost coy. He had been too busy with the postwake-up medical checks to get to the bridge before rollover, so he had missed the unobstructed

104

view of the planet. He had been in the Stalin Lounge when the ship had turned into alignment for the braking burn, and by the time he got to the bridge the ship was backing into Mars, the bridge pointing sunward with the bridge glass opaqued.

Now the *Mary Poppins* was quiet again, and they had Mars on video image in the Stalin Lounge. But Jeffries preferred the real thing, even half-hidden. He sat wrapped in a sleeping bag in the cold little South Observatory with Ahab on his lap, watching the red planet slowly grow behind the engine heat shield. He had hated Venus, but Mars seemed to awaken something in him, a longing he had never known before and still couldn't identify. All he could see were the poles, shrunken at midsummer, and the cloudless desert horizons at the planet's edge. It was enough.

Bass and Kirov were on the bridge, Jeffries knew, preparing for the braking burn. They didn't need any help, and if they did they could call on Fonda-Fox. He makes a better ship's officer than I do, Jeffries admitted to himself. He's always wanted to play the role. I never did.

Are the stars out tonight?

Even though he had turned the observatory speakers off, Jeffries could hear the old Flamingos tune all the way from the speakers in the Stalin Lounge, where the rest of the voyagers were hanging out, drinking tea and going through nine months of messages. The air pressure was only five pounds, one-third Earth normal, but over the eighteen-month hibernation, the crew's ears had compensated until they could hear almost normally. Jeffries wasn't surprised. HT serum had remarkable and still unexplored curative and healing effects: wasn't (and here he thought of a TV and Movie Star too famous to be named) still hosting the Academy Awards after who-was-counting-how-many years?

"Dr. Jeffries, are you asleep?"

It was the kid, Greetings, in the doorway.

"Oh, your speakers are off. Captain Kirov is calling you

from the bridge. I think she wants you to explain how come Beverly Glenn won't wake up."

The Stalin Lounge had pictures on the "walls," Astrakhan rugs on the "floor," and even a silver and porcelain Russian stove with an imitation mica window in its door that glowed cheerfully. It was cozy and almost warm. Fonda-Fox munched dry cereal and nuts and played with the live exterior video projector while Beverly Glenn snored peacefully near the ceiling. Unable to wake her, Jeffries had moved her into the lounge from Hab #3, hoping that the warmth and activity might do what the wake-up skin patch had failed to do, and stir her to consciousness.

Still, she slept on. Glamour filmed her as she slept near the ceiling, her face framed in golden ringlets. He wasn't going to wait until they landed on Mars to start booking image for the film, and the *Demogorgon* on his shoulder kept turning in her direction as if it had a mind of its own. They used to say in Hollywood that there were faces the camera loved, and the *Demogorgon* was more than a camera. Its love was obsessive.

But Glamour was worried: no matter how much image he booked of Beverly Glenn sleeping, it wouldn't edit into action if she didn't wake up. There were certain things even the *Demogorgon* couldn't do.

Glamour pushed expertly off the ceiling and during his long glide got a tracking shot of Fonda-Fox playing with the star projector, looking into the ball like a fortune-teller. Fonda-Fox image was money in the bank.

"Want to see something beautiful?" Fonda-Fox said as Greetings came back into the lounge. A touch of the projector button replaced Mars on the screen with the view "north," showing the Milky Way like a dropped wheel of stars, rolling away. "The dark spot there is called the Horsehead Nebula," Fonda-Fox said. He hit the magnifier twice. "See? It's a hundred million million miles away."

It looked more like a goat's head to Greetings, who was beginning to think astronomy, like astrology, was based on wishful thinking. "How did you learn all that?" she asked to be polite.

"My uncle," Fonda-Fox said. "When I was a kid he gave me a deep sky reflector."

"Was he a Movie Star?"

"I had a regular family too. He worked for the Post Office."

"I can't imagine what it was like in those days," Greetings said. "The government doing everything for you. Building streets, delivering mail; how did people develop any initiative at all? They must have been like robots."

"Wasn't all that bad," said Jeffries as he passed through on his way to the bridge.

"Well, look who's here," Kirov said to Jeffries. "Close the door behind you."

"We just found out that Markson is no longer at Pellucidar," Bass said. "I thought it was a little weird when I saw the press release faxed through from 'Voyager Pictures.' The studio gave us his new number. I got his answering machine a while ago."

"Where are the others? We're trying to keep this quiet until we figure out what's going on," said Kirov.

"They're back in the Stalin Lounge," said Jeffries.

Bass played the message back for Jeffries. A still image showed Markson in a smaller office, at a smaller desk. On the Hollywood Hills behind him, the sign had apparently been repaired, and now read HOLLYWOOD. "Hello," said a woman's voice. "You have reached the office of C. W. Markson, president of Voyager Pictures. Please leave a message after the—"

"Kirov, is that you?" said Markson's voice. The image flickered and went bad.

"We're getting live!" Bass said. He blanked the screen, and the same image of Markson came up, in the same office with the same hillside through the window. Now he was sitting on instead of behind the desk. The vid was clear but the audio exploded with static. "Hello, Mars XXXXXX lawyer to screen my calls! You're probably wondering XXXXXXXXXXXXXX and now you know. Voyager is XXXXXXXXXXXXXXXX perhaps I should say, *us*. Pellucidar went through some major management adjustments XXXXXXXXXXXXXXXXXXX pick up our option. This was . . ."

"Option? I thought we had a contract!" said Kirov. Like all the Texas-trained cosmonauts, she had taken a three-week course in entertainment law.

"My God, he's been fired," said Fonda-Fox from the door, where he had just appeared with Greetings and Glamour. "And if he's been fired, we've all been fired."

Glamour's *Demogorgon* hummed contentedly.

"XXXXXXXXXXXXX told you on the wake-up message but XXXXXXX worry you XXXXXXXXXXX our new package together. We're going to pick up a distributor soon. As a matter of fact, I am on my way to Cannes tomorrow. With all the publicity we've been getting XXXXXXXXXXX"

Through the window behind Markson, the HOLLY-WOOD sign began to tremble and the hills began to shake. "Look, they're having an earthquake!" Greetings said.

"Hardly," said Fonda-Fox. "That's not a window, it's a wall vidloop. It's flickering. Markson is calling from some cheap office complex, maybe not even in Beverly Hills." He turned away disgustedly.

"XXXXXXXXXX about Beverly Glenn. I'm confident she's awake by now, since I can't sell a package in Cannes without two Stars. But enough XXXXXXXXXX"

At 29.4 minutes round trip, communications were more like mail than phone. Kirov assigned Jeffries to deal with Markson, and instructed Bass to try and get Mission Design, while she and Fonda-Fox checklisted the preparations for the MOI (Mars Orbital Insertion) braking burn, Greetings made coffee and kept an eye on Ahab and Beverly Glenn, and Glamour circulated among them with the *Demogorgon* purring on his shoulder.

"I finally got Sweeney," Bass told Kirov. "He's still at Stadium Solutions (thank God) but it's only Friday afternoon on Earth, and he can't get any computer time until the weekend. He's going to call us back."

"The weekend? Will we have time to run the numbers for the braking burn?"

"Barely."

"The nearest I can figure is that she's a canceler," Jeffries told Markson. "Sometimes it doesn't show up on the blood test. It means that she develops an immunity to the antidote to the HT. Cancelers are usually phototropic, which means she will wake up, but on her own internal clock. I have a stronger antidote, but it's retained in the tissues, and I'm afraid if she takes it she won't go back to sleep again. That would be a disaster on an eighteen-month return voyage. I'd rather wait and see if she will wake up on her own. Meanwhile, I've put two more skin patches on, and we'll see."

Jeffries signed off, and hurried back to his vigil in the South Observatory. They were backing into Mars at over 25,000 mph and already it loomed larger than the Earth seen from the Moon. With Ahab on his lap, Jeffries watched it grow. He wanted to see the great Valles Marineris, where they would land, but he could make out only a dark shape on the west horizon. As the planet slowly turned and the area came into view, it was hidden behind the rear engine heat shield.

"You lost your boyfriend when we lost Pellucidar," Markson told Greetings, "since he was their contract player. But I was able to negotiate a dignified ending to the whole affair as part of my severance agreement." The static was gone now but the picture was bad. Markson held up a newspaper and Greetings could barely make out the headline:

LONG-DISTANCE HEARTBREAKER:

DEAR JOHN FROM SPACE STOWAWAY

BREAKS BOYFRIEND'S HEART

"That's the good news. The bad news is, your parents have separated again. Your father is living in Portland again, and your mother sends—"

Sweeney was eating from a carton in front of a small screen and a large keyboard. "I've faxed the figures through if you want to check them," he said. "Though they're foolproof if I do say so myself. If you just punch them we should have a supersweet and clean MOI, even allowing for an error of three percent. That is, if that Daewoo fires." He made a face. "You can't get decent Chinese food in Santa Monica. I'm bringing you in right under Deimos as it's passing over Phobos, so we can use the gravitational harmonics from the two moons to even out the stresses of the capture. This maneuver got me my Ph.D. from San Diego. Let's hope it works in real life. You will end up in a matched orbit with Phobos. Burn is at seven-eleven Candor, repeat, Candor Time. Markson is complaining about phone charges so I'll call back in, let's see, forty-eight minutes. But first let me read you my fortune cookie . . ."

As he headed back to the bridge from his manual check of the Daewoo ignition junction box, Bass stopped by the South Observatory. The cat was there, floating above the seat of the barca, but not the doctor. The planet was so close now that the heat shield only covered its center, like a penny laid on a Reagan dollar. Toward the western horizon the dark line of the terminator was eating a darker, spidery crack. Bass looked at his dicktracy: 6:55 P.M., Candor Time. Sunset at Candor Chasm. They were no longer on Beverly Hills Time; they were synchronized with the region of the planet on which they would be landing. Bass flicked the earcom on his dicktracy and highlighted Jeffries on the tiny menu screen.

"Hey, Bones, you want to see Mars, you should come to the South Observatory and look now," he said. "After orbital insertion we'll be in too close to see the whole planet this good."

"Can't do it," Jeffries commed back. "I have to get everybody strapped down for the burn. If the cat's there, bring him forward." And don't call me Bones, he added after switching off.

Everybody was Beverly Glenn. As he strapped her into one of the two auxiliary barcas that folded out from the birch-paneled wall of the Stalin Lounge, Jeffries took another peek down the front of her jumpsuit. The soft, silky hair between her breasts was getting thicker every day. He pulled down one bunny slipper. Hair was also growing on the tops of her feet.

AAAHHHH OOOOGAAA
AAAHHHH OOOOGAAA

"All hands on bridge," Kirov said on the intercom. "MOI braking burn in seven minutes, forty-four seconds."

The *Mary Poppins* left Earth with an initial velocity, from delta V, of 38,867 mph, corrected to 37,677, holding to a precise 38,786 at the beginning of Venus Transit. The crack-the-whip around Venus had increased its velocity to 41,089 mph, or 105 percent of initial. But in the long, slow coast "uphill" from the sun after Venus Transit it had dropped back down to 16,987 mph. Orbital matching speed was 9,345 mph (or four kilometers per second), which meant that the braking burn needed to be far less violent than the initial delta V had been. At least, that's what Bass and Kirov had said. So Fonda-Fox was unprepared for the shock as the Daewoo nuclear engine fired a mile to the "south" and the stars through the bridge glass began to shake violently as if the very heavens were tearing apart.

"Reeaaaaaawr!"

Fonda-Fox grabbed the cat as it flew by him toward the

rear of the bridge, torn out of Greetings's arms by the deceleration.

"Six point five kilometers per second," Bass read calmly to Kirov. "Six point two, five point eight, four point nine." He was neither worried nor not worried. He knew they would either slide into orbit at 5,978 kilometers; or miss, and skip off the atmosphere like a stone from a pond to sail forever between the stars; or crash into one of Mars's sullen little moons; or crease its dry sand with a ten-mile-long trench, for a ship the size of the *Mary Poppins* wouldn't burn in the atmosphere, or—

"Oh look!"

Greetings pointed outward. A black hole ate the stars and then was gone. "Deimos," said Kirov. They had just passed under the outer of the swift, dark moons of Mars.

The ship groaned and shuddered as the burn continued. The cat was flattened against the rear bulkhead. Joints creaked and lights flickered. From the Stalin Lounge there was a sound of glass breaking.

Then the lights went out and the Daewoo died at the same instant. The silence was sudden and terrifying.

Bass held a flashlight on the board while Kirov punched in the codes for an orbital trajectory check. Sweeney was patched in on the phone line, but he was fifteen minutes behind. She wanted to know *now* if they had made it.

"Voyagers, give me a count!" she called out.

"Bass here."

"Greetings here."

"Fonda-Fox."

"Lou."

"Where the hell's Jeffries?"

"I'm here."

"Then why the hell didn't you answer?"

"We're in the slot!" Bass crowed as the figures came up. "Wrong side of Phobos, I think. But other than that, perfect orbit."

"Everybody sit tight, I'm going to align the ship," said Kirov.

"What the hell was all that turbulence?" Fonda-Fox asked.

"Could have been worse," Bass said. "Some kind of gravitational harmonics. We just slipped between two moons like a . . ."

He felt the hair on the back of his neck stand up. Everything was turning red. The bridge seemed to catch fire as the *Mary Poppins* turned slowly over like a world, and Mars, like a burning sunset sky, came into view.

Whang! Whang! Whang!

The lights were flickering, and somewhere back in the axis tunnel a fan was hitting its frame. Greetings, Jeffries, Glamour, Fonda-Fox, Bass . . . even Kirov, all were holding their breath. Then the lights came on, too bright, and from every speaker in the ship, from the other side of a hundred million miles of night, came the lonesome howl of a Gibson electric and Chuck Berry's voice:

> *. . . Hello, operator,*
> *give me Tidewater 4-10-0-0*
> *Tell the folks back home it's the promised land calling*
> *and the poor boy's on the line*

GREETINGS'S DILEMMA, which she naively thought was unique to her but which has been common to stowaways for thirty-one centuries, ever since the first dock waif curled up in a coil of rope on a felucca bound east across the Indian Ocean, was whether to try to be useful or stay out of the way. She resolved it, as have stowaways for centuries, by trying to do both at once. Staying out of the way was easy on a ship as big as the *Mary Poppins*, especially in zero g, where you could float like a ghost from room to room, half-hoping, half-dreading someone would see you. Bass seemed to find her invisible, like a proper ghost; and Dr. Jeffries paid little attention to her once her arm had healed. She felt like the reverse twin of Beverly Glenn, whom everyone noticed and who noticed no one at all. Greetings watched everything that went on, and yet went unseen unless Kirov happened to catch her out of the corner of her eye. Kirov always found something for her to do.

"Greetings, quit daydreaming and bring me *The Best of the Everly Brothers* from storage."

Greetings left the bridge and kicked off down the central axis tube, through the Stalin Lounge, toward Hab #3, storage. On her way, even though it wasn't exactly on her way, she looked into the South Observatory. The little round room was flooded with orange light. She wasn't surprised to see Dr. Jeffries sitting in the center barca with Ahab on his lap. The two spent all their spare time in here. Dr. Jeffries had been avoiding the ship's company, sleeping long hours alone in the

South Observatory, as if determined to go in dreams where he couldn't go in the flesh.

Mars was still covered with the planetwide dust storm that had struck the day they had gone into orbit. Now that the ship was aligned, the planet was seen equally well from the South Observatory and the bridge. Only 3,700 miles away, it almost completely filled the sky. Greetings had seen the old *Viking* and *Mariner* photos on disk in the Stalin Lounge, and she knew there should be mountains and canyons (but no rivers or seas), snowcaps and even a few clouds. Instead, because of the storm, Mars was like a pastel drawing some kid had smudged with the side of her fist. Some sloppy kid.

"Want another thermos of coffee?" she asked. Dr. Jeffries put away ten or fifteen cups a day. But he shook his head without turning around and Greetings went on her way.

The Everly Brothers were in a locker at the entrance to the dark, spooky Hab #3. On her way back to the bridge, Greetings looked in on Beverly Glenn in the Stalin Lounge. Drifting near the ceiling in a bright yellow jumpsuit, like an ornament, she snored quietly. Green and blue wake-up patches were stuck on her ankles, on her wrists and on her neck. Her beard was blond and fuzzy like peach down. Checking both doors to make sure no one was coming, Greetings looked down the front of the Movie Star's jumpsuit. She had just gone through puberty herself, and the downy hair between Beverly Glenn's perfect breasts fascinated her. It was mysterious—but she found it no more strange than the idea of menstrual blood or her own hair "down there."

When Greetings got back to the bridge, Kirov was bent over the positional scanner, trying to locate one of the two fuel-processing units that had been sent down to the surface of Mars twenty years before. Her face looked split like a clown's: one cheek ruddy in the orange glow of Mars, the other pale from the gray light of ashheap Phobos, looming only ten kilometers off the starboard bow of the *Mary Poppins*. Bass was working with Sweeney, checking the coordinates of the lander hidden on the other side of Phobos. Glamour drifted near the ceiling filming, or booking image, as he called it. He was always booking image. Maybe he was the ghost, Greetings thought. Maybe that's what ghosts did. Maybe live people were just actors in their movie.

"I'm getting a beep here." Kirov said. "Must be the *Agnew.* The *Gagarin* was lost years ago. And what's this? The Everly Brothers. Thanks, kid."

For thirty-six hours the *Mary Poppins* had circled Mars alongside its inner moon. The ship was not in an orbit around Phobos; the twenty-mile-long football-shaped satellite was too small to capture it. The ship was in the same Mars orbit as Phobos, side by side, as was the *Tsiolkovsky* hidden on the other side of the moon. It was an unstable configuration; the *Mary Poppins* was drifting toward Phobos at slightly more than eleven meters per day, and thus would collide with it in one hundred days. But by then, for better or for worse, they would be long gone.

The question was: would the storm lift in time for them to get down to the surface and back before they had to return to Earth? Or as Markson put it almost daily: will there be a film in the can?

Mars, 5,978 kilometers "below," seemed almost close enough to touch, but there was nothing to see except a scour of reddish dust clouds. The planet was as featureless as Venus had been; worse, in fact, since the clouds had neither shape nor depth. Even the ice-covered polar caps were hidden from view. All that was visible was the snowcapped tops of the 80,000-foot (25,000-meter) Tharsis volcanoes—Olympus, Arsia, Ascraeus and Pavonis Mons.

Sweeney's fortune, faxed through complete with misspellings, was taped to the screen over Bass's console:

ALONG AWAITED MEETING MAY PROVE DISSAPOINTING

* * *

"How long can it last?" Greetings asked.

Bass shrugged that Bass shrug. "This is the Martian summer. Storm season. Maybe a month, maybe a day, maybe a week."

At the ceiling, Glamour groaned. They had 19 days (M) before their return window opened, and 22.6 before it closed. Three weeks to get down, book enough image to make a film, and get back up to the *Mary Poppins*—and already two days were gone.

Three days.

"Shouldn't you save your film for Mars?" Jeffries asked as he changed Beverly Glenn's wake-up stickers. He only came into the Stalin Lounge to attend to her, always looking annoyed, as if he preferred to be alone with Mars and Ahab.

"Can't run out. It doesn't use film," Glamour said from behind the *Demogorgon*.

"It uses optical disk space," explained Fonda-Fox, who was in the middle of a 3-D Scrabble game with Kirov. "And it's erasable. Every two or three days he compresses the image into 340,000K bytepaks and sends it back to Earth. Then he starts over."

"But where are you sending it?" Bass asked from the ceiling, where he was scanning through the back issues of *Hot Rod* magazine with a remote. "I thought Markson wasn't with the studio anymore."

"He's rented disk space at a U-STORE-IT in Pasadena," said Greetings, who was cleaning the outside of the samovar with a laser swab. "I overheard him telling his secretary to hold the bills for Disney-Gerber."

Four days.

"This is a disaster! First Beverly Glenn and now Mars won't wake up. I had some interest in two Stars going to Mars, but now, with only Fonda-Fox awake, and with you guys not even landing but just circling, we're talking Best

Circular Travel Documentary here." Markson was speaking
from a phone booth in Cannes, and he looked disheveled
and hurried. Behind him, barely visible in the signal dis-
torted by the sun's gravitational field, a reporter shouted in
French and tapped on the glass with a Euroyen. "Kirov,
Sweeney tells me you are preparing to go out into space to
check out the lander, the *Tchaikovsky*. Is there any way
Fonda-Fox could go? That way, with a Guild-certifiable
Movie Star on the first EVA in Mars orbit, I can at least talk
to the press without looking like a total fool. Otherwise I'm
dead meat here in Cannes. Momento, goddammit, I'm on
the phone!"

Kirov looked at Bass, who looked at Jeffries, who looked
at Fonda-Fox, who looked excited for the first time in days.
"I'm game," he said. "I'm EVA certified. I did an outdoor
sequence a few years ago for a film called *High Orbit*."

"I thought that was a double," Glamour said from overhead, where he was filming.

"It was supposed to be, but I paid him off."

"Okay," said Kirov, "but it's the *Tsiolkovsky*, not the
Tchaikovsky." She sent the message to Markson's hotel file,
since the reporter had found two friends and the booth was
rocking, and it was clear Markson wouldn't last the 14.8 minutes it would take for the message to reach Earth.

Five days.

Kirov was first out the outer air-lock door. Fonda-Fox
started to follow and then pulled back, fighting to control his
breath. He had felt no fear 250 miles above Earth, but now
he was hanging 3,700 miles above an unfamiliar planet. This
was different. From the corner of his eye he could see Glamour filming through the air lock's "eye." The *Demogorgon*
could edit out a little uncertainty, but if he didn't follow Kirov
now . . .

Three thousand seven hundred miles straight down.

Kirov turned and extended one massive glove. "Keep your

eye on the ship," she said as she pulled him around the corner. "Ignore the scenery up there."

The "up" did it. Fonda-Fox felt the universe realigning itself in his head, to the great relief of his stomach; the red planet below changed to a red sky above; under his feet he could see a million stars but they were too far away to fall into.

A few meters aft of the air lock on Hab #3 there was a non-air–locked door. Kirov had to bang it with a wrench to open it. She went in and pulled out a space scooter. It was shaped like a wheelless motorcycle with one long Velcroed pillion seat, a searchlight attached to the handlebars, and a hydrazine power plant. She snapped in a battery pack and watched the lights go on. She hadn't ridden one of these in twenty years. Her grin lighted up the inside of her helmet as she patted the seat behind her.

Fonda-Fox waved to Glamour, now filming from the bridge, as they motored off into space.

Phobos was too small to curve space for an easy ride around, so Kirov cut half a pentagon with ten-mile sides around the gloomy, potato-shaped moon. To Fonda-Fox it seemed that they were crabbing sideways, and getting nowhere. There were no landmarks on Phobos to mark their progress, just dark gray craters dusted with dark gray dust. All the same. Then over the gray horizon, startlingly white, the lander appeared.

"What's its name?" Fonda-Fox asked.

"The *Tsiolkovsky*. The *Konstantin Tsiolkovsky*." It was named after the Soviet father of rocketry, but in fact it was at this stage all glider. It was a blunt needle, the size and shape of the old DC-3 airliner without the wings. Its delta tail, carried low on the rear, was smaller than a rocket's fin. Its narrow, straight wing, half again as long as the fuselage, was carried pivoted lengthwise along its back. Below the nose rode a twenty-foot-diameter disk like a radar pod. The blunt tail was covered with a streamlining cone, which, reversed, would become the main engine's thrust cone. Small solid-fuel rockets were fitted to the nose and the wing for orbital maneuvers and the de-orbit burn. Even with all these protuberances, the bone-white *Tsiolkovsky* looked sleek and bright next to Mars's brooding vampire moon.

There was only one air lock, far forward, just behind the flight deck. They locked in, but didn't unsuit. While Kirov topped off the fuel cells and booted the systems self-tester, Fonda-Fox looked through the ship. Where the *Mary Poppins* was plush, the *Tsiolkovsky* was spare. The tiny flight deck in the nose held only two seats. Behind them, two more web and tube barcas were bolted to a rotating shaft. There was a small square window on either side of the empty main cabin. At the back, behind the last bulkhead, a tangle of pumps and tubes, lines, wires and hoses looked as impossibly complex as the rigging on a clipper ship. Fonda-Fox drifted back and read the WARNING decals and ATTENTION! stickers. He was looking at the forward end of an ancient twentieth-century Rocketdyne engine.

"The F-1," said Kirov. "The most powerful and dependable rocket engine ever made. The Chrysler hemi of space. The *Tsiolkovsky* de-orbits with a jettisonable solid rocket, then glides down, dead stick. Good old-fashioned NASA technology. Then the F-1 hauls her back up. With the wing and heat shield off it only weighs nine thousand six hundred pounds, a ton and a half on Mars."

"But isn't there something missing?" Fonda-Fox asked.

"We add the toilet," Kirov said. "It's back in storage in Hab #3. And the galley and stuff."

"I mean the fuel."

"The fuel is waiting on the surface. Diesel plus liquid oxygen. You're standing in the tank. We live in here while we are on the surface, then divide it—two thirds for diesel #2 and one third for LOX. Then we set the ship on her tail and fly out, with all of us squeezed into what's now the flight deck. That little space over there."

"Seven people?"

"Six. The kid stays in orbit. With the cat."

"You're kidding."

She was not kidding.

"Found the *Agnew*, so our landing site's confirmed, that is, if this storm ever clears up, come on," Bass said to Markson.

"Is that the fuel dump? I thought Kirov already found it," said Greetings.

"Redundancy check," said Bass. "I want to find it, too." According to the locational scanner, the *Agnew* was right where it was supposed to be—in a narrow belt of dunes at 2,345 feet (less than 1,000 meters) elevation above Mars datum, near the west entrance to the Candor Chasm, part of the Valles Marineris canyon system. Situated a few miles south of the Martian equator, this was one of the lowest and warmest spots on the planet.

"There was a Russian processor, too," Bass explained, "just for good measure. Both had kero stores and oxygen processors. But the *Gagarin*'s chute didn't open all the way. It hasn't put out a signal since it went down twenty years ago."

"Good show," said Markson, 31.212 minutes later. "Now all we've got to do is get permission from Disney-Gerber. Come on."

"Disney-Gerber? What do they have to do with it. The UN owns the *Tsiolkovsky* and the processors, and we have salvage rights, come on."

31.345 minutes later, Markson said, "Where have you guys been? Disney-Gerber won their court case last year. Plus, just to make sure, they bought the UN four months ago. Aren't you reading the *Hollywood Reporter*? Or am I wasting good money faxing it up every Friday, come on?"

"Look! Here they come!" said Greetings.

Braking with an almost visible spume of nitrocellulose from the solid-fuel boosters pinned to its nose, the *Tsiolkovsky* glided past the bridge of the *Mary Poppins* at less than thirty meters. Kirov and Fonda-Fox waved from the tiny flight deck. Bass and Greetings waved back and went to the air lock to meet them. Glamour grunted and kept filming.

A hundred yards back, in the South Observatory, Jeffries watched the small ship lock on to the air lock. Designed to soar, not just glide, in the thin Martian atmosphere, the *Tsiolkovsky* was sleek and beautiful. With its wing slung along its back like a bow, it actually looked capable of going somewhere. How ironic, now that there was nowhere to go.

For after five days, the planet below was still cloaked in its robe of dust. It was as though, Jeffries thought, Mars had pulled a veil over her face just when he was close enough to touch her cheek. He brooded with the cat in his arms, feeling betrayed.

Six days.

"For medical reasons," Jeffries said. "For psychological reasons. For humanitarian reasons, dammit. For the same reason that we can't leave Beverly Glenn awake on the trip back. Kirov, you ought to know you can't leave a teenager all alone for three weeks on a mile-long spaceship two hundred million miles from home."

Greetings had been trying not to cry; it was the two hundred million that did it.

"One hundred and eighty," Kirov said. "Stop crying, kid. And at this point, even if the storm stopped tomorrow and Glenn woke up, it would only be two weeks. And she won't be alone, she'll be with the cat." They were in the *Tsiolkovsky*, attaching the gravity toilet to the rear bulkhead. "Look around, Jeffries. This isn't the *Mary Poppins*. The *Tsiolkovsky* is a small ship, designed for four. Six is already stretching it past the limit."

"This ship can glide with twice the weight," said Jeffries. "It's already carrying an F-1; what difference does one hundred five pounds make, or forty pounds, which is all she'll weigh on Mars?"

"It's not going down, it's coming back up that's the problem. And there, the forty pounds matters twice. It's forty pounds of fuel we can't carry, and forty pounds of meat the rest of the fuel has to lift."

"There's plenty of fuel on the surface, in the *Agnew*. You said so yourself."

"Yes, but the *Tsiolkovsky* will only hold so much. And the F-1 will only lift so much. It'll be tight at best."

"We have a movie to make," Glamour muttered. He felt sorry for the kid, but only a little. He had been in the movie business long enough to know that sentiment, logistics and shooting schedules didn't mix. All the obstacles to *Voyage to the Red Planet* seemed concentrated in Greetings's tear-stained, sniffling face.

"Look, kid, it's not like you haven't been living on the ship for over a year," Kirov said. "It's just a question of waiting, relaying messages, watching over things. Somebody has to feed the cat."

"Besides, if the storm doesn't clear none of us will be going down anyway," Bass added.

Seven days.

Breaking all rules of procedure, Bass and Kirov took an EVA together. They rode the scooter 9.8 kilometers to the dusty, cinder-covered surface of ashheap Phobos. Unheralded and uncelebrated, the first human foot (Kirov's) touched down on a surface other than that of Earth or its dead twin. There was little to see on Phobos. The horizon was a quarter of a mile in any direction, and the ash underfoot was almost as dim as the fabric of space itself. It was impossible to walk since they were for all practical purposes weightless, but with nothing to hold on to. There were no large rocks, these presumably having been knocked off by the larger hits that made the craters. Kirov found water ice under the ash in a tiny crack and brought back a chunk the size of a Coke bottle. They melted it that evening in the samovar in the Stalin Lounge and drank Phobos tea. Jeffries and Bass mixed a couple of cubes with Johnnie Walker Red. Jeffries held his milky lump up to the light and wondered: "What if we found a fly frozen in the ice?"

"I'd hurry and finish my drink before it melted," said Bass.

Eight days.

Greetings looked up from the screen where she was watching a rerun of *Family Ties*. "What if—?"

"The storm doesn't end?" Fonda-Fox said. "Guess we'll call the movie *Gone With the Wind*."

"No, what if Beverly Glenn doesn't—? Why couldn't I—?"

"Wake up? Take her place? But my dear, you're not a Movie Star," Fonda-Fox pointed out. "We don't have a Guild-certifiable movie if we don't have two Stars. And if it's not Guild certifiable, it's not licensed for theatrical release. And if it's not licensed for theatrical release, it's not Academy Award eligible. And if it's not Academy Award eligible, it'll go straight to TV and then to tape. You wouldn't want that, would you?"

"No, of course not, but—"

"It's nothing personal. It's a question of Birth, not Talent."

"But where did Movie Stars come from anyway?" demanded Greetings. "They were once just ordinary people too, like everybody else. It doesn't seem—"

"Fair? It doesn't seem fair because it's not fair. It's not supposed to be fair. Look at [and here Fonda-Fox named a Star beloved of millions] and ask yourself why him and not you. He can't act and neither could his mother. But she happened to be the daughter of an old girlfriend of [and here he named a Star whose exploits were legend], and so under Guild rules . . ."

Fonda-Fox was so used to being filmed that when the *Demogorgon* cut off he felt a sudden chill. "Where are you going, Glamour?"

"To call Markson. I've got an idea."

* * *

Nine days.

As impatient as a lover, Jeffries floated, wrapped in a sleeping bag in the dark South Observatory, and watched. He dozed. He woke. He dozed while far below the red planet turned. Every seven hours Olympus Mons appeared on the horizon, with its plume of snow showing immodestly through the dust clouds like a nipple through a gown. Soon it was followed by the other Tharsis volcanoes, three of them in a row. Six times as high as Everest, the highest mountains in the solar system, they were the only features visible on the surface, the only marks that clocked the planet's turning and the ship's turning around it.

Ahab, unsleeping, sat weightless on his lap.

Nine days.

Bass was keeping busy to avoid getting depressed. Just in case the storm cleared and the other Star woke up, the *Tsiolkovsky* was made ready. Bass fitted out the interior of the lander with a galley, and Fonda-Fox, who was getting used to EVAs, helped him wire and arm the retro-rockets. The wing pivot was loosened and the wing's leading-edge lift-enhancer slots were checked. "They're called lesznos," said Bass. "Named after the town in Poland where they were invented. Greatest thing since the airfoil: supposedly they triple the lift under the speed of sound. Of course, they've never been tried in the Martian atmosphere."

"Of course," said Fonda-Fox, who had seen enough movies to recognize that Bass's pessimism was part of an ace pilot's good luck ritual.

"If they don't work, we drop like a stone," said Bass.

"Like a stone," said Fonda-Fox, a warm feeling of security seeping into his bones.

Ten days.

"I'm with her mother," Markson said, "and we're working on it. Disney-Gerber is interested enough to finance the search, based on the composite footage Glamour sent down two days ago. It will mean going to New Mexico, and..."

"Whose mother? What search?" Greetings asked from the corner of the Stalin Lounge, where she was cleaning the samovar with a laser swab.

"Ssshhh!" said Glamour.

"We're checking out an alternate plan since Beverly Glenn won't wake up," whispered Fonda-Fox.

"...doesn't wake up, I guess the kid can go down in her place, but..."

"Omigod!" said Greetings. At least she wouldn't be left on the ship alone.

"...will sign a contract unless I can show them some surface footage. So unless the storm clears it's a moot point, come on."

Eleven days.

Kirov glided into the South Observatory and, without asking, squeezed a cup of tea out of Jeffries's thermos. Negatively ionized, the tea stuck to the bottom of her positive cup. The room was as cold as a cathedral, and featureless, dust-shrouded Mars filled the heavens like a stained-glass window.

"Were you named after your father?"

"Huh?"

"Was your father Sundiata Cinque?" Kirov asked.

Jeffries looked at her wonderingly. "How did you know that? Where did you ever hear about him?"

"I'm from the Soviet Union, remember? In high school we studied the Black movement and US political prisoners. At least we did until the US and the Soviet Union became such pals. I remember reading that he had been arrested after the 1995 uprisings, when the African Brotherhood and all the other underground groups were..."

"He died in prison. That's all I ever knew."

In the early morning of the twelfth day, Jeffries had his dream.

The planet was in darkness, as it was three times a day, only this time, as dawn came 3,700 miles below, Mars emerged over the horizon as perfect as if newly made: canyonlands of an immense variety of reds and mysterious, dusky almost-blues; low peaks and braided riverbeds remembering water; layered mountains crested with thin dioxide snow.

It was like a dream. But *it was no dream: he lay broad waking.*

The cat, Ahab, woke him up. The dream was still there. Mars had laid aside her robes and lay unclothed before him, more ravishingly beautiful than he had dared imagine. To the north was the bluish ice of the pole, making clouds where it met the plains and the cyclones of the high Martian summer. To the south, the other pole was hidden beyond the planet's smooth shoulder. Straight below were the volcanoes of Mars, and beyond them to the west, the Valles Marineris, four times as deep as the Grand Canyon, as long as a continent and a hundred miles wide. Jeffries could see the shadings of reds and yellows, purples and even blues on the still dark canyon walls as it unrolled underneath; first the labyrinthine chasms of Candor and Hebes, where they were going to land; then the thousand-mile trench of Coprates; then another thousand miles of canyon as the *Mary Poppins,* racing with Phobos, outran the day, and the planet below was swept into darkness again. Jeffries must have slept; for it seemed only moments later that dawn was painting the haze on the horizon again. He was looking down on the moonlike plains west of the Tharsis. Even in the darkness he could see Argyre, with its deep, sinuous memories of rivers etched into the sands. There was Hesperia, quiet now, soon to be dusted with hurricanes kicked up by the sun's warmth: a plain broader than a sea, and as lonesome. The sun's first light was just striking the peaks of the Tharsis volcanoes as the *Mary Poppins* sped over them. First was Olympus Mons, bigger than the moons of Mars, ringed with cliffs and with a caldera at the top as wide as a nation. It was so high that its peak would be in daylight for an hour before the sunlight brushed the lower slopes. Then came the eastern slope sisters, Pavonis, Acraeus, Arsia, even in midsummer arrayed with dioxide snow. The *Mary Poppins* was traveling east so fast that the westward-moving dawn seemed almost stationary. The eastern slope of the Tharsis was half-lit by the terminator, still a hundred miles to the east. Ragged white clouds blew out of the canyon and up the slope in what Mars meteorologists called the "dawn wind." It was almost noon at the eastern end of the Valles Marineris, three thousand miles away, and the expanded hot air chased the cold air westward at a hundred miles per hour.

There were the dune fields at the head of the Candor Chasm, where the *Tsiolkovsky* would land: pink in the first light of the dawn. Jeffries punched up superX on the barca's armscope and found the *Agnew*'s squat shape in the dunes. While to the east, down in the canyon . . .

He thought he saw a flashing light. He turned the scope but couldn't find anything. Holding the scope stationary, he closed one eye and let the other race with the ship's trajectory across the flat canyon floor. Scraps of mist . . . a flat-topped mesa . . . and in a cleft between high red cliffs—a blinking light? a gleam of metal on the sand? Whatever it was, it was gone. More likely, a trick of the morning light as the *Mary Poppins* raced into the dawn.

Jeffries stretched and checked his dicktracy: 6:04 A.M., Candor Time. The others were probably still asleep. He was reluctant to leave his vigil but anxious (and this surprised him, for in general he only tolerated his shipmates) to share this vision that filled the sky. The storm was over.

He turned to go and wake the other Mars Voyagers. "How long have you all been there?" he asked, surprised. For they were, all five, clustered in the doorway, gazing in silence and wonder at the red planet that was at last in their reach.

7

"IF THE AIR on Mars is so thin, how can we expect this thing to fly?" It was Fonda-Fox who asked but they all (quite naturally) wanted to know.

They were taking the *Tsiolkovsky* down in the morning.

"We have three things working for us," said Kirov. "The Martian atmosphere, though thin, is relatively constant to a higher altitude and doesn't fall off as rapidly as Earth's. Also, don't forget, the gravity is only a third of Earth's; the same lesser gravity that makes the air thinner makes the ship weigh less. It also means the ship will be flying faster. The atmosphere is so oxygen poor that we'll be able to enter at and maintain a much higher speed without burning up than the NASA gliders on Earth. The ship itself is a lifting body, and when we begin to open the wing at a little over Mach one, we'll be able to glide. Then when we open the lesznos, the specially designed leading-edge slots, we'll even soar."

"Hopefully," said Bass. While Fonda-Fox and Greetings transferred the last of the supplies into the lander, he was cutting his toolbox to the bare minimum, selecting what he called his Desert Planet Tool Kit—a roll of duct tape, a tube of blue Permatex and a pair of needle-nose Vise-Grips.

"Our initial entry will be with retro-rockets," Kirov went on. "We'll lose most of our speed through aerobraking, then we'll drop the heat shield at three hundred thousand feet and start to extend the wing, which opens"—Kirov illustrated with her two crossed forefingers—"like a pair of scissors. It will be

129

fully open by the time we're under fifty thousand feet and under a thousand knots. Then we'll open the special Polish soaring slots . . ."

"Feet, knots," said Fonda-Fox. "I thought this was a metric voyage."

"We'll come back up metric," said Bass. "Going down, we go the oldtime way."

"See you in two weeks," Greetings said. Then she whispered: "I'm sorry I wished you would never wake up!" She wasn't really, but she knew Beverly Glenn would understand. The Movie Star lay curled up against the ceiling of the Stalin Lounge, her face framed in the golden curls of her hair and beard. While Greetings whispered in her ear, Dr. Jeffries checked her pulse and listened to her breathing through the little microphone built into her dicktracy.

"Sleep tight," Jeffries said, satisfied. Except for the fact that she wouldn't wake up, Beverly Glenn was in perfect health. Many people had slept longer than eighteen months at the Career Spacing Clinic in Beverly Hills; one actor waiting out a contract had snored for fifty-four months. "So long, Ahab," Jeffries said. He made sure the cat food timer and robot vacuum zero-g cat box were powered up, and put the cat in Beverly Glenn's arms. "Look after my patient, will you?"

"Good luck, darling! We've got it all fixed up through your XXXXXXXXXXXXXX." Through the snow and static, Greetings could see her mother standing next to Markson in front of his desk. The office seemed slightly larger. The HOL YWOOD sign was visible again through a real window behind them. "I've got composite approval from XXXXXXXXXX pending our papers from the New Mexico State Police," said Markson. "And XXXXXXXXXXXXXXXX your test shots, of course. Disney-Gerber wants to see surface XXXXXXXXXXXXXXXX the contract."

"What are they talking about?" Greetings said. She wished her father were there. He always managed to slow down her mother's frantic pace—which was perhaps why her efforts to get them together again never worked.

"Let's show her," said Fonda-Fox.

Glamour punched a button on the *Demogorgon* and the whine changed to a whirr. "Look through the finder," he said.

Greetings peered into the lens and saw figures fast-forwarding. Then there was Beverly Glenn in her yellow jumpsuit like a golden-bearded sleeping beauty. Then a jump cut, and there was Greetings in her blue coveralls cleaning the Stalin Lounge samovar with a laser swab. Then the frame split and both images came up; Glamour turned a knob and the two figures blended . . . a heavy-breasted blonde, un-bearded, in a green suit, waved at the camera, a little stiffly—

"Hey!" said Greetings. "That's me! At least, that's my face. Sort of. But not my hair. And not my—"

"It still needs work," said Glamour. "It's a composite."

"Omigod! Does this mean I get to be in the movie?"

"Partly," said Glamour. "Maybe."

"Not quite," said Fonda-Fox. "First we have to get Guild approval. And that means checking out your blood-line. That's why Markson and your mother are flying to Santa Fe."

"Hey, how come I'm the last one to find out? Not that I mind, but—"

"Because you're under eighteen," said Fonda-Fox. "Markson has to deal with your mother. If you were a Movie Star, it'd be different. Since both my parents were Guild members I came of age at—"

A bell rang. The center air lock "on" light was blinking. It was time to leave the *Mary Poppins* for the *Tsiolkovsky*. "All aboard," said Kirov, who as a Texas-trained cosmonaut was not above mixing metaphors. "Point 'em up and head 'em out."

* * *

From half a mile, the *Mary Poppins* was a blaze of lights, like a skyscraper at dusk; from three miles, distant but still beckoning, like a farmhouse on a winter night; from twelve, as meager and cold-looking as a small town seen from the plains. Bass maneuvered the *Tsiolkovsky* away with gentle blasts on the bolted-on solid-fuel orbital maneuvering engines. Kirov listened raptly to the last figures from Sweeney at Mission Design (already fifteen minutes cold). Glamour filmed Fonda-Fox and Greetings at the starboard port glass, watching the *Mary Poppins* dwindle to a tiny collection of faraway lights, to a star, to nothing. Jeffries noted his shipmates' wistfulness with professional satisfaction: it meant that they had bonded successfully to the ship. The *Mary Poppins* was now as much "home" as Earth.

The *Tsiolkovsky* was tiny. Kirov and Bass were jammed into the flight deck; Jeffries took the Third Officer's jump seat behind them. In the open main cabin, between tied-down boxes of food and supplies, Fonda-Fox and Greetings found seats and strapped in beside Glamour.

"Firing retros in twenty seconds," Bass called out.

"Hey, listen to this," Kirov said. She switched on the cabin speaker:

"The awesome privilege of XXXXXXXXX red planet XXXXXXXXXXXXX behalf of all XXXXXXXXX XXXXXXXXXXXXXXX United States it is my XXXXXXXX XXXXXXXXX where no Movie Stars have ever . . ."

"Firing in fifteen seconds," said Bass.

"Thank you, Mrs. President," said Kirov. "On behalf of the Soviet people and Pellucidar Pictures . . ."

"It's Voyager Pictures now, I think," said Greetings.

"And the American people," said Fonda-Fox.

" . . . we go in peace for all humankind. Over and out."

"Ten seconds," said Bass. The front of the ship was blind because the heat shield covered the glass, but the red light of Mars flooded through the side ports as the ship turned, giving everyone's face an underlighted spookhouse glow.

"And may the Force be with us all," said Jeffries, and

laughter crackled like lightning through the nervous atmosphere.

"Five," said Bass. "Four, three."

"Zero," whispered Kirov as the little forward rocket roared. "We now descend to Mars. Mr. Bass, you are at the helm."

8

ENTERING OR LEAVING the heavy atmosphere of Earth, trapped in its ponderous coils of gravity, is a strenuous and violent business that had always been, to Jeffries, the most unpleasant aspect of space flight. Mars was, in contrast, a piece of cake. There was a mild, eighty-second braking blast, tugging them all forward in their barcas. Through the starboard window Jeffries could see the cigarette-ash–colored chunk of Phobos growing smaller. Against the blackness of space it was a gray smudge, more like a note for a moon than a moon. Then as if awakened it rose, suddenly, out of sight and was replaced by the horizonless bulk of the red planet, sliding into sky.

"Rollover complete," said Bass, fishing for a good piece of Red Man.

"Check," said Kirov.

"How's our burn?"

"Forty-two seconds to go. In line and flying fine." Kirov's Texas accent thickened when she was flying.

There was a sudden silence after the blast. Embarrassed, Glamour quit humming "Over the Rainbow." Kirov looked for a rock tape but the bin was empty. Jeffries had been in charge of packing the cultural supplies . . .

"Jettisoning de-orbit engines," said Bass. There was a thud as the explosive bolts blew the little solid-fuel rockets off the top of the fuselage.

"In line and flying fine," said Kirov. Now it was only a matter of waiting. They would start hitting the Martian at-

134

mosphere at 800,000 feet (151 miles, or 244 kilometers). Then they would know if they were going too fast or too slow and any corrections would be aeronautical—dead stick.

Bass felt a hand on the back of his own and he smiled at Kirov beside him. Twenty years late, they were landing on Mars.

"Markson on the line," said Jeffries, who was monitoring the radio.

"Markson? Where's Sweeney?" Kirov asked. "He was getting me some more figures."

"He had to go to work. His ride came by, and he couldn't wait for you to call back. Markson just called on the other line from Santa Fe."

"Well, tell him to call back tomorrow. Tell him we're busy landing on other planets."

There was a snore from the back. It was Fonda-Fox. Generations of learning to nap on location were bred into every Star. Beside him, Greetings sat with her eyes wide open under tightly closed lids.

Thirty-eight minutes and twenty-one seconds after the braking burn, Bass felt a slight pressure of gravity in the seat of his pants. At 38:44, the ship began to vibrate as if picking up a wind. At 39:02, the heat shield began to redden, then glow.

"Shield temperature 507 degrees centigrade," Kirov read off the console. "At 125,914 meters. Speed 17,895 kilometers per hour."

"What do you think?" Bass asked.

"Your call," Kirov said. "I think we're in the envelope."

It depended on how well the shield held up. It was glowing cherry red now, and there were no white spots that could mean a developing hole.

"699 degrees. 120,780 meters. 16,410 kph."

"Give me feet and miles per hour," Bass said.

"I thought you were a NASA man."

"I'm also a glider pilot, dammit, and this rocket is turning into a glider. We like feet and miles."

"Heat shield at 1,304 degrees Fahrenheit. Altitude 389,000 feet. Air speed 9,787 mph."

They were not slowing enough, and heating too fast. Bass eased up a fraction on the elevators, so that the body of the ship would slow its trajectory, hopefully dumping some of the heat.

"1,078. 371K. 9,100."

It worked; they were planing on the edge of the thin carbon dioxide mantle of Mars.

"955. 375. 8,950."

No good. They were staying too high too long and the heat shield was time as well as temperature critical. If they planed too long, it would fall apart like an overcooked Christmas turkey. Bass steepened the descent.

"915. 322K. 8,756."

Better. Steepening the dive increased neither the heat nor the speed. The thickening atmosphere dumped off as much heat as it created. It was like flying a rock but it was like flying. The heat shield was decaying, but slowly.

"712. 301K. 6,538."

Bass grinned as he felt the ship shudder. They were falling, but now the planet was reaching up to catch them in her long arms.

"I can feel it," said Greetings. "In the seat of my pants!"

"Oh no," said Jeffries, afraid to turn around.

"I mean gravity!"

"693. 290K. 5,777."

"Where are we in reference to the terminator?" Bass asked.

"Four hundred miles west, on an east-north heading," Kirov responded.

"Perfect." The plan was to hit the landing site just before the Martian midmorning, when the updraft that would lower them to the ground would be at its best.

"645. 278K. 4,553. Heat shield temperature dropping."

"582. 223K. 4,132. Why don't you dump some more speed, Bass? This is taking too long. 556. 211K. 3,987. Beautiful."

"Arm EBs," Bass said.

"Explosive bolts armed. 412. 201K. 3,766."

Two hundred and twenty degrees centigrade was the line at which they could drop the heat shield. Sweeney had calculated they would hit it at 61,000 meters. Not far off, Bass admitted reluctantly. There was something dangerous about things going too right. It tempted fate.

"393. 199K. 3,625."

"Pop your top, Natasha."

Kirov pulled the pin and the heat shield blew off in a wild, silent flurry of sparks. There was a snort from the back as Fonda-Fox sat up, startled. Greetings had opened her eyes. Only Glamour seemed unperturbed, swinging his *Demogorgon* around to catch the new red light streaming through the narrow, twin DC-3–style front windscreens.

"Wing time," Bass said, easing the lever forward to two degrees. Adjustable from its resting, parallel position to 90 degrees relative to the fuselage, the wing was designed to generate lift at 5 degrees plus. Two more touches on the lever brought it to 6 degrees. Bass could feel the life in it. He touched the stick, and the *Tsiolkovsky* turned slightly to the right, then back to the left.

"You're flying," Kirov said.

And so they flew. They soared. They rode the long air down through the Martian dawn, west, with the sunrise behind them. Twelve degrees; 20 degrees: Bass cranked out the wing slowly so that the ship gained lift as it lost speed, keeping the drop rate steady at an almost soaring glide aspect of 16:1. Not wanting to overtake the terminator, he spiraled in a fifty-mile-wide circle, waiting for the sun to catch up. Eastward, 144,000 feet below, two 50-mile-wide parallel canyons led off to the horizon, deep and painful-looking like claw marks, their depths veiled with thin morning fog. This was the Valles Marineris, almost three thousand miles long, and deeper than four Grand Canyons. The slow-moving dawn revealed the labyrinths at the Valles's western end, where the claw marks ended in a maze of canyons and mesas like cracked glaze, now straight below; then, as the dawn moved still farther west, the smooth lava plains of the Tharsis plateau, higher than two Tibets and half again as vast. The *Tsiolkovsky* was banking to starboard, and behind her in the rear cabin, Kirov could see the voyagers piled up at the tiny starboard window, taking turns looking out over Glamour's *Demogorgon*, two at a time. Mars was spread out below them, strange and beautiful. Bass felt a flutter as he cranked the wing out another notch to 48 degrees and spiraled down to 110,000 feet. There it was again: the updraft he had been looking for. It had been thermally tracked for years and was as regular as the tides on Earth. It was high noon at the eastern end of the Marineris canyon but barely down in the west; and the *Tsiolkovsky* was feeling the updraft of the sun-warmed, west-flowing air as it howled out of the canyons and rose over the Tharsis. Bass nosed the little ship down to gain speed, then flew due west, over the long domed plain. The glide ratio was 20:1 in the updraft, even at over 100,000 feet. The high plain was still in darkness as the canyonlands disappeared behind. Then far ahead, appearing pink over the black horizon, were the ghostly summits of the great shield volcanoes. The *Tsiolkovsky* dropped slightly, and as he cranked the pivoted wing out another notch to bring the nose up, Bass saw over his shoulder three faces and the *Demogorgon* in the flight deck door: Greetings, Fonda-Fox and Jeffries stood watching the volcanoes appear from the top downward as the sun rose, as if it were painting them on the sky. "Pavonis Mons," Kirov said, pointing to the great dome dead ahead. "Arsia Mons" (three hundred miles to the left of it, and more flat topped); "Ascraeus Mons" (three hundred miles north, its flanks rougher and more mountainous). The *Tsiolkovsky* rushed soundlessly at almost one thousand miles per hour toward Pavonis Mons, and as they passed just ten thousand feet over the peak, they could see the crater, at eighty thousand feet—a bowl spilling over with white clouds, washing away westward in the morning wind. Fonda-Fox had flown over Kilimanjaro once, and he remembered feeling that the barren crater below was almost like another world, un-knowable in its light and dark and lifeless cold. Now he had the same feeling: only this one *was* another world.

No one spoke. The cabin of the *Tsiolkovsky* was still; even the air was hushed, since they were still outrunning the speed of sound and the only noise came from the vibration of the ship's airframe.

Then Pavonis Mons was gone, behind them, and they were still descending, whipping through the ice cloud that blew off the summit. Bass banked to the right, turning north, and as the ragged cloud dropped behind, there in front of them, itself just emerging from the dark side of the planet, was the largest volcano in the solar system, two hundred miles across its great humped summit; the upper slopes dusted with snow, white at the top, reddened at the lower margins by the dust storm that had raged around its lower flanks but never touched its higher reaches.

"Olympus Mons," said Kirov.

Even as she spoke, the mountain was clothing itself in light. It was fringed at the bottom with twenty-thousand-foot sheer cliffs, fluted red and ocher in the Martian dawn.

It stayed with them like a ghost continent off their left side for the next hour as they flew due north over the Tharsis plain.

AT JUST UNDER 1,000 mph, the asymmetrical wing was cocked at just over 61 degrees, relative to the fuselage; and seen from the surface of Mars 45,000 feet below, the *Tsiolkovsky* would have looked like a giant pair of scissors, half-open, flung by a mad tailor. The glide ratio stayed flat as the speed dropped, the wing opened, the thin dioxide atmosphere thickened (perceptibly now, according to their instruments) and the rising sun warmed the plain below. The world below was all in light, from horizon to horizon. The hydraulics groaned as Bass cranked the wing out another notch, to 64 degrees. Now the ship pulled a little to the left, which was the forward side of the wing, but Bass trimmed with the tail and sailed on.

Sailed on.

The plain was reddish gray and almost featureless far below, and Bass felt relieved as the descent took on some of the comfortable boredom of flight and the voyagers left the cabin door for their seats. The grooved and tumbled slope of Ascraeus Mons slid by fifty miles to the east, whippet clouds streaming out of the summit caldera like vapor flags, quickly disappearing. The clouds were above, not below the *Tsiolkovsky*.

"We're below the mountaintops," Kirov said. The news made the voyagers nervous. For two years space had been home, and now they were leaving it, descending back into the world of worlds.

As Ascraeus Mons dropped behind, Bass turned the *Tsiolkovsky* eastward and started down the long north slope of the

Tharsis. Thirty-five thousand. Thirty-one thousand. Twenty-nine thousand. The wing was at 68 degrees, which was as far as it could be extended until they dropped below the speed of sound. The ship rocked gently in the rising, icy air. Glamour was back at the window with the *Demogorgon,* with Jeffries and Greetings looking over his shoulder. Fonda-Fox was snoring again.

Coming from nowhere behind them, there was a thin, eerie whistling. Bass looked at Kirov and she nodded. It was the wind. "Six hundred seventy-four miles per hour at twenty-two thousand feet," Kirov read. Now they knew by actual experience the speed of sound on Mars: their sound had caught up with them. Bass cranked the wing out four clicks, to 72 degrees. He opened the leszno leading-edge lift-enhancement slots a notch, and the wind howled, and welcomed, and lifted them. They soared. Another notch and they floated, shuddering as the *Tsiolkovsky* lofted on down the high desert air. The plain ahead and below was rough, gray rather than red: serrated with lava flows swept free of dust by the wind howling out of the Valles Marineris. At first, with the de-orbit rockets, they had traded fuel for speed; then in the upper reaches of the atmosphere, heat for speed; now they wanted their speed, for it was all they had to trade for lift, and as his airspeed dropped to 590, 575, Bass could feel the alarming thinness of the Martian atmosphere for the first time—so unlike Earth's damp, fat winds. This air was like thin ice. The controls were soft, slow, as if connected by elastic bands to the stick in his hand. He turned and soared across the ugly scours of the Ceranius Fossae badlands.

"17,500," Kirov said. "Sit down, Greetings. This is not space flight; we're soaring now and you can't gawk around the cockpit door."

Bass opened the wing the last two notches to a full 90 degrees and felt a welcome punch in the seat of his pants. They were actually gaining altitude slightly; he nosed further to the right and gained more. He had found the lower part of the dying wave updraft that washed the north slope of the Tharsis. Now all he had to do was follow it around to the edge of the canyonlands, where it would still be a torrent.

"Look," said Greetings, who had not sat down at all. "Twins."

Ahead were two volcanoes, perfect Fuji-type cinder cones, unlike the rounded shield giants. These were smaller but steeper—comfortingly Earthlike with their Japanese profiles. Bass steered between them, opening the lesznos a little more, and the five hundred mph that had seemed like soaring at twenty thousand feet was more like ridge-running at seventeen thousand. The two peaks were only five thousand feet below. Bass was looking for lift, and he had to ride low to find it. He followed the long slope around, between the volcanoes, to the east. The air was turbulent but weak, and Bass trimmed the slots while he reached above the console for a pinch of Red Man from the foil pack wedged there. Kirov watched him, thinking how strange it was that after almost two years of weightlessness, weight did not seem more strange. She tested her own arm and it didn't feel weak: the HT had done its work well.

"16,250. 412," she said.

"Getting low and going slow," Bass answered. The ship tipped again and as he trimmed it, he looked back and saw the voyagers crowded again at the port window. The *Tsiolkovsky* sailed over the perfect cone of Ceranius Tholus. The mountain was marred by a long lava trail down the north slope, leading to what had once been a lava lake larger than the summit caldera itself. The lava lake was dreamy with mist, grayer than the ice clouds that brushed the mountaintop. To the east, a giant dust-filled crater extended north to the horizon, shallow but wide enough to swallow both mountains. Bass wheeled south of it and the plain was smooth again, like gray asphalt that needed sweeping: dusted with the red dust of dusty Mars.

"Where is it?" Bass muttered, but not aloud. Then the wing shuddered and there it was: the dawn wind. Bass threw the stick to starboard, opening the lesznos all the way, dropping the nose in a speed-grabbing shallow dive, and the *Tsiolkovsky* streaked off due east as if a turbo had kicked in. Greetings and Fonda-Fox cheered. Glamour grunted and the *Demogorgon* whined. Jeffries was glued to the window, grinning like a kid at Mars.

"11,314. 435," Kirov said. "A long clear shot at the landing site, Mr. Bass."

The leading-edge lift-enhancer slots that hung the *Konstantin Tsiolkovsky* on the dawn wind of Mars had been perfected by the clubs of the Polish soaring capital, Leszno, and tested over Europe and America. The legendary Carolus had soared nonstop from Leszno to Cork to Catalan and back. Bass himself had flown a fixed-wing, open-cockpit leszno-rail down the Kittatinny-Blue Mountain front from Pine Bush, New York, to Hancock, Maryland, in one wild nine-hour ride. But no one had known how well the lesznos would work in the dioxide vapors of Mars.

Until now.

For an hour they sailed south and east, following the smooth downslope of the Tharsis. With the slots open, the air lifted the ship at precisely its drop rate, holding both elevation and speed steady at 10,200 feet and 415 mph. Below, the plain was broken only once, by Tharsis Tholus, another Fuji-type cone, which swept by four thousand feet below at 10:41 A.M. (M). They had been soaring almost four hours; they had left the *Mary Poppins* almost six hours earlier. On the horizon Bass could see the dark labyrinths of the canyonlands. The *Tsiolkovsky*'s two thousand-mile approach circle was about to close and it was time to start looking for the landing site.

10

"1,610. 266."

Fonda-Fox woke up frightened.

"1,520. 257."

The soothing schuss of the wind had turned to a menacing howl that came not only through the air but through the soles of his feet. It was strange to wake up with weight. He could feel the straps of the seat under his butt. The little ship was rocking and rolling from side to side. Jeffries and Greetings were at the right-hand port, while Glamour filmed through the front windscreen between Bass and Kirov. Fonda-Fox unstrapped and pulled himself to his feet. After two years of weightlessness, he had expected to feel weak, but his legs and arms felt strong as he walked to the front of the *Konstantin Tsiolkovsky*, holding on to the strapped-down cases of supplies to keep his balance. At the entrance to the flight deck, he stuck his face over Glamour's whining *Demogorgon* and in between Bass and Kirov.

The Captain was in the co-pilot's barca, reading speed and altitude figures from a changing digital display, while Bass fished for tobacco with one hand and flew the ship with the other. The howl of their passage deepened to a relaxed thrumming, like the *OOOOOMMMMMM* Beverly Hills kids used to make in kindergarten before naptime.

"Hate for Sweeney to miss this," said Bass.

"1,366. 231. I'm going to get my marsuit on," said Kirov. "Jeffries, come with me."

"Jeffries is in back, by the window," said Fonda-Fox.
"Then you come. You're even better."

Red ground was racing by. Greetings saw something move
in the rocks, like an animal. It was chasing them, and she
almost cried out. But then she saw it was only the shadow of
the *Tsiolkovsky*, leaping over the rose-colored rocks. They
were racing up a long, shallow valley toward a notch in the
horizon; there were dark maroon dunes near the notch, and
beyond them something dark and menacing, like the sea.

"865. 224," said Jeffries, whom Bass had called forward to
replace Kirov as co-pilot. "I can see something down there."
Far ahead, what looked like a squat little house sat amid the
dunes.

"That'll be the *Agnew*," said Bass.

Kirov finished zipping up the back of Fonda-Fox's marsuit
while she called out orders: "Greetings, strap down! Bass, I'm
channel four on your earcom. Fonda-Fox and I are suiting up
in case we need an emergency EVA. Glamour, you can shoot
but strap down, dammit. If you break that camera there'll be
hell to pay."

"157," said Jeffries. "We're stalling."

"Don't see any airstrip yet," said Glamour.

"Want to be stalling, that's the plan," said Bass. He was
going to take the *Tsiolkovsky* down in the spectacular, harrier-
like maneuver that Carolus called the Polish Stairway Stall.

The Valles Marineris canyon system has been compared to
the Grand Canyon because it is deep and dry and red; but in
its size and in its role on the planet, it resembles more nearly
the Amazon basin. It's a weathermaker. A vast, fan-shaped
system of branches and subcanyons and side canyons covering
211,000 square miles, the canyon is so long that the eastern
half is in high sunlight while the west is still in darkness; the
temperature differential creates a torrent of wind coming west
out of the canyonlands from dawn to midmorning, slowing by

noon to a river, still strong. This is not the thin air of sun-warmed thermals, but thick, heavy, cold air pushed out by warmer air far to the east. The *Tsiolkovsky* had ridden the high crest of this wave a thousand miles since Bass had found it making his turn around the Tharsis volcanoes and heading into the sun. Now, close to noon, the wind was gone from the higher altitudes; but near the ground it was still strong enough to float the *Tsiolkovsky* all the way down to the sand.

Theoretically.

As he raced up the slope on the cold river of air, Bass could see the shadow of the ship running before him, and he was pleased with its sailplane figure, the wing half again as long as the fuselage. He waggled the wing, welcoming himself to Mars, as Jeffries read out the figures and then pointed out the *Agnew* in the dunes ahead.

Kirov was barking out orders and Bass knew she had left the faceplate of her marsuit open.

"151," read out Jeffries.

"134."

"112."

The dune field was straight below. Bass gentled the *Tsiolkovsky* up the long slope, slower, slower, slower. He opened the lesznos the last notch, all the way to eleven, the spectacular finale trick of the Polish soaring champions, which in a good headwind could hold them hovering for as long as the pilot could balance on the wind, and in the right hands could ease them straight down on their belly, not their tail.

The Stairway Stall.

The *Tsiolkovsky* came to a stop one hundred feet in the air.

Snap/one, snap/two: with the heel of his hand, Bass rocked the stick, so that the ship danced like a leaf, side to side, while his fingers searched through his Red Man, looking for that one last, sweet bit.

"Ninety-three."

"Is that speed or altitude?" Bass joked.

"Altitude. And we ain't talking miles but feet."

"Eighty-one." Dropping too fast. Bring up the nose. Fishing for air. Like roller skating on a cloud.

"Fifty-eight," said Jeffries.

"Is that your age or your IQ?"

"Forty-three."

Fishing for air.

"Thirty. Whoah."

The ship was oscillating. Walk it, walk it down.

"Eighteen. Whoo."

There's a cushion of air by the ground. Drop the nose, then the tail. Find it.

"Eleven, ten, nine—"

And the gravity that had held the *Tsiolkovsky* for the past five hours was gone again, disappearing like water poured into the sand, and they were dropping way too fast, and Bass still fished for air.

"I get no reading!" Jeffries said, and Bass pulled up the nose and the *Tsiolkovsky* stood up slightly; he waited for it to fall again.

"That's okay.. " Bass could feel the great wing thrumming; he smacked the knob again to close the lesznos and tensed for the jar of contact—but there was nothing, just a soft flow of gravity flowing back into his bones like shading into a drawing, and he knew he had just made the softest landing of a forty-year career.

"We're down," from the back.

"We're down," from the front.

Bass smacked another knob to close the trailing-edge flaps so the wing wouldn't rip off in the wind. Then he leaned back and grinned. Mars! He reached for Jeffries's arm (wishing for ceremony's sake it was Kirov's) and was surprised to see the doctor half-standing, looking alarmed toward the back of the ship.

The floor was tipping up like the deck of a small boat in a storm.

"What the hell's happening?" Bass demanded.

"The lesznos didn't close!" Kirov shouted. "I can see them from here."

Bass smacked the leszno knob in frustration, but the ship kept rocking. It was getting worse. The same wind that had set them down was trying to pick them up again, or at least tear the wing from the ship.

"I can cut the wing loose," said Bass. "But—"

"But it's our solar collector," said Kirov. "We can't let it blow away. We're going out to try and walk the slots down."

Fonda-Fox was already turning the wheel to open the inner air-lock door. "Jeffries, get your earcom on," Kirov said. "Give us the weather on earcom #4."

"What should I do?" wailed Greetings.

"Do? Quit hollering. And close this door after us." Kirov and Fonda-Fox were already in the air lock, sealing their facemasks.

"Air pressure exterior, point six millibars," Jeffries read. "Temperature, minus two centigrade. Wind speed, 177 kilometers per hour."

"You have a collect call from a Mr. Sweeney," said the operator on the flight deck radio. "Will you accept charges?"

"Yes," said Bass, wondering if she knew to wait thirty minutes for an answer. She had probably already hung up fifteen minutes ago. "Go help Greetings with the air lock," he said to Jeffries.

"Don't we have to make sure there's no contamination and all that?" Greetings asked as she strained against the wheel and the curved door slid shut.

"Ancient history," said Jeffries. "There have been twenty years of unmanned landers, sample tests, etc. It's certain now that there is no life on Mars for man to mess up. Fortunately. Or unfortunately. Or whatever. There they are, Bass. I can see them through the window, climbing up from the air lock to the wing."

*   *   *

"Slow but steady," Kirov said as she followed Fonda-Fox's turquoise-suited figure straight up the handholds from the air lock. The surface of Mars lay still untouched below them. The long, straight wing was a vibrating canopy over the *Tsiolkovsky*. "Tune to earcom #4 if you can hear me. Are you cold?"

"I'm cold," said Fonda-Fox.

"The marsuit has a heater but it takes a few minutes to work."

"It's the star-shaped knob on your dicktracy," Bass put in.

"I'm okay, let's do this first," said Fonda-Fox. "What do we do?"

"Just walk on the edge to force the lesznos down," Kirov said. "Bass, they're all still half-open. Must be sand. Can you see us?"

"No, you're on top of the wing. Wait. Yes, I can see your shadow!"

Cold, Mars was cold, even through the thermo-Spandex marsuit, Mars was cold. Fonda-Fox could feel it on the backs of his hands through his gloves as he walked the wing. The wind wasn't so bad. Even howling at over 150 kph (according to Jeffries on earcom #4), it was so thin it felt no worse than a strong seabreeze. Here where there was no sea. Here on Mars!

"Can you walk okay?" Jeffries asked.

"No problem," said Fonda-Fox. He looked behind him toward the other end of the wing, which was tipping up toward a cliff leading to a ruby sky. Kirov walked the leading edge, carefully stepping onto the top of the gill-like lift-enhancer slots and riding them down like little six-inch elevators. Fonda-Fox copied her, doing the same thing on his end of the wing.

"Have to step each one!" Kirov complained to Bass. "Shouldn't they all work together?"

Halfway out, the wing began to give up and lie down. Fonda-Fox cheered and walked backward. His end was already on the ground. Kirov was almost at the end of hers.

"Amazing how easy it is to walk," Fonda-Fox said. "After two years in zero g."

"It's the HT," said Jeffries, who was patched in with Bass on earcom #4.

"Slow and steady," said Kirov.

"Sweeney just called," said Bass. "I told him we were okay."

"Slow and steady," said Kirov.

Fonda-Fox waved at Kirov and she waved back. They had made it! The wing was drooping, no longer vibrating; and by the time Fonda-Fox rode down the next-to-last little elevator, his wingtip ten feet away was buried in the sand. He looked back. Kirov's wingtip, 120 feet away, was also in the sand. She waved, about to step off. Knowing she was entitled to the honor, Fonda-Fox stepped back—lost his balance and tripped on the last leszno; and fell three feet and 160 million miles onto the coarse red sand, becoming quite by accident the first Movie Star, and indeed the first human, to set foot on the red planet Mars.

BOOK
THREE

Stones, stones,
nothing but stones!
—SHELLEY

"THE *Konstantin Tsiolkovsky* has landed on the planet Mars. We come from Earth on a voyage of peace and understanding for all mankind."

Kirov had come back into the ship to officially declare the ship had landed, but Sweeney's operator had hung up, confused by the time delay. Kirov called Markson's Beverly Hills office and then his hotel in Santa Fe, but they both hung up, thinking it was a bad connection. "To hell with it," she said, handing the phone back to Bass, who left the historic first message on Markson's home answering machine, after the beep. Then Bass shut down the flight systems and powered up the environmental probes while Kirov and Fonda-Fox helped the others into their marsuits. Everyone wanted to get out and have a look around. The officers wore white and the rest wore colors: Fonda-Fox in turquoise, Greetings in orange, Glamour in bright red.

Jeffries should have been in the turquoise and Fonda-Fox in white, thought Kirov, as the Movie Star helped her drag the air freshener and the sunlight converter toward the air lock, where they would be tipped through and lowered to the sand outside.

"How cold does it feel?" asked Jeffries, who was helping Greetings put her boots on.

"Not bad," said Kirov. "It's almost forty degrees out there. Bass, just leave a message and come on. Aren't you getting into your marsuit?"

"In a minute," Bass said. As a boy, he had always been

the last one out of bed on Christmas morning. He enjoyed the anticipation more than the event.

Glamour went out the air lock first. No one witnessed his undersized feet hitting the sand. Indeed, he hardly noticed it himself, he was so anxious to film each of the others making the first step onto another world, down the short aluminum stair. First (this time) came Kirov, then Jeffries, then Greetings, followed by Fonda-Fox, who displayed, even here, on the far side of the sun, the legendary gallantry of the Movie Star.

Then they ran through it once more, just to make sure.

It was quiet at last inside the *Tsiolkovsky*. Bass stripped off his coveralls, then pulled his white Spandex marsuit over his thermal underwear. The suits were not pressurized, but they were tight against the skin. The heating coils (which it was expected would not be needed in midsummer) were powered by shoulder-mounted solar panels that looked like epaulets. The plastic air tank fit like a fanny pack and weighed only eight pounds (2.6 pounds M). The helmet was elastic, tight-fitting like a twentieth-century flier's leather hat, with a diver's-type face mask forming a pressurized area over the eyes. The gloves had an extra warming circuit, since they were tight and it was feared they might interfere with circulation.

Bass adjusted each glove individually, pressurized his mask, and opened the inner air-lock door. He wheeled it closed behind him, then unsealed the oval outer door, pushing it since the ship's five-pound air pressure wasn't enough to nudge it open. He stepped through the outer door, into the pale light, down the short stair, onto the sand, and it was just as he had always known it would be.

Mars lay all around him.

The *Tsiolkovsky* had landed belly-down on deep sand, pointed due south and uphill toward red dunes that spilled through a rocky notch. Somewhere in the dunes was the *Agnew*, half a mile away; and beyond the dunes, through the notch, was the Candor Chasm, the "Shining Canyon" of the Valles Marineris. To the east, behind the ship, a long stone slope became a cliff, and rose four thousand feet, dusted with snow toward the top. In front of Bass, to the west, the plains of Mars stretched out, featureless and uncratered for half a hundred miles—reds, volcanic grays, buffs and oranges—one of the longest views on the planet. The Tharsis was more than a plateau: it was actually a continent-sized bulge on the planet itself. The plain, which sloped upward toward the north, was smooth as far as Jeffries could see except for the southernmost of the small Tholus volcanoes, Tharsis Tholus, a perfect cone on the horizon to the north; and to the west of it, peeking over the curve of the horizon, the awesome dome of Ascraeus Mons, eighty thousand feet high, its thin snows gleaming white in the high sunlight.

Mars.

Mars at last.

On earcom #4 he could hear the happy jabber of his fellow voyagers. He turned them off and cracked his face mask, just a little, just for a second, just to hear the howl of the wind.

"Help me with this thing," Kirov said. Greetings took hold of the rear rack of the air freshener and together they dragged it to a low spot in the sand. It was the size of a small washing machine. Kirov popped in a sunlight disk and the engines whined as two legs burrowed deep into the Martian sand, looking for water ice. The freshener would process some of the water whole, and break the rest of it down into oxygen to add to the ship's system. Meanwhile, Fonda-Fox set aside the manual he had been reading and dragged the smaller digital sunlight converter across the sand; he plugged it into the wing, which had been lifted from the ship and set against a small dune facing south.

"This thing makes our air?" Greetings asked, slapping the air freshener. "Where are the batteries?"

"No batteries," said Kirov. "Doesn't need them. It runs on a CD system. The wing acts as a solar collector. The converter Fonda-Fox just set up digitizes the sunlight and stores it directly on compact disks. Then we play it back to run the air freshener here, as well as the ship's heating and vent systems, which Jeffries is supposed to be setting up. Where the hell is he?"

"Up there," said Greetings. "On the hill."

Jeffries looked behind him. Even at 100 mph, the wind was too weak to wipe away his footprints following him up to the top of the dune, and by the time he reached the top, it had died completely. The gravity felt the same as on Earth, even though it was only one-third Earth normal. The human body had an uncanny capacity to adapt to whatever weight conditions prevailed, making Jeffries wonder if space travel were not part of the genetic heritage of humankind.

It was high noon at midsummer and they were at the equator, less than two thousand feet elevation above Mars datum. Once the cold night air had been pushed out of the canyon below, this was one of the warmest places on the planet, with the densest, moistest air. The dicktracy on Jeffries's wrist read .5 pounds per square inch (as opposed to Earth's 14 and the ship's 5), and a temperature of 34 degrees Fahrenheit (1 centigrade). The air pressure was rising with the temperature. That was odd; he wondered if it could be significant. He knelt and scooped up the sand and let it run between his fingers, conscious for the first time of his white, skintight gloves. His fingers had still not completed the voyage from Earth; like the robot landers of the last century, they could poke the red planet but not truly touch it. What is the difference between us and the *Viking* fifty years ago? Jeffries wondered. We can walk on the planet but we still can't touch it; we're just poking it with a shorter stick.

He knelt and picked up the sand again. Or his gloves did. After all this travel, he couldn't personally touch the sand. The only planet in the universe he could touch was Earth. He couldn't *not* touch Earth. He was made of it. He was Earth touching Earth.

He was not made of Mars.

So what the hell was he doing here?

"Jeffries, is your receiver on earcom #4?" Kirov demanded.

"It is." By the detached wing, he could see Kirov and Fonda-Fox fooling with the air freshener. Bass was at the rear of the *Tsiolkovsky*, pulling off the cone-shaped engine cover, revealing the ship's blunt, businesslike tail. Glamour was on top of the ship, sitting on the now-useless wing rotor track, filming Greetings against the coarse red sand. She looked up at Jeffries and waved. He waved back and started down, resisting the impulse to run for the sheer hell of it, puzzled by his own happiness. Why did he feel so glad to be on Mars?

Glamour booked 22K of the kid against the sunwashed sand, then climbed down and filmed her against the sky. Then he sent her off to help Bass and just booked horizon, 12K worth, then 12K more. He was beginning to understand, finally, why they had come to Mars. The light was so strange that he might have been in the system of a different star, or even in a different universe altogether. The sky was pink, but a pink unlike any he had ever filmed on Earth, where pink was a warm color. This Mars pink was a high, cold, dead pink that passed imperceptibly to maroon and then ruby toward the vault of the sky, even near the noonday sun. There were no clouds. The light seemed bright to eyes that had adjusted for a year and a half to the gloomy inside of a dacha-colored spaceship; but according to the *Demogorgon*'s meters it was actually a little dim. It was thin light, like paint with too much water.

But Glamour could correct for that later. With the *Demogorgon*, he could correct for anything.

It took Kirov and Bass two hours to go over the *Tsiolkovsky*, seam by seam. It was undamaged. Bass had that one essential quality of a good pilot, luck, and he counted on it as did, he often suspected, the ships he flew. The ship had landed flat like an airplane, but it would have to be winched up into a vertical position before taking off in eleven days.

"Shouldn't we go up in the dunes and have a look at the *Igloo*?" Greetings asked.

"You mean the *Agnew*. Tomorrow," Kirov said. "Today we stay around the ship. I want to monitor the air freshener, make sure it's making both water and air. Plus I want to take a shower. Fonda-Fox, is everything buttoned down there?"

Fonda-Fox gave her the thumbs-up. Kirov closed her clipboard with a satisfying click and patted Bass on the rear, NASA style. She hadn't felt this good since Baikonur. The ship was sound. The crew was safe. She was on Mars.

"Greetings, Mars Voyagers," said Markson, or Markson-tape, or Markson-past, for even if he was "live," he was speaking from 14.7 minutes (M) ago. The delay was accompanied by a distortion and a flatness in the transmission, as if the Mars Voyagers were looking at a faded print of an old movie on a poorly received channel.

Markson was followed by a string of politicians and celebrities. Johnny Carson, Jr., invited the Mars Voyagers to his show as soon as they got back. Vice-President Kennedy invited them to the White House and congratulated them on an achievement comparable in history to the signing of the American Constitution.

"How come there are no Russians?" asked Kirov. "Let's turn it off and enjoy our first evening together on Mars. We can play it back and watch it later."

"Oh, wow, look!" Greetings said as she poured a bowl of cereal. After almost two years in zero g it was a luxury to be able to pour—to watch the Froot Loops march in lockstep through the air from box to bowl.

"Hey! Where are my rock tapes?" Kirov said. "Where are the movie disks; where are the book disks?" She turned accusingly toward Jeffries, who had loaded the library onto the *Tsiolkovsky*.

"You said cut everything to the bone," he said.

Kirov held up two CDs. "Charles Mingus and William Shakespeare. This is it? Nothing more?"

"Each contains everything that came before," Jeffries said. "And much of what came after as well."

"Collect call from a Mr. Sweeney?" the operator broke in. "Will you accept the charges? Hello? Hello? I'm sorry, Mr. Sweeney, there doesn't seem to be anyone there. Would you like to check that number again?"

2

THERE IS SOMETHING about waking up on a new planet. The first sighting, the long approach from space, the fiery descent through the atmosphere, the historic first footstep—all are so melodramatic, so shaped and colored by the entire history of discovery and exploration, so written about and celebrated as to lack both subtlety and surprise. But waking up, that's something else. A new light taps at the eyelids. A new gravity pulls at the blood. When the night's dreams fly away in the daylight, where do they go on a world undreamed-in before, where there are no drifts of old dreams filling the gutters like dry leaves? A new world. And the consciousness, which the ancients used to think was newly created every day, almost seems truly to be so here on Mars, as the realization steals over you that you are no longer on the world whose turning awakened your fathers and their fathers for a half a million years, but on another.

So it seemed to Dr. Sundiata Cinque Jeffries.

"Rise and shine," called the Captain. Wan sunlight slanted over the clifftop and through the east port, and a quick check of the electrics showed that it was enough to flood the digitizer that filled the solar CDs that powered the *Tsiolkovsky*'s internal systems and external air freshener. Bass and Jeffries suited up to go and find the *Agnew* across the dunes. Greetings, still playing Cinderella, cleaned up after breakfast and got dressed with Fonda-Fox. Glamour was eager to start filming in the weak-tea Martian light.

"What about makeup?" Greetings asked.

Fonda-Fox laughed. "You've seen too many old movies. Makeup is all dithered in digitally now, after the image is shot."

"Let's go, Bones," Bass said.

"I'm right behind you," said Jeffries. "And don't call me Bones." Their job was to find the diesel #2 fuel that would carry them back to the *Mary Poppins*. Kirov would stay with the *Tsiolkovsky* and try to reach Sweeney in Pasadena and Markson in Santa Fe.

Walking was easy; the sand was coarse and heavy, like river sand. Everything lighter had long since blown away. There were red drifts against every stone and between the ripples on the ground. The sand came in three colors: red, dark red and light red. They were unmixed, as if the wind blew them from three continents and they would not combine.

"Now give him a hug like you're seeing him for the first time in twenty years," said Glamour. Startled, Jeffries looked over at Bass, who trudged on unhearing. It was Glamour on earcom #3, directing Greetings and Fonda-Fox. Jeffries switched through earcom #4, #5, #6 until he found Bass's steady breathing on #11. Bass didn't want to talk and neither did he. After the continual jabber of the ship, silence was a relief. Even when they saw the lander a hundred yards ahead, neither did more than point and nod.

They were almost upon it before they noticed that something was wrong.

"Sweeney sends his best," Markson said. "He would be here in Santa Fe with me except he's moonlighting in an animation studio since he lost his job at Stadium Solutions. He would call but I can't afford to give him a phone card until we get a signed contract, but it shouldn't take long—because look at this!"

Markson waved a piece of paper. At his side, Mrs. Gentry looked as proud and shy as a new bride. Standing on his other side was a New Mexico State Trooper in full regalia.

"This is our documentation for composite Star certification," Markson said. "Thanks to Mrs. Gentry here and Lieutenant Briggs of the New Mexico State Police. Now all we need is the rushes and I think Disney-Gerber will bite. How soon can you get me some Mars footage? Lou, are you there? Come on."

"Greetings, are you there? I know you're there," said Mrs. Gentry. "I don't understand why she won't answer her own mother."

"Greetings and Glamour are out shooting," Kirov said. "We'll have to call back this evening. Over and out."

She hung up. Talking with Earth was always frustrating. She didn't like being out of touch with Mission Design. It was lonesome in the ship, so she suited up to join Bass and Jeffries in the dunes. It was against regs for all three officers to leave the ship, but who was watching?

The *Spiro Agnew* and the *Yuri Gagarin* had been sent from Mars orbit to the surface two days apart, two weeks before the end of the twentieth century. The *Gagarin*, deflected by an unopened parachute vent, sailed off and was lost. The *Agnew* landed on target in a field of dunes at the Candor Chasm's western entrance. It carried 1.3 tons of tools and parts, including a lightweight all-terrain vehicle, 5.6 tons of diesel #2 fuel, and a small solar plant (nondigital) to process twice that much oxidant (liquid oxygen, or LOX) out of the thin Martian atmosphere over the next four years (M), or until the joint US-Soviet mission landed. Bass had helped fit the *Agnew* out for launch and had been in Houston when its readings had come in. Four years (M) had passed, and then four more. In fact the *Agnew* outlasted both NASA and the Baikonur Institute, and when its last messages had been logged its tanks were full and it was still processing LOX to replace that which was boiling away out the overflow.

Kirov had confirmed the *Agnew's* location from orbit by its radio signal ID, and Jeffries had located it visually after the storm had lifted. Bass had seen it flying in. Patterned after the early moon landers, it was a squat, businesslike little unit, like a twelve-foot-tall coffeemaker on three legs; unmistakable in its outline and detail.

And this wasn't it.

"This doesn't look right," Bass said as they approached across the sand. It was too big. The *Agnew* looked at least twenty feet tall. And there was no gleam of metal, no shine of plastic or foil. It was dull, like barn wood or mud.

The closer they got, the worse it looked.

"Holy shit," Jeffries said. He stopped, not sure if he wanted to believe what he was seeing. Bass never hesitated, though. He walked right up and kicked the end of one of the *Agnew*'s extended legs and watched it crumble into clay. Reaching up, he grabbed at a lump that had at first seemed to be an external pump housing, and it broke away in his hand.

He crumbled it between his fingers.

"It's dirt," he said.

Bass walked around the oversized clay *Agnew*. It was complete with a cluster of clods for each of its three small tanks, a mud model of its solar unit, a short clay ridge for each of its three outstretched legs. There were two knobs where the LOX pump rotor vane pitch control was accessed. On the prototype, twenty years before, Bass had learned to tune them by setting the intake (left) at slightly over half and then upping the outtake until the gauge above the panel stopped bouncing or until the pumps whined at a steady D note.

But here nothing bounced; nothing whined. Bass broke off the left knob and crumbled it into powder between his fingers. The right knob was printed with a crude "Я". Angrily, Bass smacked it with the heel of his hand and it dropped into the sand. He started to break off something else, but Jeffries caught his hand.

"Cool it," he said. "There's no point in tearing it up, at least not until we learn what it is or . . ."

"Or who made it?" Bass stepped back and they both looked around uneasily. Then they both jumped as a voice rang in their ears:

"Who made what? Where are you guys?" It was Kirov. She had tried all the channels before finding them on ear-com #11.

"We're at the *Agnew* and we've got a problem," Bass said.

"What do you mean you're at the *Agnew*? I've been at the *Agnew* for ten minutes waiting for you. You guys are lost. Look up, I'm setting off a flare."

Bass scanned the horizon looking for the little signal rocket's trail. He was surprised to see it blast up from behind the next dune.

Jeffries was already on his way up the steep sand slope.

"Will somebody tell me what the hell's going on?" asked Bass.

"Come look at this," Jeffries said. On the other side of the dune, he saw Kirov with her arms folded, tapping one toe, standing beside a smaller, shinier and very real *Agnew* gleaming in the noon (M) sun.

3

THERE IS NO MORE financially rewarding, socially exciting, technically challenging, or artistically tedious business than film. Fonda-Fox liked acting, but the actual moments of acting—the work of solving a problem, getting into a scene or situation, discovering a character—were few and far between in Hollywood. It was bad enough in the old analog days, when shooting was mostly a business of being paid fantastic sums to wait on light, wait on props, wait on wind or weather or on the temperaments of others. Digital made it even worse: now scenes were only roughed in, to be corrected later in edit. The *Demogorgon* promised to be the last straw. With its awesome memory bank, internal self-editing capabilities, tachyon delays and video loops, the digitizer completely freed the image on the screen from the real world that "sent" it, reducing the actor to nothing more than a prop to be booked in a variety of poses and settings, to be later dimensionalized and dithered and screebed, made older or younger, turned left or right, kissed or killed depending on the story line, which was often purchased long after the image had been booked. The work that had been something less than acting was now not even acting like acting. All the cameraman had to do was book enough image and later the editors could make the image do anything they wanted. If it weren't for the Guild, there wouldn't be any need at all for Movie Stars or even actors.

Fonda-Fox had watched enviously as Bass and Jeffries

started up the dunes to find the *Agnew*, and even more enviously as Kirov had followed half an hour later. Now that the actual location filming had begun, his days of playing Fourth Officer were over. He was stuck on "on set" with Glamour and Greetings, walking in circles in the sand.

"Mr. Fonda-Fox?" Glamour always called the actors "Mister" when he was officially playing Director.

"Sure, sorry." Fonda-Fox took Greetings by the hand. As they trudged in circles, the powdery sand rose in clouds around their feet—clouds that were gone almost as soon as they appeared, with little air to sustain them. Greetings had on her face that look of mixed anticipation, pleasure and pain that Fonda-Fox had seen on so many movie sets. She had to pee.

"Glamour? Can you guys hear me?" a voice broke in. It was Kirov.

"Hey!" Glamour complained. "I thought you were going to stay off earcom #3 while we were working."

"Sorry, Lou, but we need your help up here. We have a problem with the *Agnew*. Bring a shovel."

Even though the Martian sand was light, it took Fonda-Fox, Glamour and Jeffries an hour to dig out the buried side of the *Spiro Agnew*. When Kirov had come on the unit, after taking a wrong turn through the dunes, only half of it had been showing. Dry clay was clinging to the struts and tanks like leaf fungus on a log, hiding its contours and giving it a stuccoed look.

While the men dug, Kirov sent Greetings back to the ship to try and call Sweeney. Then she and Bass crossed the dune to look at the other, or, as she called it, *Faux Agnew*. "Spooky," was all she said. She broke off a piece. It was made out of the same white clay that covered the *Agnew*, only in the one it simulated the shape that in the other it hid.

"I've got Sweeney's wife," said Greetings, breaking in on earcom #4. "She says he's helping his cousin paint motel rooms in the Valley. She says he got fired from Stadium Solutions. She says . . ."

"Get his cousin's number and keep trying," Kirov said, switching off the sound and heading back across the dune.

Dug out of the sand, the real *Agnew* looked as if it had been attacked by a fungus. The LOX tank was bright and clean, and steaming a little from the overflow. The lower part of the fuel, or diesel, tank was covered with ridges of powdery white clay. Jeffries peeled off a few samples while Bass checked the gauges on the power unit. They both read 99.43 but he didn't trust them. He knocked on the fuel tank with his knuckles, but it was impossible to hear through a marsuit in the thin atmosphere. He stepped back and swung at the tank with his shovel. Kirov shook her head. It rang too high, like a bell far away. It sounded empty, but there was only one way to be sure. Bass lay on his back, scooted under the tanks and, pulling a clutch-head screwdriver from the top of his boot, unscrewed the panel that covered the *Agnew*'s backup analog gauges.

"Just as I suspected," he said. "The fuel tank is less than half-full," he said. "We can replace the LOX from the processors, but unless we can find some more diesel #2 fuel, we're in trouble."

Fonda-Fox, alarmed, looked at the three officers. Jeffries looked thoughtful, but he always looked thoughtful. Bass looked worried, but he always looked worried. Kirov didn't look worried, but she never looked worried. Fonda-Fox decided not to worry. He had been in enough movies to know that problems like this existed only to be solved.

"Lunchtime," Kirov said. "Let's go back to the ship. Fonda-Fox, leave that shovel here, nobody's going to steal it. On second thought, better bring it."

While Greetings prepared a lunch of liver paste on just-inflated white bread, and Kirov and Bass tried to locate Mission Design, Jeffries checked out the Mars Voyagers, looking for ill effects from the long morning EVAs. Although the air pressure was low, Mars wasn't like space. The Thinsulate elastic marsuits kept the skin from decompression blistering, and body heat was enough to keep everyone warm—at least here at the equator in midsummer. There didn't seem to be any ill effects either from the suits or the long periods of outdoor activity.

Then, as an afterthought, he called the *Mary Poppins* and patched into the system monitoring Beverly Glenn's vital signs; she was sleeping peacefully.

Meanwhile, Kirov had reached Sweeney. "We can replace the liquid oxygen," she explained. "The air freshener is pumping it right now out of the soil, and we can cool it to a liquid. We can pump hydrogen, too. But diesel fuel is organic, and there's none of that on Mars. Somehow it leaked or got leached out of the tanks. We need you to come up with a fix. Is there any way we can convert this F-1 to run on hydrogen?"

"Negative," Sweeney said thirty minutes later. "It'll only run on diesel #2. We've definitely got a problem here. The *Agnew* was the backup to the Soviet fuel unit, the *Gagarin*, which blew off course landing and was lost. If we could only—"

"This *Gagarin*," Jeffries said, remembering the light he thought he had seen from orbit. "Ask him if it could have landed inside the canyon, say, about twenty miles?"

"Lunch," said Greetings. With a packing crate as a table, she set out paper plates and napkins. Outside the tiny window, Mars was as still as a beach without an ocean.

"Possible," said Sweeney, thirty minutes later. "I have all the old NASA figures on disk, but the problem is running them through our revised ecosphere program. I need a Cray and it's the weekend. But what the hell, this is an emergency! I'll head down to Stadium Solutions and call you back from there in a few hours. Over."

"I thought he got fired," said Bass.

"Hurry up and pass the ketchup," said Glamour.

"Isn't it nice to eat in gravity?" said Greetings, smacking

the bottle. She had no doubt that Kirov would find an answer to the fuel problem. Kirov was the Captain, after all.

After lunch, while they waited for Sweeney's return call, Jeffries set up a mini-lab out of a crate and examined the clay samples. They were white, not snow white but dead white, like the undersides of mushrooms and about the same consistency. They looked almost alive but not quite. Under Jeffries's pocket knife, the clay flaked in thin sheets. It had a familiar smell that brought back memories of his grandmother's house in Atlanta.

Baking? No. Wax? No. Jeffries closed his eyes and let his mind drift. He could see his grandma's frilled curtains filled with sun. And on the table, the old ornamental kerosene lamp . . .

Jeffries broke off a piece of clay and took a bite. "Found it," he said.

"Found what?" asked Kirov from the flight deck, where she was waiting to hear from Sweeney.

"The fuel. It's in the clay," said Jeffries. "The clay ate it."

"Take over, Bass," Kirov said. She climbed over the crates to the back of the ship and pulled two marsuits off the wall, tossing Jeffries one. "Let's you and me go for a walk."

The video came up showing Sweeney in a large computer room, with screens behind and above him, all lighted. He was wearing a white Dacron shirt and blue gabardine NASA-style pants; his penholder read "Morton-Thiokol."

"I ran the figures and it's possible," he said. "What you saw in the canyon could have been the *Gagarin*."

"What who saw in what canyon?" asked Glamour.

"What's a gagren?" asked Greetings.

"Hooray," said Fonda-Fox.

"Ssshhh," said Bass. He was taking the call with Fonda-Fox and Greetings looking over one shoulder and Glamour filming over the other.

Sweeney went on: "I ran a series of possibility configurations based on the wind figures and temperatures you have given me, and in two out of six simulations the *Gagarin* landed against the North Wall beyond the Candor Mesa. That's thirty-five kilometers, or twenty-one miles, east and a thousand feet, or three hundred meters, below you, down in the canyon. The question is, can you get down there? I'm faxing through the extrapolated two out of three location, but in the meantime I can show you on this map."

Sweeney turned with his remote toward a large screen and brought up a map of Mars. He started clicking through screens past contour maps of volcanoes, badlands, icecaps and braided canyons. Then suddenly he tossed the remote away and raised his hands over his head.

"What's the matter with him?" Fonda-Fox asked.

Sweeney was backing up against the video array, hands raised. A man in a blue uniform was pushing him down against the console while another, with a drawn gun, put his out-stretched fingers toward the screen so violently that Greetings jumped back and fell back across a packing case.

"Somebody do something!" she cried. "Somebody help him!"

"No way," said Bass. "Whatever is happening to Sweeney already happened fifteen minutes ago."

"Life on Mars?" Jeffries said as he and Kirov trudged through the dunes above the *Tsiolkovsky*. The late afternoon sun was lengthening their shadows across the sand. "I wouldn't call the clay 'life.' It seems to be a replicating, not a reproducing form—a sort of crystal structure that can 'grow.' The catalyst seems to be the diesel fuel. My guess is that the activated clay seeks out the highest form of organization around, and replicates it."

"The *Agnew*."

"Yeah. Ordinarily it duplicates itself. But since it has no genetic history or memory, its own form would be no more familiar to it than any other, so when something more interesting turns up . . ."

"You get life on Mars."

"Not life. Something even more interesting. Something between a salt crystal and a primitive prokaryotic cell." They came out of the the the dunes; ahead was a long sand slope to the notch overlooking the canyon. Kirov started tramping up it and Jeffries had no choice but to follow.

"One of the hypotheses in the Dual Origin theory is that it all starts with a replicating crystalline structure. Of course all this is just a theory. I don't have tools for a really good structural analysis. What I intend to do is fax through a cross section of a sample tonight, so that . . ."

"That's what I wanted to talk to you about," said Kirov. She was twenty feet ahead, so he couldn't see her face; but with the earcoms they could talk as if they were walking side by side. "How come you didn't tell anyone you had seen the *Gagarin?*"

"I didn't exactly see it," Jeffries said. "I thought I might have seen it."

"But you didn't tell your fellow officers."

"There was nothing to tell. I forgot all about it. What are you driving at?"

"The clay. I think we should keep this under our hats for a while," said Kirov.

"You mean not tell Sweeney."

"Not tell Sweeney. Not tell Markson." Kirov pulled ahead again. "Look at it this way. Suppose we did discover life on Mars, or a missing link or a wannabee cell, or whatever. Would we want the first people to know about it to be Disney-Gerber or Kashawahara-Globus or whatever superconglomerate ends up owning this film?"

"Who would you tell? The Soviet Union?"

"You could do worse. And there are other countries, socialist countries less backward than the US."

Even in Mars's one-third gravity, the long slope was a killer. Jeffries's face mask was beginning to fog up and he lifted it off his chin just for an instant; and felt a delicious blast of frosty, never-before-breathed air. Mixed with the oxygen from his tank, it smelled tangy and exotic.

Kirov must be getting tired too, he thought. She had stopped again. But this time she was standing funny, with one hand on her hip and the other raised to her face mask, leaning forward, not resting; and when he caught up with her he saw why. She was in the notch, overlooking the Candor Chasm of the Valles Marineris, a canyon dwarfing anything he had ever seen except, perhaps, the spectacular skies and seas of faraway Earth. The floor was only a thousand feet below them, at the bottom of a sandy slope. Ten miles across, the South Wall rose in cliffs fifteen thousand feet high, rising to twenty thousand in the distance. The cliffs were striped by colored bands and fantastic wind-carved bluffs. The North Wall was less high, at least here at the mouth of the canyon; but deeper in, it rose to at least ten thousand feet. Both walls were red and pink, the same color as the sky in its lower reaches, so that in the distance the horizon was almost as soft as the sea's. From a deep notch near the top of the South Wall, a feathery spray plunged down two miles: a cascade of what they both at first thought was water but then realized was sand and dust, a dry "waterfall" fed by the dunes above. The canyon floor was dark, flat, cracked and crazed into a jumble of ravines. Smaller feeder canyons, each as large as the Grand Canyon, led off to the north and south in the distance. In the center of the chasm, Candor Mesa squatted like a Martian sphinx, guarding the far reaches.

When he heard the call-waiting beeper, Jeffries looked at his dicktracy. They had been standing overlooking the canyon for almost ten minutes without a word.

Kirov opened the earcom circuit.

"Sorry to break in," said Bass, "but Sweeney just called with some locationals. He says the *Gagarin* could be down in the canyon, near the North Wall."

"That fits with what I saw," said Jeffries. "That would put it just on the other side of that mesa."

"Good," said Kirov. "You two go down in the morning. I'll stay with the ship."

"Aye-aye," said Bass. "Meanwhile, the bad news is, Sweeney's in jail. I'll explain when you get here."

They turned and started back down toward the *Tsiolkovsky*. To the west, beyond the whitecapped dome of Arsia Mons, the horizon was pink, darkening above to purple and black. There were only a few clouds, straight overhead: ribbons of rose cirrus. The whole display shimmered like the northern lights, then darkened quickly, almost with a shudder, as if a lid had closed.

Sunset on Mars. Kirov unclipped her light. As they trudged back down through the dunes, she wondered if they had settled anything.

"You should have been here," said Greetings. "They broke in and arrested Sweeney. He's in jail."

"He's the one that broke in," said Bass. "Apparently, after he was laid off at Stadium Solutions, he kept a key. He set off the alarms when he was running our program through their mainframes, and they got him for breaking and entering."

"Ssshhh," said Fonda-Fox.

Markson was on screen, standing in front of his desk, looking harried. "—until Monday morning when he's arraigned and they will set bail. That's the bad news," he said. "The good news is that the rushes Glamour sent look pretty good. I've sent the new composite image to Disney-Gerber. Did I tell you they were interested? Meanwhile, the New Mexico State Police are—"

Kirov turned away, bored. "What in the world are you doing?" she asked Bass, who was leaning over a pile of red and green plastic and rubber parts.

He pointed at the label on an opened crate and she bent down to read it: *Isuzu: one three-wheeled all-terrain vehicle (ATV): reciprocating plastic hydrogen engine: 1,200 cc.*

"Think it'll run?" he asked.

4

THE NEXT MORNING, after a breakfast of egg paste and canned biscuits, as soon as the dawn wind had begun to die, Bass and Jeffries threw two extra tanks of air and two empty plastic drums into the bed of the Isuzu three-wheeled truck and started through the dunes toward the entrance to the Candor Chasm. Bass drove and Jeffries straddled the seat behind him, holding on to his waist.

The little ATV pop-popped as it wound between between the dunes, its open pipes making barely a whisper in the rarefied air of Mars. After a while it settled down to a smooth rumble as Bass tweaked the injectors and got the hydrogen/oxygen mixture right. They passed the *Faux Agnew* and then the *Agnew*, surrounded by sandpiles where it had been dug out. To the left, the east, the stone slope rose in a smooth swoop to the stars that dotted the rose-black sky. Even at midmorning it looked like dawn on Mars. Or sunset.

Jeffries tried to remember what Earth's sky looked like.

The dunes got looser after the *Agnew*, and Bass shifted down. The oil temperature needle started to climb, so he turned up the fuel mixture, making it a little rich. That meant the truck was fuel cooled and twice inefficient. Not that it mattered: both hydrogen and oxygen were by-products of the *Tsiolkovsky*'s air freshener. It was kerosene, diesel #2, they were worried about.

Bass wondered if they would ever see Earth again.

Past the end of the dunes they reached the gap, where a

174

steep sand slope swept down into the Candor Chasm. Far across the canyon the dustfall streamed; rivers of mist clung to the canyon floor a thousand feet below. Jeffries had seen this view for the first time yesterday with Kirov, and he expected Bass would stop and look, as they had, transfixed. But he was wrong.

"Hang on." Bass kicked the ATV down into low and stood up on the pegs, blipping the throttle and then letting the two-cylinder plastic V-twin brake them as they pitched over the rim and started down the long slope, down into the mysterious, open-before-them heart of Mars.

"Those guys sure don't talk much," Kirov said to Fonda-Fox. She had kept her earcom tuned to Bass's on #6, but she had heard only the faint pop-popping of the Isuzu's engine; then it too was lost as they descended into the canyon and out of range. While Glamour filmed Greetings in all the variations of Martian light and shade, Fonda-Fox and Kirov were filling the air freshener's power intake with disks loaded with sunlight from the solar collector. Then they put the "empties" back into the solar collector to be reinitialized and loaded with fresh, digitized sunlight.

"I got two extras here," Fonda-Fox said.

"Bring them inside, we'll use them for 'firewood' tonight." The residue left behind on the emptied disks was usually enough to keep the stove inside the ship flickering. While they waited for the air lock to open, Kirov looked up toward the dunes, as if she could see past them into the canyon.

"Worried?" Fonda-Fox asked, knowing he wouldn't get a straight answer. He had been in enough movies to know that the Captain always kept her worries to herself.

"Worried?" What a question, Kirov thought. There was no assurance that the *Gagarin* had ever made it into the canyon. Or that Bass and Jeffries would be able to find it. Or reach it if they did. Or that there would be any diesel #2 left in it. Or that they could get the fuel back out of the canyon. "I don't worry," she said. "I learned long ago that worrying was a waste of time."

Bass drove down the long sand slope in broad, swooping S curves, then put the three-wheeler up into second, then third, when he hit the hard clay at the bottom. As he drove east toward the mesa, the flat canyon floor narrowed until the high walls on each side blocked the lower sky; the sky above was deep black-pink, the almost-magenta of space, seasoned with more stars than they had seen since entering the atmosphere two days before.

The Isuzu could do about forty on the flat. The smooth rumble of the twin-cylinder plastic engine throbbed through the seat as Bass found a speed he liked. The ground was smooth, blown free of sand by the dawn wind, except for little drifts here and there like sugar spilled onto a table.

As they passed to the left of Candor Mesa, a flat-topped monument as high as Pikes Peak, the canyon narrowed and the sky overhead seemed darker. Jeffries looked at his dicktracy and saw that it was 10:20 A.M. (M); they had been riding for almost an hour on the canyon floor. The air pressure was 1.9, twice as high as in the dune field where they had landed. They were heading north and east; spires and castellations of pink and rose lay ahead, and behind—Jeffries looked back and saw that the sand slope was barely visible, a low point in the farthest horizon.

The beat of the 1,200-cc V-twin slowed. Ahead, white mist clung to the ground in rows, like cotton in bloom. Bass steered between two rows, and then when they began to angle off, cut across one. The ATV bumped slightly, and Jeffries saw that the mist rose out of narrow seams or cracks in the canyon floor. "Stop and let me get a look at this," he said.

Bass stopped and Jeffries got off. Along the seams, little clay buds grew, the size and shape of mushrooms. He broke off two and put them into his specimen bag. They were the same dead white as the clay he had collected back at the *Agnew* ·

"You mean this is all we do all day?" Greetings said. Glamour shrugged and kept filming. "Walk up and down? Look at each other? I thought we would have lines to learn, scenes to rehearse. Is it because I'm not really a—"

Fonda-Fox could see through the mask of her marsuit that she was close to tears. "It's not you," he said, taking her hand. "It's just the way it works. It's all digitized. Once they have stored your image for a critical threshold of K, they can remix and redesign it to do almost anything. A smile? It can be put together. A fall? Patch it in. Of course, it's still you—"

Greetings pulled her hand away. "There's no acting *at all?*"

"That's nice," Glamour said. "The Bette Davis bit with the hands on the hips—I could use a few more K of that."

"There hasn't been for years," Fonda-Fox said. "The truth is, most of the Stars in the Guild can't act. It's been bred out of us. We're like dogs that can't hunt. The few who can, do their acting in summer stock."

"Summer stock?" Greeting asked. "What's that?"

"Summer stock? It's—"

"Say that again," Glamour said. He moved to where he could get her face through the mask. "I like that. Get real close; now look up into his eyes and say it, Miss Buffalo."

"Summer stock," she whispered.

"Say it back to her. Say it like lovers."

"Summer stock."

"Summer stock."

Bass rode straight across the plain toward the canyon wall, angling across the seams, scattering the thin mist and crunching through the lines of little buds. It felt wrong to Jeffries, vandalistic, like driving a truck through a field of beans.

It didn't bother Bass at all.

Jeffries checked his dicktracy. It was noon (M) and they had been gone almost two hours. The air pressure was 2.1, almost half the atmospheric pressure in the ship (which at 5 was one-third Earth ambient of 14.5). The temperature was a balmy 39 degrees. Jeffries resisted the impulse to tear off his face mask and breathe unhindered the cold air of Mars.

The engine temperature seemed especially sensitive to the denser air, and Bass was able to run the V-twin a little leaner and still keep the cylinder temperature at a level the plastic could tolerate. Only a mile or so ahead, he could see the entrance to a feeder canyon where, if Sweeney's computers and Jeffries's intuitions were right, they would find the *Gagarin*.

The mist was heavy: when they rode over a seam, it clung to the tires and then spread about behind them in a trail that gradually disappeared like seafoam.

The cliffs of the North Wall ahead were not sheer like the South Wall, but ragged and wild, like pure color carved into shapes by the wind. Jeffries tapped Bass on the shoulder and pointed. At their base, near an opening in the cliff wall, was a squat, familiar shape. The *Gagarin*? Or a *Faux Gagarin*?

"Wish we could eat outside," Greetings said. It was noon on Mars and they were inside the *Tsiolkovsky* having lunch.

"A barbecue," said Kirov, remembering her NASA days in Houston. She was trying to raise Bass on the ship's radio, but everything was blank since he had descended into the canyon.

"A picnic," Greetings said. "Like in the movies. People sitting around on those canvas chairs, eating fancy catered food. Or was that all bullshit too?"

"That was real," Glamour said, between mouthfuls of chicken paste and freshly inflated bread. "I was raised on movie food."

"You worked as an extra?" Fonda-Fox asked.

"I didn't but my aunt Megan did. Us Hollywood little people took care of one another, and you English had a hard time keeping us counted."

"What do you mean, 'you English'?" Fonda-Fox asked. "I happen to be Jewish."

"Nothing personal. We called all the oversized people English. Pass the chicken."

The chicken paste was made for zero g. Only Kirov liked it; only Kirov had spent her teenage years in and out of zero g.

"Beverly Hills calling Mars," Markson said. "Listen up, I have the good news you've all been waiting for."

Like the *Agnew*, the *Gagarin* was a tin can on three legs, about the size of a Chevy van set on end. Bass shut off the Isuzu and approached it cautiously, almost superstitiously, as if he thought his own eagerness approaching the *Faux Agnew* might have been what turned it to clay.

Jeffries stood back and watched. The *Gagarin* was clean. There was none of the leaf clay that had formed on the *Agnew*, nor were there any clay buds on the ground nearby. The buds seemed confined to the cracks in the canyon floor farther from the wall. Bass whanged the side of the unit's tank with the side of his hand, and was rewarded with a dull thump that even Jeffries could hear.

"It's real, anyway," Bass said. "And it even sounds full."

"Does it have a beacon?" Jeffries asked.

Bass opened a small panel and shoved in a battery pack. "It does now." He lifted a plastic plate, and under it numbers began to dance in a blur. Then they settled at:

LOX: 6.65

KERO#2: 45%

"Well, it looks like we might see Earth again," said Bass. "Between this tank and the *Agnew*, we have just enough fuel to take us back up to the *Mary Poppins*. Now all we have to do is get it out of this canyon."

While Bass hooked up a filler hose to the fuel drum in the

bed of the ATV, Jeffries looked around. If the *Gagarin*'s beacon hadn't been on, what was it he had seen? The Soviet unit was at the mouth of a deep, narrow canyon that fed into the side of Candor Chasm, under a high stone cliff scoured and pitted by windblown sand. The parachute that had lowered it the last three hundred feet of its journey from Earth twenty years before had long since blown away.

Jeffries had the strangest feeling: as if he had been here before. Perhaps it was because he had traced his way up the canyon with the telescope.

"I guess what I thought was a beacon was the reflection of the sun on the tank," he said. Even as he said it, he didn't believe it.

"Must have been," said Bass. "No juice to run it. I'm still waiting for the batteries to soak up enough to start the pump. Can't just slip in a disk. This thing was built back before they had sunlight digitizers. Where you going?"

"I want to look up the canyon, around the corner. To see if there is any more of that clay around."

"Just stay in touch on earcom #4."

"Will do."

Greetings's mother was beaming. She was standing beside Markson, holding a copy of the *Hollywood Reporter*. The headline read: GUILD MEMBERS STRANDED ON MARS.

"What's so great about that?" Greetings asked.

"You're the Guild member," Fonda-Fox said. "They've gotten you half-membership, enough for the composite—"

"Ssshhh," said Glamour.

"The good news," Markson said, "is that the rushes you sent were very bankable, plus we have been able to track Greetings's ancestry back to [and here he named a Movie Star known less for his talent than for his squandered career] who, it turns out, under the name of 'Eddie Eagle,' wintered in 1969–70 just north of Taos."

Greetings's mother looked coyly toward the floor and

seemed, though it was hard to tell from sixty-five million miles, to blush.

"But that doesn't make him my grandfather!" Greetings said.

"They don't have to prove that," said Glamour.

"All they have to do is prove that he *could have been* your grandfather," continued Markson, as if he had been listening. "You know how things were back in the Raging Sixties. Under the Commune Paternity Act, we only—"

"Does that make me a Movie Star?"

"Of course not!" said Fonda-Fox. He looked a little insulted, but only for a moment. "But it does mean that your image can be legally combined with Beverly Glenn's to make a composite."

"It means we can make a movie," said Glamour and Markson at the same time (fifteen minutes apart).

"She's up and pumping!" Bass sounded far away over earcom #4. "The first drum's already half-full with beautiful sweet-smelling diesel #2. We'll be out of here in twenty minutes. What about up the canyon? See anything, Bones? This thing has an auto-shutoff, so I can come up and join you if—"

"No, no," said Jeffries. "Don't bother. I'm on my way out. Nothing here but sand and stones."

"No clay? No *Faux Gagarin?*"

"Nada. I'm on my way back out."

"No lost cities, huh?"

"Disney-Gerber loves the rushes, and their marketing and publicity department is already putting together a profile on Noreena Pellucidar," Markson said. "Meanwhile, Greetings, your salary has been negotiated with your mother's agreement, but with one stipulation, that you pay—"

"Who's Noreena Pellucidar?" Greetings asked Fonda-Fox.

"Greetings, honey, this is your mother. We've had to agree

to pay your grandfather's, well, your possible grandfather's, back dues from 1967 to 1989, when he died. Now that comes to—can you hear me?"

"That's the name of the composite," Glamour said. "Noreena Pellucidar."

"Why doesn't she answer me? She used to do this when she was a teenager."

"I've explained, Mrs. Gentry," said Markson, "that because of the great distance—"

"Don't give me that. I can see her standing right there, ignoring me. I know she used to stand like that on the other side of her door and pretend not to hear me."

"You're awful quiet," Bass said, as they headed back across the plain.

Loaded with six hundred gallons of diesel #2 fuel, the Isuzu rolled as smoothly as a Cadillac. Cold mist boiled out of the seams in the clay. Some of the seams were three inches across, but they hardly jolted the fat, squashed tires of the three-wheeled truck.

"The seams are wider," said Bass. "Like they're opening up. And the clay buds seem bigger." He slowed without stopping so Jeffries could pluck one for his specimen bag. "Don't you want a sample?"

"Oh. Sure."

Then they were out of the plain and in the shadow of the Candor Mesa. The canyon floor was as smooth as glass. Bass kicked the ATV up into third and the 1,200-cc plastic V-twin throbbed happily.

"Look," Bass said. Steering with one hand, he pointed up with the other. In the rose-black at the top of the sky were Mars's two racing moons. Phobos, about one fourth the size of Earth's Moon, and half as bright, was heading east. Deimos, just a bright spot little bigger than a star, was heading west. Even as Jeffries watched, they passed; and Bass, sighting the sand slope far ahead, opened the throttle, racing the westbound moon.

* * *

"Put your cheek against my arm," Fonda-Fox said. "Now sight along as if it were a rifle. Have you ever shot a rifle?"

"Of course," Greetings said, insulted. "I see it."

"That's Deimos. The bigger one is Phobos."

"They're so fast. They're so—shy." Greetings wondered what it would be like to grow up on a planet where the moons were shy like squirrels, and playful. Would lovers pay any attention to them?

Glamour was filming Kirov, who was watching the sun sink toward the horizon. He wished he could use her smile in the composite; she had a Russian Mona Lisa smile that only appeared when things were going well. But of course that would be against Guild regulations.

The setting sun moved too fast and looked too small, like a cue ball for a child's pool table. Kirov looked from it toward the dunes. She had been watching for the past half hour, and just as the too small sun set, she was rewarded with a high plume of red dust. She knew as soon as she saw Bass standing on the pegs, waving, that they had found the *Gagarin*.

"More good news," said Markson, 29.5 minutes after he had heard about the diesel fuel in the Soviet unit. "Did I say good? I meant great. Now all we have to do is get Sweeney out of jail, which I'm happy to say is being taken care of by the legal staff of Disney-Gerber. Now let me hear from Dr. Jeffries. I have a scientist here from Smithsonian-Nabisco, a subsidiary of Disney-Gerber, by the way, who is interested in that strange clay that imitated the *Agnew*." The image pulled back to show a lanky white man in Reeboks and Levi's, holding a clipboard.

"Nothing on that yet," said Jeffries, dimming the screen while Kirov nodded at him. "Over and out."

The photon load on the disks from the sunlight digitizer was so heavy that even after they were used up by the air freshener, there was sunlight left. These used "firewood disks" played back on the video made a nice imitation of a fire. After supper the voyagers sat drinking Scotch (Johnnie Walker Black, which Jeffries had decided was worthy, along with Mingus and Shakespeare, of descending to Mars), watching the flames dance across the screen.

"Cheers," said Fonda-Fox, raising his glass. "Here's to our ticket home."

"Cheers," said Kirov. "Here's to our movie deal."

Jeffries raised his glass silently.

"One question," said Glamour. "How come you didn't tell the Smithsonian-Nabisco guy about the clay?"

"Yeah," said Greetings. "Didn't you say it might be some kind of wannabee life?"

"It could be the most important scientific discovery of the century," said Fonda-Fox. "Doesn't it belong to science?"

"Science!" scoffed Bass. "Those people aren't scientists, they're marketeers."

"I told Jeffries to keep his mouth shut," said Kirov. "Suppose we have discovered life on Mars? Do we really want to hand it over to some Hollywood studio's publicity department?"

"You would hand it over the Soviets, I suppose," said Fonda-Fox.

"Don't get huffy! I don't know. If Russia was Communist, maybe. But we haven't had communism in Russia since— Anyway, I agree that whatever we find belongs to science. But not to Disney-Gerber."

"I never thought of it like that," said Greetings.

"I don't think Russia's any better," said Fonda-Fox. "What do you think, Bones?"

"You guys said it, not me," Jeffries said. "And please don't call me Bones." He finished off his drink and walked back to his samples. He pretended to be working so the others would leave him alone. Hearing Kirov and Bass defend him, he felt rotten: for he wasn't just hiding things from Hollywood, and he wasn't just hiding the discovery of the clay.

A few hours ago, around the corner of the canyon, out of

sight and sound of Bass, he had found something so astonishing that he had turned down his earcom so Bass wouldn't hear his excited breathing.

It wasn't American; it wasn't Russian; it wasn't clay.

It was alien. And he was the only human on Earth or Mars who knew about it.

5

"WHAT TIME DO YOU show?" Kirov asked.

"Nine-thirty-six A.M. (M)," said Bass.

"What do you see?"

"The usual. The dawn wind has almost died, even up high. Angel Dust Falls is coming off the South Wall straight down. Man, that's something to see. Mist is rising off the floor of the canyon, but it doesn't rise very far. Only a few feet. Then instead of dissipating it rolls in long strings over the ground. Rolling this way up the slope it looks like sticky air."

"Stinky ears?"

"Sticky air." Bass and Jeffries were on the idling ATV at the top of the sand slope, getting ready to go down into the Candor Chasm for the second load of diesel. "I said it looks like sticky air."

"I can't understand you but good luck," Kirov said. Her signal was weak and Bass knew they would lose it entirely on the canyon floor.

"Roger. See you guys at dinnertime." Bass stood up on the pegs, kicked the Isuzu into gear, and started down the slope. Jeffries, even more silent than usual this morning, leaned against him, holding on. Long ropes of fog rolled up the slope, looking to Jeffries like giant, tangled DNA strings. He watched his dicktracy as Bass drove straight through one. In his marsuit he couldn't feel anything, but the air pressure bumped from 1.7 to 1.9 and back down, as if the instrument had been jarred.

At the bottom of the slope Bass kicked the three-wheeled

ATV up into third and headed east across the wind-rippled sand. It was like driving along railroad ties and even in the low gravity of Mars, bone-jarring. "I call this Ripple Run," said Bass, who liked to give everything a name. Where the Candor Mesa split the airflow like a boulder in a stream, the canyon floor was swept clean, and they picked up speed as they passed to the south of the mesa. As they approached what Bass called the Field of Seams, he slowed and wound through in second, trying to avoid the wider cracks.

"They're narrow now," Bass said, "but I think they get wider later in the day."

Jeffries got more samples for his bag. Yesterday's clay buds were already sand, and new ones had grown up on and around them.

It was dark in the shadow of the mesa; then they were in the sunlight again, crossing the last wide stretch of sand toward the North Wall. Ahead, the morning sunlight was painting with fantastic colors the castellated formations behind the *Gagarin*, where Jeffries had been walking yesterday when he had stumbled upon the stairway under the sand.

"You're even quieter than usual today," Bass said.

"Huh? Oh, sorry. Just thinking."

The first time he stubbed his toe, around the corner of the canyon, Jeffries had thought it was just a rock under the sand. Then there was another; then a third, with very unrocklike regularity. He looked ahead and behind, and the ripples leading up the canyon almost took on the shape of stairs. With the side of one boot, Jeffries cleared away the sand at his feet and found a wide red stone step. He knelt and brushed it clean, and placed his hand flat on the stone. It was as smooth as marble but whether from age, or use, or design, he could not tell.

He turned off his earcom, afraid Bass would hear his heart pounding.

He stood up and looked around; the steps led up to the crest of a low rise where the canyon opened up. Controlling his breathing, Jeffries put his earcom back on as he climbed the steps. Bass was humming and singing to himself. No problem.

Going on up the hill was easier now. Jeffries almost ran, matching the long steps. Mars steps! At the crest, the little canyon opened up, fanlike, into an amphitheater. On the high stone wall to his left were black holes in what almost seemed a regular pattern, like windows. And on his right only a few yards away he saw, or thought he saw—

"She's up and pumping!" Bass had said over the earcom. "The first drum's already half-full with beautiful sweet-smelling diesel #2. We'll be out of here in twenty minutes. What about up the canyon? See anything, Bones? This thing has an auto-shutoff, so I can come up and join you if—"

"No, no," said Jeffries. "Don't bother. I'm on my way out. Nothing here but sand and stones."

"No clay? No *Faux Gagarin?*"

"Nada. I'm on my way back out."

"No lost cities, huh?"

"Huh?" What he had seen, or thought he'd seen, was a silver pyramid on the sand. When he looked away, it was gone. Then when he looked back, it was there. It was only there when he looked directly at it, a pyramid the size of a tent, as bright as a drop of mercury in the sun.

"Bones, are you okay? You sound funny. I'm coming up there."

"No, I'm okay. Must be the channel. Let's switch to earcom #5. I'm heading back down the canyon now."

That was yesterday. Today, Jeffries left Bass setting up to pump more diesel fuel out of the *Gagarin*, and he started up the canyon with his specimen bag.

"I thought you said there was nothing up there."

"There's not. But I want to get some rock samples."

"And leave me to do all the work!"

"Doesn't take two to pump gas."

Around the corner, Jeffries bounded up the stairs They

seemed to fit his legs precisely. It amazed him, today, that he hadn't seen them right away yesterday, since the sand that covered them only softened and didn't hide their shape. Today, the amphitheater and the rock wall that enclosed it looked even less natural than before, and more created or carved.

He stopped at the top of the stairs and only when he saw the silver tent, thirty feet away across the sand, did he realize he had hoped it wouldn't be there after all. The stairs would have been quite enough.

It was a four-sided pyramid, some ten feet tall. Jeffries looked a little to one side, and it was gone. It simply didn't exist in peripheral vision at all. He looked back at it, and there it was. It flashed in and out of visibility as fast as he moved his eyes: and he realized he had found the light he had seen from orbit.

It was more silver than silver itself, the silver of stars or video signal. If it was an illusion, it was an active one; for when he took a step toward it, it suddenly was closer, and bigger. Much closer. Another step and Jeffries had somehow moved from thirty feet away to ten. It didn't seem that the pyramid had moved at all. Another step and it was close enough to touch.

He didn't want to touch it, though. It seemed far more alien than the stone steps of Mars.

He picked up a handful of sand and tossed it. Instead of going through the silver image of the tent, as he had half-expected, the sand slid down the side.

He pitched another handful of sand, and it did the same.

"Is it warm up there, Bones?" Bass said. Jeffries jumped. The voice on the earcom sounded coarse and intrusive.

"A little." Jeffries looked at his dicktracy. "Fifty-four point seven degrees. Amazing!" he said, trying to sound amazed. It wasn't hard.

He walked all the way around the pyramid. As he turned each corner, he could see two sides, the one he was leaving and the one he was approaching, yet he had the distinct feeling that he was seeing the same two sides over and over. It was the same going back. The silver structure looked like a pyramid but "felt" like a two-sided, one-edged figure, even though Jeffries couldn't think of how that might be . . .

There were no windows or doors. Every side was the same.

Jeffries touched the side of the pyramid and though it gave a little, it was as hard and smooth as plastic. Then on an impulse, he pulled off his glove and touched it with his bare finger.

As soon as he touched it, he was inside.

"Bones? You all right?"

"All right?"

"Is something wrong? You're breathing funny."

"I—stubbed my toe. And please don't call me Bones."

"Sorry."

On the inside, the pyramid seemed much larger than it had looked from the outside. Jeffries was standing halfway to the center, nowhere near the wall that had admitted him. Now he could see all four sides of the pyramid; it was twenty feet high in the center (not ten), and the walls were cream-colored, not silver. The floor was sand, the same sand he had been standing on all along. Or was it; was he still on Mars? Jeffries checked his dicktracy: 55 degrees, 1.9 pound pressure, the same it had been "outside." His bare right hand stung a little from the low air pressure, but not too bad. He bent over to look for his glove, but it wasn't there. When he straightened he noticed, directly in front of him, a small spire in the exact center of the pyramid. Had it been there all along? It was about three feet tall, a four-sided spike of clear glass or crystal. Jeffries was standing on one leg, trying to decide whether to take a step backward or forward when directly above the spike, hovering in the air, a man appeared.

"Are you about done?"

"Done?"

"Collecting rocks or whatever. I'm topping off; I need some

help down here. We have to load this baby and hit the road. I'm worried about those seams opening up to where you can't even drive across them."

"Okay, got you," said Jeffries. The man was wearing a cream-colored one-piece suit with long sleeves. He looked friendly somehow. His dreadlocks came to his shoulders. He was talking but there was no sound. Or was there? Jeffries realized that he couldn't hear, since he was insulated by his face mask from the Martian atmosphere.

"Are you sure you're okay? You're breathing hard again."

"I'm telling you, there must be something in the circuit, there's nothing wrong with me. And I asked you, please don't call me Bones."

"I didn't!"

"Okay. Ten minutes, okay?"

"Five."

Jeffries took one step back, and the man disappeared. He stepped forward and the man reappeared. He walked around the spike and tried the same sequence on the other side. The figure always appeared facing Jeffries and making the same gestures. He was a hologram, a recording. He was very patiently explaining something that apparently mattered a great deal to him: or at least that's how it seemed to Jeffries because the man's eyes were wide open and his hands moved fast.

His hands, when they slowed down, were different sizes.

Jeffries backed toward the wall of the pyramid and it "opened" before he reached it—he was "outside" and the pyramid was only ten feet tall again, and twenty feet away from him. And his glove was at his feet.

Jeffries put his glove back on. His fingertips were stinging, but he was smiling as he hurried back down the canyon to the *Gagarin*. It wasn't until he saw Bass's familiar and yet unfamiliar pink face behind the mask of his marsuit that he realized why. The figure in the pyramid was Black. Not only human in appearance, but African.

* * *

"This makes twelve hundred gallons," Kirov said as she and Fonda-Fox helped roll the drum from the back of the ATV and set it beside the *Tsiolkovsky*.

"Leaving only six hundred, or one more trip to go," said Bass. "But let's get started earlier tomorrow. Those cracks definitely open wider in the afternoon. On the way back today one of them was over a foot wide."

"The planet is breathing," Kirov said.

"Breathing?"

"That's what Sweeney calls it," Kirov said as they crowded through the air lock, all four at once. "I faxed him through the readings from the air monitor on the ATV, and he made a profile. He says the so-called 'sticky air' is an oxyplastate compound, a sort of heavy oxygen that comes from inside the planet. Even after it dissipates, it seems to increase the air pressure way beyond what the weight of the atmosphere itself would account for, at least temporarily."

"Sweeney's out of jail?" asked Bass.

"For now, at least," said Fonda-Fox. "Stadium Solutions dropped the charges after Disney-Gerber bought Stadium."

"Apparently the cracks open and close in some kind of tidal harmony with the moons," said Kirov. "Sweeney's running figures on that right now. My theory is it's when the moons are in opposition on different sides of the planet. Or maybe the oxyplastate itself pushes them open. It's supposed to be pretty heavy stuff."

"I can vouch for that," said Bass, taking off his gloves. "I took my gloves off today while I was pumping the fuel." He held up a fingertip; it was red, as if it had been lightly scalded.

Jeffries was relieved that his own decompression blisters didn't show up against his darker skin. He hadn't yet decided how much of what he had found he wanted to reveal.

"If the pressure got much higher down there we could almost breathe!" Bass said. "Right, Bones?"

"What about specimens?" Kirov asked, turning to Jeffries. "Have you all found anything interesting in the canyon. A *Faux Gagarin* maybe?"

Jeffries hesitated only for an instant. "Nothing but stones and sand," he said.

"But what a view!" said Bass. "Tomorrow's the last trip. The *Demogorgon* should get a few shots of the canyon."

"It's not in my contract," Glamour said. "And the *Demogorgon* doesn't go where I don't go."

Jeffries was quiet through dinner.

After the turkey paste tubes were put away, Markson called and showed a videotape of his first news conference with the president of Disney-Gerber, a twisted old man whose shiny suit fit like an exoskeleton. While he and Markson answered reporters' financial questions, a screen behind them showed maps of the solar system, stills of the *Tsiolkovsky*, panning shots of the Martian landscape, and a group shot of the Mars Voyagers inside the lander, waving at the video camera.

"Where am I?" Greetings asked. "And who's that blonde? Omigod, that's, that's—"

"That's her," Glamour said proudly. "That's Noreena Pellucidar. Her first public appearance."

The composite Star was sitting on a packing crate between Fonda-Fox and Kirov. Greetings had expected to see her own face on Beverly Glenn's body, like in the first rushes; but the Guild-certified composite Movie Star on the screen didn't resemble either of them very much. She had Greetings's green eyes, Beverly Glenn's cheekbones and an odd Mona Lisa smile. She was as voluptuous as Beverly Glenn, but her hips were smaller. Her lips were full, and when she threw back her head to laugh her teeth were bad.

"That's not my smile," Greetings said.

"That's not Beverly Glenn's smile, either," said Fonda-Fox.

'Isn't that Kirov s smile?" asked Bass.

"Of course not," said Glamour, making a mental note to fix the teeth. "That would be illegal."

"Where you going?" Kirov asked Jeffries, who was pulling on his marsuit.

"Out for a walk."

JEFFRIES'S REAL FATHER hadn't been a doctor; he hadn't been anything, and then he had been a revolutionary, whatever that was. He had left Jeffries's mother before their child was born, and Jeffries hadn't laid eyes on him until he was captured, in the raids on the Black nationalist underground the week the Philippine War began. Jeffries was nine when his father sent for him and a mysterious "aunt" took him to the prison for the first time.

The Mars night air was cold and thin (9 percent and .09 atmospheres), and Jeffries wished his marsuit had a battery heater as he walked up into the dunes. He hadn't thought about his father twice in twenty years, and now he had come up twice in a week: when Kirov had mentioned him, and now today.

Perhaps it was the dreadlocks. The elder Sundiata and his comrades had grown them in prison.

Jeffries was eleven when his mother remarried and moved to Cincinnati, and twelve when he learned his father had been killed in the Atlanta Riot of '99. His stepfather, not his mother, told him. He remembered feeling only relief that he wouldn't have to go and visit him again in the brightly colored visiting room filled with candy machines that didn't work, guards in high chairs, and crying Black babies. He was the only kid whose mother didn't come with him.

They hadn't had much to say to each other. Even at nine, Jeffries was embarrassed by his father's long silences. His stepfather had been equally remote and inaccessible, but that was different. He had a philosophy that fit the world: make it work for you. This philosophy had served Jeffries well enough in college, in the Navy and in business; but now for the first time, with the discovery of the pyramid and the hologram, not to mention the steps and the clay, it didn't fit. It didn't cover events.

Where was he supposed to go with all this? And why was he feeling like a kid, thinking his father would know?

Was it the dreadlocks, the superficial resemblance? Or was it the window on an alien, a *non-American* world: for his father had been anything but American. He had left Jeffries— had left Sundiata—only the request that he not change his name. He hadn't said don't shorten it. Sundiatas didn't get far in the Navy.

Jeffries's butt was cold.

He squatted on his heels on the side of a dune and looked out over the Tharsis plain, dark under an unfamiliar sky. The *Konstantin Tsiolkovsky* was a single spot of light on a world of darkness, under a million brilliant stars. Earth was not distinguishable, not even imaginable, in that display. The triangle of yellow light that spilled on the sand from the port side window of the *Tsiolkovsky* looked as close and warm. A shadow moved inside and Jeffries felt a sudden, unexpected— unwanted, really—rush of kinship with the men and women who had come here with him, and with those who had stayed behind. People of Earth. For half a million years, they had looked out from their planet as from a prison cell; alone, they had talked to the animals and peopled the skies with gods. And now there was a footprint on the beach. Now they were no longer alone.

And only he knew it.

Jeffries had spent a lifetime keeping his distance from people, and now he felt as if they were standing around him, waiting for him to speak. Kirov had backed him up on not sharing the clay samples, at least not right away, but there was no question of keeping this a secret. It belonged to every-one on Earth, the living and the dead, but who represented humanity? The US government? Not highly likely. Smithsonian-Nabisco? The Soviet Union? The UN?

For the first time in twenty-five years Jeffries wished his father had lived. Maybe his philosophy would fit this world-sized problem.

He looked up at the sky. Which one was the home of the man in the pyramid? Jeffries felt sure that it wasn't Mars. No, the man with the dreadlocks was a voyager like himself . . .

"Jeffries!" It was Kirov on the earcom.

"Okay, okay, I'm on my way in," he said.

"We just got a call from the *Mary Poppins*. It's your patient, Beverly Glenn. She woke up and she wants to talk to you."

7

"SHE'S REMARKABLY CALM for someone whose ship is about to crash into a moon," Jeffries whispered to Kirov while he monitored Beverly Glenn's heartbeat from the on-screen display. It was morning. The Star had fallen back to sleep shortly after last night's call, and this was Jeffries's first chance for a comprehensive remote physical.

"What's he saying?" Beverly Glenn asked.

"You know how doctors are, they mumble," said Kirov.

"It's almost nine, Bones," said Bass on the earcom from outside, where he was fueling up the Isuzu for the final trip to get the last load of diesel fuel.

"Ten more minutes," said Jeffries, who was going with him. "And please don't call me Bones. Ms. Glenn, can I ask you to disrobe so I can get a visual? If you want, I'll send the others outside with Bass."

"Don't be silly." Already out of her jumpsuit, Beverly Glenn was unsnapping her bra. "Greetings and the Captain are both girls. I've got nothing Glamour hasn't filmed before and Fonda-Fox is a Guild member. Family, in fact. We're what, FF? Second first step-cousins? And call me BG, please."

As Jeffries examined her visually for muscle tone and spectrally for bone loss, Fonda-Fox and Kirov, interrupting one another, continued with their rundown of the last two years. Beverly Glenn's spirits were good but Jeffries had expected that. Career Spacing was a rejuvenating experience, and the longer people slept, the better they felt when they woke up.

She seemed comfortable with her silky body hair; at least she hadn't bothered to shave it. It grew in golden clumps at the base of her spine, on the backs of her knees and around her ankles; on the backs of her hands, between her breasts and on her chin. Her eyes looked bright, her teeth were good and her skin was clear except for the three deep scratches, now reddened with Mercurochrome, down her left cheek. She had been awakened by Ahab, driven into a frenzy by the alarms that had gone off when the ship drifted to within half a kilometer of Phobos. Sweeney's figures had been wrong. The *Mary Poppins* was orbiting Phobos in a steadily decreasing spiral, and in less than two days the mile-long ship would hit the Martian moon.

"According to Sweeney's latest figures, from last night we have forty-six point eight hours (M) to get to the ship and align it for delta V," Fonda-Fox said, winding up his tale. "Otherwise . . ."

"Except for the scratches, she looks fine," said Jeffries, pulling on his marsuit. "Career Spacing has cured her asthma and toned up her skin. Meanwhile, I'm out of here. I'm taking a camera today."

"You're sure there's nothing I can do from here?" Beverly Glenn asked, getting dressed.

"Afraid not," said Kirov. "All the orbital maneuvering engines were detached and used to brake the *Tsiolkovsky*. You have alignment engines but that's all. That means we get one shot with the *Mary Poppins*—the nuclear shot. We have to be aboard for that one, and we will. We plan to be off-planet by dark. Bass and Jeffries are on their way down into the canyon to get the rest of the fuel, and Glamour's wrapping up the filming."

"Ah, the movie . . ." Beverly Glenn looked wistful. "I had forgotten all about it."

"She sure is a good sport," Greetings said as she and Fonda-Fox air-locked out for the last day of filming.

"About being left behind in orbit?" said Fonda-Fox. "According to Jeffries, there's a euphoria in the HT. Hopefully, we'll get to her before it wears off."

"I mean about being left out of the movie. About being amalgamated into a composite Movie Star."

"Oh, that. I'm not surprised. Being a Star has always been a mixed blessing to BG, and I think she's glad to share the burden a little."

"So you knew her . . ." Greetings had started to say, " . . before she was a Movie Star," then she realized how silly that was and finished: ". . when she was a kid."

"Oh sure. My second mom and her first dad made several movies together. They were even married at one point, I think; but that was back before either of us were born. There go Bass and Bones!"

It was almost noon and a few solitary clouds were gleaming high in the ruby sky. The Tharsis volcanoes guarded the west, each with its plume of cloud. As they stepped down from the ship onto the sand to begin filming, Greetings and Fonda-Fox saw the ATV disappear into the dunes, leaving behind a little vapor trail of white puffs.

"He doesn't like it when you call him Bones," said Greetings.

While Glamour, Fonda-Fox and Greetings were outside the ship filming, Kirov showed Beverly Glenn how to work the *Mary Poppins*'s radio bank and called Sweeney at the new Redondo Boulevard headquarters of Mission Design. With the connection patched through the mother ship, the signal was better than usual. It was the clearest Kirov had seen Sweeney since leaving Earth. He was better-looking than she'd remembered.

"I'm afraid the error isn't in my figures," Sweeney said. "I wish it was. But there's a periodic mascom-type anomaly under the surface of Mars near the edge of the Tharsis. Near where you are, in fact. My theory is, it's a bubble of heavy gas that moves through channels and caves under the surface.

It's apparently tidal, and it causes the opening and closing of the seams and the releasing of the heavy oxygen or 'sticky air' Bass noticed. It may even *be* the 'sticky air.' It's affected by the moons but it affects them in turn, increasing what we call their 'virtual mass.' That's why the *Mary Poppins* seems to be spiraling into Phobos, a body much too small to attract it so strongly. It's actually spiraling into a harmonic gravitational node point, a nonexistent virtual body with the combined mass of both moons and the mascom. Unfortunately, that 'virtual body' is located only point-six kilometers from the center of Phobos. So for all practical purposes . . ."

"He's saying the ship *is* or *is not* going to run into Phobos?" Beverly Glenn asked. She was drifting over the control panel on the bridge, nibbling trail mix out of a plastic bag. The ship was cold and she was wearing an orange sweater, holding the cat in her arms.

"Is," said Kirov, turning down the volume on Sweeney. "Get the rest of what he says on tape. I've got to go outside and winch the ship upright. We have to be ready to go as soon as Bass and Jeffries get back with the last of the fuel."

"Anything I can do from here?"

"Monitor the radio. Feed the cat. Generally stay cool. You're doing pretty good at that."

High in the rose-black sky, two moons played like kittens. On the floor of the Candor Chasm of the Valles Marineris, the air was calm and heavy. Tendrils of mist curled up from the opening cracks like willow shoots along creeks, growing miraculously fast. Even though it was only 10:00 A.M. (M), the seams were already a foot wide and Bass had to weave among them, picking his way carefully. The clay buds swelled, gorged on heavy oxygen. Jeffries bent down and snagged one for his bag and was surprised at how heavy it felt.

Rattling in the back of the ATV were the two 300-gallon drums for the fuel that would take them off the planet and back to the *Mary Poppins*.

Then they were out of the mist. Bass pointed at the cliffs

along the North Wall. The late morning sun was only just now penetrating to the stone battlements behind the *Gagarin*, illuminating the spires in a rainbow of colors, all of them red.

Jeffries booked a still image of the wall with the videodisk camera he had brought along for this last trip. He still hadn't resolved who, if anyone, to tell about what he had found up in the canyon. In the daylight, with emergencies all around, it seemed less important. He felt as if events were running away with him, and it was a good feeling.

He checked his dicktracy: 2.4 atmospheres, 48 degrees. It was going to be, for Mars, a hot one.

Kirov tied the winch to a boulder and the cable to the nose of the *Tsiolkovsky*. The nose of the ship pulled up only two feet, then fell back as the stone pulled loose. The second boulder was the size of a car, and it, too, pulled loose, but more slowly. The third was the size of a one-car garage. It held as the *Tsiolkovsky's* nose rose upward 10, 15, 20 degrees. Then the ship started to fall back as the stone plowed forward through the sand. "Help," called Kirov; and Greetings, Fonda-Fox and Glamour, *Demogorgon* in hand, jumped onto it to add weight. The electric come-along groaned as the ship hung in the balance, and Kirov shoved a fresh sundisk into the converter. Twenty-two, 24, 30 degrees; the ship started rising again and Greetings hugged Fonda-Fox and cheered while Glamour, still booking image, filmed their cheers. Once above halfway, the weight of the F-1 in the tail made the rest of the pull easy. Greetings's and Fonda-Fox's cheers died as the ship rocked into its final position, though at first they didn't know why. Somehow, the rocket pointing toward the sky changed the look of everything around it. The low dunes that had become as familiar as a yard now looked alien and strange; the needle-shaped *Tsiolkovsky* poised for takeoff looked swift and light. Their little house on the prairie had become a spaceship. They were not homesteaders. They were voyagers, very, very far from home.

* * *

As soon as he had helped Bass hook the lines to the *Gagarin* and start the pump, Jeffries headed around the corner of the canyon. "I want to get some rock samples and some photographs, okay?" he said as soon as he was out of sight, expecting Bass's complaint. But today, their last on Mars (hopefully), there was no complaint.

The stone steps were covered again with the sand that fell like dew every night, but the pyramid was as clean and bright as ever, as if it inhabited a dimension unaffected by the winds of Mars. And perhaps it did: Jeffries took two pictures from each side with the videodisk camera, wondering if they would come out. He wished now he had tried before; this was his last chance.

He turned up his earcom, and he could hear Bass humming; or was that sound the pumps draining the last of the diesel fuel out of the *Gagarin?*

Jeffries checked his dicktracy—57 degrees and 3.5 atmospheres. Balmy and the highest air pressure yet, well over half ship normal. He took off his gloves and stuffed them into his belt; there was no place to clip them, since it had never been anticipated that it would be possible to remove them on Mars. His hands stung a little, but it was from excitement as much as from decompression. He touched the silver wall and was, suddenly, inside.

He photographed the little crystal spike while walking around it, spiraling inward.

When he was about twelve feet away, the figure appeared, wearing the same buff jumpsuit, making the same gestures and, as far as Jeffries could tell, the same speech. The figure's forehead looked uncommonly high, as he was partially bald; his skin was an ash blue-gray without a trace of brown. Was that biological, or was it the holo? His eyes were—but there was no word to describe the color there. His dreads were between black and gray and came almost to his shoulders. His African-ness was in the dreads and the dark skin only: his features were more Oriental; no, Mayan; no, not really human at all but different, alien: and Jeffries felt a chill as the full import of the word fell over him like a shadow.

As he circled the figure, taking pictures, the figure continued to face him, but without appearing to turn. This somehow seemed perfectly natural, as if the figure did not occupy the same space, or even time.

But what was the holo saying?

Jeffries stepped back and the figure disappeared. He checked his dicktracy—3.4—and cautiously lifted his face mask. He sniffed once, twice; the air smelled sharp and sour. Without giving himself time to think it over, he breathed deeply and air filled his lungs in an slow, icy rush: unfamiliar, never-before-breathed. Jeffries grinned. He was breathing the air of Mars. It was as exhilarating as leaning into a freezer on a hot summer day.

Wearing his face mask on top of his head like a cap, Jeffries stepped forward toward the spike until the figure appeared again. He pulled his earcom loose and, for the first time, heard the voice: a kind of slow singing, sweet and sharp at once, a sound so utterly alien that he felt it couldn't come from the figure in the holo. Though it looked human, this was no man. Yet the speech was somehow *comforting*, in its cadence if not its tone, as if—

"What do you figure he's saying?"

Jeffries turned. Right behind him, inside the pyramid, also with his face mask raised, stood Bass.

"Now that the *Tsiolkovsky* is on her tailbone, we're getting a proper mass reading," said Sweeney. He was standing in front of the bank of new terminals Markson had written into the Disney-Gerber contract, looking simultaneously pleased and worried. He was wearing a new wrinklsilk sport coat, but he still had the classic NASA blue gabardine pants, white drip-dry shirt and plastic penholder in his pocket. Kirov found all that reassuring. "The *Tsiolkovsky*'s total weight is 14.3 tons (M), which gives you a payload of 722 kilos (M) with a projected thrust of 3.33 newtons at a duration of 3.5 minutes. That's assuming another 585 gallons of diesel #2, allowing for pump spill. Your weight varies according to the strange mascon under the surface, so your delta V is at seven-forty-five (M), which gives you Phobos rendezvouz at . . ."

"What's he saying?" asked Greetings.

"Will you shut up so I can hear," said Kirov.

"He's saying," whispered Fonda-Fox, who had played this scene in several movies and was now pleased (he supposed) to be playing it for real, "that we are going to make it by the skin of our teeth."

"What're you doing here?"

"Same thing you're doing here."

"Where'd you come from?"

"Same place you came from. Down the canyon where you left me. Did you think I couldn't figure something was going on?"

"Well . . ." said Jeffries. There didn't seem to be much else to say. "Tell me this—what do you see?"

"What do I see?" Bass stepped forward. Even standing beside Jeffries, he sounded far away in the thin Martian atmosphere. "Do you mean, do I see a late-middle–aged redneck with tobacco-stained teeth? Is this a projection keyed to our individual psyches? No, I see a hologram of a Black dude with fancy dreadlocks in a jumpsuit."

"Okay, okay." Jeffries looked at Bass again and realized he was glad to see him. He squeezed his arm; even through the marsuit, it felt reassuringly human. "I guess it's a little late to say I was trying to figure out how to tell you about this."

"A little, but what the hell."

"Anyway, I'm glad you're here. It was all getting too—" The alien had disappeared. "Don't worry, he comes back," said Jeffries. "If we start walking around him, like this, he starts over."

"What happens if we walk around him in the opposite direction?"

They tried it. The figure appeared and began speaking

again, and pointed at the wall. A three-sided window appeared, a smaller reverse image of the triangular wall. As the holo figure pointed, the window moved along on the wall like an icon on a computer screen.

Seen through the window, the amphitheater was cleared of sand. The stairs ringing the space, all of bright red stone, were swept. The window (or was it a screen?) rose higher to show the openings in the red stone wall, flickering with what seemed to be fires within. The voice was gone, and now instead of speech Bass and Jeffries heard a cluster of high tones, an intricate harmony of three, then six, then eight at once, weaving in and out, up and down, then dying one by one, each leaving its memory lingering on the air. Then all was gone but a single tone, full and low and somehow very sad.

"We're looking at a ruin," whispered Jeffries.

"Huh?"

"We're looking at a ruin, like Rome or great Zimbabwe or Uxmal. We're looking at an exhibit."

The window blinked out and was gone as the last note died; the man with the dreadlocks was gone again.

"If this is a ruin, then where's he from?" Bass asked. "Maybe he's not from Mars at all! Maybe he'll show us."

"Maybe. Maybe not. Would an exhibit at Uxmal show the campus of Mexico City University? Or UCLA? What's that beeping?"

"The alarm on my dicktracy," said Bass. "It's keyed to the pump and it means the drums are full. It's time to head back to the ship."

"You mean everything?" asked Greetings.

"I mean everything," said Kirov on the earcom.

"Okay!" The teenager flung the coffeepot and the coffee, the CDs of Mingus and Shakespeare, the extra boots and the first-aid kit, out the hatch onto the sand. It was sort of fun. The *Tsiolkovsky* was surrounded by concentric circles of junk.

"What about these inner panels around the windows?" Fonda-Fox asked.

"Rip 'em."

"What about these seat cushions up here on the flight deck?"

"Rip 'em."

"What about the *Demogorgon?*" asked Glamour, who was outside on the sand, filming Kirov attaching the thrust cone to the F-1.

"Use your imagination," Kirov said. "According to Sweeney, we're still 680.4 kilos (M) overweight. So we either leave it, or one of us."

Jeffries had the still video images, but he wanted something tangible to take with him—if, indeed, any of what he saw was tangible. He walked up to the spike in the center of the pyramid and touched it; it was cold and hard. The figure appeared, but it was a different figure: another man, in blue this time, slightly more African in appearance. His voice was deeper and less musical, almost harsh. He held a basketball-sized globe in each hand: one of Mars and one of Earth. He held them out at arm's length and released them and they hung, spinning slowly.

Jeffries took a picture of each.

Bass couldn't take his eyes off the figure's outstretched hands; he had three fingers on his left hand and four on his right, one of them an opposable thumb. The right hand pointed and Bass turned and looked behind him at the wall. Through the triangular "window" he saw not sand and stone, but stars: darkness and stars.

The globes seemed more solid than the figure, but when Jeffries reached for one his hand went right through it. Mars was identifiable by its great shield volcanoes, but the globe had gray-green patches around the equator and the icecaps were larger. On the Earth globe, North Africa was green and most of Europe was covered with ice; the northeastern part of North America was covered by an ice sheet centered approximately on Montreal. Kansas was a small sea or a large lake, depending on one's point of view.

"A museum exhibit," Jeffries said. "From a long time ago."

"Or a long time in the future," said Bass. "Let's go, Bones. We have to get back to the *Tsiolkovsky*."

At least the crystal spike was real. Jeffries touched it and the figure and the globes disappeared. The top two inches of the spike made a miniature pyramid, like the top of the Washington Monument, that appeared to be separated from the lower shaft by a narrow seam.

"Twist it," Bass said. "No, to the left."

The top came off in Jeffries's hand and suddenly they were out in the sunlight. The pyramid itself was gone. They were standing on the sand, outside, on Mars, face masks lifted, without oxygen! Watching Bass, Jeffries took a deep breath: the air was the same as it had been in the pyramid. Cold and sour. It was thin in the lungs, but it would do.

The spike on the sand, the pyramid—all was gone. The miniature pyramid in Jeffries's hand, a model of the larger one, was all that was left. Feeling like a thief, he stuffed it into the pocket of his marsuit and followed Bass down the sand-covered ruined steps.

Bass was pleased with himself: who would have guessed that right-hand threads would be a universal constant?

"As you can see from the video display," Sweeney said, "we're in orbit around Phobos now—that is, we're in virtual or apparent orbit, since we're not actually orbiting Phobos but rather the gravitational harmonic node near its center— though for all practical purposes it's the same thing—making one transit every three point nine hours (M). I can track it exactly because there's one of the old Russian hoppers on the surface, and we have transited it twice since eight this morning. Each time we pass it, we're closer. When we hit, and I'm afraid that's not an *if* but a *when*—"

"Don't you just love the way he says *we*?" said Beverly

Glenn, from the bridge of the *Mary Poppins*.

"I'm glad," Kirov said. "It means he identifies with your plight." She turned the sound off and shunted Sweeney direct to disk. Nobody wanted to hear what would happen if they didn't get off-planet by sundown, when the *Mary Poppins* collided with Phobos in 5.4 hours (M). Everybody already knew.

"How're you feeling? How's Ahab?" Greetings asked Beverly Glenn. She looked so great in her yellow jumpsuit; Greetings was so proud to be her composite partner.

"See for yourself, little sister." Beverly Glenn punched in the Stalin Lounge screen showing the gray and orange cat sleeping on the ceiling with one eye open. Like Beverly Glenn, Ahab looked completely at ease in zero g. Watching them, Greetings felt strange herself not being able to float. She wondered if the feeling of being handicapped by gravity would ever go away.

"I love the way BG calls you 'little sister,'" Fonda-Fox said.

Greetings blushed. So did she.

"Don't strap them together, Bones," said Bass. He and Jeffries were securing the drums in the bed of the three-wheeled truck with long cords.

"Why not?" Jeffries said. "If we lose one, we might as well lose them both. We need all six hundred gallons to get off-planet, don't we?"

"Yeah, but still—a long shot's better than no shot at all," said Bass as he primed the ATV's injectors, flooded the cylinders with pure hydrogen and kicked the starter switch. The engine's roar sounded far away in the thin Martian air.

"I asked you not to call me Bones," said Jeffries, climbing on behind him.

The pressure began to drop as they rode back across the canyon toward the Candor Mesa. At 2.3, regretfully, they put their face masks on; at 2.1, their gloves. Inside the pyramid, barefaced and barehanded in the presence of an alien artifact,

Jeffries had felt a brotherhood with Bass that he hadn't felt with any man in years. Now that they were isolated in their marsuits again, the feeling was gone. Jeffries felt in his pocket for the crystal tip he had taken from the spike. It reassured him that something significant had happened.

"I can't believe you're not pissed off at me," he said. It felt weird to be talking on the earcom again.

"Why would I be pissed?"

"Once I realized what I had found, I just didn't know where to start or who to tell."

"Forget it," said Bass. "I don't blame you. I understand."

"I wanted to tell somebody. It's just that everything is so commercialized these days, even science. How can I turn this over to Disney-Gerber?"

"Look, I understand. But you can trust Kirov. Really. I don't know about the rest of them, though. Fonda-Fox—"

"There's nothing even remotely comparable to it in human history!" said Jeffries. "It means we're not alone in the universe."

"Yeah, well, I'm not sure I don't wish we were," said Bass as he slowed; they were approaching the Field of Seams. "Did you see that? What's that on your hand?"

"A snowflake."

8

"NO WAY," said Sweeney. "He's going to have to leave the *Demogorgon* behind. We have your weight down 1100 kilos, but even with the extra 300 gallons of fuel Bass is bringing back, you are still 151.6 kilos over margin. We've got you slotted out of there at seven-twenty-seven (M), right after sundown, in a 143-second window, on a trajectory that docks with the *Mary Poppins* in less than one orbit. That gives you— let's see—an 80.6 minute (M) margin at the ship. Now if—"

"Is Glamour still sulking?" Beverly Glenn asked.

"He'll get over it," said Kirov.

Glamour was filming Greetings and Fonda-Fox tearing the ship apart, while from the other end of his camera he was faxing image up to the storage banks on the *Mary Poppins*.

"Aren't you glad you didn't go down?" Beverly Glenn said to Ahab as he rubbed his furry cheek against hers. "They would leave you behind for sure!"

"Snow on Mars," said Bass.

It fell up, not down. Giant snowflakes rose from the seams and spun upward, then hung in a rooflike cloud just thirty feet off the canyon floor; a few, like the one Jeffries had caught, floated free of the others, evaporating as soon as they hit the sand.

Bass kicked the Isuzu into gear and rode straight through, under the cloud. The light was ivory; it was as if they were riding into an ice cave. Each rising snowflake was the size of a poker chip.

Jeffries saw on his dicktracy that the pressure was rising again. He pulled off a glove and reached out and caught another snowflake; he could feel rather than see the cold mist that bore the flakes upward. Overhead, the cloud roof was a blurry mass of white, like a roof of blossoms. It seemed to mark the upper limit of the heavy oxygen, or "sticky air."

"Keep your face mask on," said Bass on the earcom. "We have no idea what this pressure's going to do. The seams are still opening, I think."

The Isuzu's fat heavily loaded rear tires ballooned as Bass bounced over the six-inch-wide cracks, angled across the foot-wide cracks, and swerved to avoid the two- and three-foot-wide seams.

"Hang on," he said as he opened the throttle. The front wheel jumped an almost three-foot-wide crevasse, and the rear tires leaped it one at a time. Looking down and back, Jeffries saw mist, snow, churning blackness...

He held out his hand for another snowflake and it disappeared even as he caught it on his bright, brown palm. He saw one tiny drop of water, the first free water he had ever seen on Mars, gleaming and then gone, even as he watched.

"Hang on with both hands, dammit," said Bass, sounding angry for the first time. "We're going to have to do some fancy riding to get across here without getting swallowed up!"

"Sweeney called again," said Beverly Glenn, "while you were outside double-rechecking the engine. Sweeney just double-rechecked our trajectory here, and according to him we have only one more orbit left, not two."

"What do you mean?" Kirov demanded. "Our launch window isn't until seven-twenty-seven. That's more than four hours from now. If you're orbiting every three hours..."

"The problem is, Sweeney says, there's a mountain on Phobos. It's only 813 feet high, but that's high enough. He says next time around, we're going to scrape it."

"Scrape what?" asked Greetings, who had just come onto the flight deck after helping Fonda-Fox throw the last of the ceiling tiles out the air lock. "What's she talking about?"

"Ssshhh!" said Fonda-Fox. He and Glamour joined Greetings, and they all crowded into the tiny flight deck of the *Tsiolkovsky* and watched the screen with Kirov. The HT euphoria had worn off Beverly Glenn—for the first time, she looked scared. Even Ahab on her shoulder had a wide-eyed, nervous look.

"Is this for sure?" asked Kirov.

"Sweeney says it's just a question of how hard, and what part of the ship hits it," said Beverly Glenn.

"When?" asked Fonda-Fox.

"At three-oh-nine P.M. (M)," said Beverly Glenn. She looked as if she were about to cry. "That's twenty-one minutes from now."

The Field of Seams formed a closed weather system, as far as Jeffries could tell. The tidal triangulation of the moons and the mysterious moving mascom under the canyons, together with the heat of the sun, opened the seams in late morning and began closing them in late afternoon. The "sticky air" rose in the form of a heavy oxygen mist or, when the air was a few degrees colder, snowflakes that hovered in low clouds.

Jeffries was too busy holding on to get more than a few stills on videodisk. Bass ran the ATV like a racing bike, drifting around the seams that were too wide to jump, some three and four feet wide. More were opening all the time, forcing them south as well as west. Running in second gear, Bass angled first southwest, then west, tacking like a sailboat through fog.

"Slow down," begged Jeffries.

"Can't," answered Bass. If they got cut off and had to wait for the seams to start closing, they'd never get the ship fueled in time for the launch window. But if he melted the little plastic engine down . . .

Bass pulled off his right glove and tossed it into the bed of the truck, then used his hand on the cooling fins to gauge

the engine temperature. Not too bad. Hitting a patch of two-
and three-foot seams, he shifted down to first and angled
across them, lofting the right wheel over with the engine's
torque and praying the left would follow.

"Hold on to the oil drums, Bones."

They were almost out from under the cloud—Jeffries
could see a bright thin red strip of sky ahead—when the
left wheel missed. It hit a soft patch of dead clay buds, and
spun, and dropped. The Isuzu's frame hit stone with a bone-
jarring crunch; Bass shifted down to bulldog, and the right
wheel groaned and caught, shattering more of the clay buds
that lined the seam; but instead of pulling forward, the
machine tipped backward; and Jeffries felt the rim of the
forward oil drum pull gently, almost apologetically from his
fingertips.

Sweeney, 14.8 light minutes away, was the last to know
when the *Mary Poppins* hit the mountaintop. Beverly Glenn,
strapped in the Captain's barca with a terrified Ahab on her
lap, was the first to know. While Kirov and the other voyagers
watched on the screen from the flight deck of the *Tsiolkovsky*,
a great *clang* rang through the *Mary Poppins*, setting off siren
alarms first far away, then getting closer.

"I felt it," said Beverly Glenn. "Hear those alarms? What
do I do now?"

"I think you just brushed it," said Kirov. "See that bank
of switches under your armrest? That turns off the alarms.
Now we just wait until we hear from Sweeney. He's patched
into damage control." She turned and looked behind her.
"Meanwhile, you guys clear out of here! Find something
to do."

Greetings, Fonda-Fox and Glamour fled.

The window of the *Tsiolkovsky*'s flight deck pointed
straight up, toward the sky, but Kirov was looking south,
through a small port in the "floor," toward the dune field,
watching for the telltale plume of dust.

* * *

Jeffries saw it happen again and again in his nightmares for the next eighteen months. The two drums were rocking back toward the tailgate. One spun crazily, dancing around the other, which for some reason was sliding sedately. Holding on to Bass with one hand, Jeffries reached and even caught the rim of the rocking drum, but it was too heavy, he knew it was too heavy; and so he wasn't surprised, only dismayed, to feel it slip from his grasp again. Then the sliding drum, with Bass's glove on top of it, hit the tailgate, opening it as smoothly as if it carried a key, and slid off the back of the ATV, into the boiling, bottomless mist. The last Jeffries saw of it was Bass's glove waving good-bye.

"Pull, baby!" said Bass as the right rear tire caught and the rear end came up. Away from the edge, he stopped, and with the engine idling, said: "You okay, Bones? Did we lose anything?"

Bass knew better already. He was trying to delay looking behind him.

What a great feeling! thought Beverly Glenn. She was on the bridge of the *Mary Poppins*, stripped to her underwear, following Kirov's instructions and throwing the switches that gave Sweeney access to the ship's primary monitoring systems. The damage control report was already in: only the heat shield had scraped, and neither the nuclear engine nor the ship's mile-long alignment struts had been damaged. The next crash would be considerably less gentle, but there wouldn't be a next one, according to Kirov and Sweeney. Within three hours the *Tsiolkovsky* would be back in orbit and the *Mary Poppins* would be returning to Earth.

If Bass and Jeffries make it back with the fuel, that is, thought Kirov. She kept her worries to herself and watched Beverly Glenn, almost envious of how well she was playing her role. Like Fonda-Fox, BG was a good enough actor to play officer on any ship's crew. Plus beautiful. It was amazing how quickly one got used to facial hair on a woman, especially on a Movie Star.

The sun was sinking fast. Where the hell were the boys? They had less than three hours before the launch window opened. If they didn't make it, Kirov had already decided what to do, though she hadn't discussed it with anyone. Without the last six hundred gallons of fuel, there wouldn't be enough to lift the *Tsiolkovsky* to orbit, so she would be spared the decision of who to leave behind. She would instruct Sweeney and Beverly Glenn to take the *Mary Poppins* back to Earth—without them.

She hoped for Beverly Glenn's sake as much as anyone's that it wouldn't come to that.

Signing off, Kirov went outside and down the ladder, to where Glamour was setting up to film his last (he hoped) sunset on Mars. Greetings and Fonda-Fox were sitting on the sand beside him. Fonda-Fox had discovered that he could lift his mask for a few seconds at a time, and inhale the cold, club soda air of Mars, if only for a breath or two. He showed Greetings and she (who tried everything) tried it.

That was how she was first to hear the faint, faraway, pop-pop-popping sound.

"Look!" She pointed up the hill toward the dunes. The Isuzu was coming over the hill, leaving a vapor trail in the icy air like a jet. "How can they move so fast!"

"Because they're only carrying one fuel drum," said Glamour, who was looking through the *Demogorgon*'s zoomfinder.

SUNSET ON MARS is as sudden as dawn is slow: the thin cirrus reefs that in the late afternoon float high over the Valles Marineris are one moment white, and the next rose, while around them the sky darkens like paint drying. The sun races for the horizon, all fire. The wind drops, and when the wind drops on Mars, it leaves an emptiness that feels like the vacuum it almost is.

In twenty-two years of location work, Glamour had noticed that it was not until you were leaving a place that you really saw it for the first time. The novelty had worn off, and the faint coloration of regret was beginning to bleed in around the edges. Maybe memory works forward as well as back; maybe his eyes were finally getting used to the dim Martian light; maybe the sun was brighter, the few clouds higher, or the air clearer than usual today; but whatever the cause, as the sun dropped on the last day (M), there was a glow and precision in the light Glamour had never seen before. The late afternoon shadows of the voyagers and their ship on the sand were Martian shadows, more delicate than those of Earth, with more mystery in their shapes and less definition in their lines.

Both the air temperature and pressure were dropping: Glamour's dicktracy showed 1.4. He had cut the tips from the fingers of his right glove so that he could fine-tune the *Demogorgon*, and now he could feel the sting. He would have to go in soon.

To the west, the sun was setting over the Tharsis plain.

A thin spray of cloud was blowing off the top of Olympus Mons, which loomed over Mars's sheer horizon like another planet, its steep lower slopes hidden.

Fonda-Fox and Greetings were on the dunes above the ship, walking hand in hand. Having booked their long shadows from the high flight deck of the *Tsiolkovsky*, Glamour dropped down to get their silhouettes against the reddening sky of his last sunset on Mars.

Kirov and Bass were under the ship working on the engine and arguing. Glamour didn't have to wonder what they were arguing about; he knew; they all knew.

"I learned this old trick from a NASA hot rodder in Huntsville," Bass said. With the needle-nose Vise-Grips from his Desert Planet Tool Kit, he was squeezing shut every other one of the F-1's 218 $5/16$-inch cooling lines.

"Fuck you," said Kirov.

"This way we steal half the LOX that is supposed to cool the engine and route it to the oxidant injection ports one loop early," Bass said.

"Go to hell," said Kirov.

"It's like adding a supercharger," said Bass, "and like any supercharger, it will destroy the engine. The question is, how long will it take to do it. For this one, about twelve minutes, and you only have a nine-point-nine-minute burn."

"You're full of shit," said Kirov.

"But that might just possibly be enough."

"I'm the Captain of this voyage, Bass, not you. What if I overrule this John Wayne sacrifice?"

"But I am the captain of my soul," said Bass. "And what's the point? Overrule me all you want, could you come to a different conclusion? You heard Sweeney. Even with the full 600 gallons of diesel #2 we were 913.5 pounds (M) over liftoff weight. And with the 300 of that gone we're—"

"Not going to make it anyway. That's why your martyrdom is such a pain. We might as well all stay together."

"A long shot's better than no shot," said Bass. "You can't

strand these folks here just because you don't want to try and fail. Either you or me has to fly them home, and you're the senior officer. There's no way around it. Plus, I've got twenty years on you, and did Jeffries mention to you about my medical condition?"

"Hand me those Vise-Grips and please shut up."

"There's no way around it," Bass repeated. He knew: he had looked at it from every side and the certainty itself was oddly comforting. He had known down in the canyon, when he looked back into the half-empty bed of the ATV, that he wouldn't be going home to his Allen County hillside. The realization had come suddenly, all in a piece, like an equation: the 300 gallons of #2 rolling into the heart of Mars's darkness; the .8 minutes of burn, or 16 miles of altitude that his weight represented; the extra 120 mph, or 12 kilometers, or 340 pounds that tweaking the cooling tubes *could, might, maybe* contribute. After years of working with F-1s, it had come to him through the seat of his pants, in shapes rather than numbers.

Jeffries had been quiet for most of the ride back, stunned by the magnitude of their disaster. "What do we do now?" he had asked finally.

Bass told him his plan.

"You're kidding."

"It's your only chance."

They were at the foot of the sand slope; Bass kicked the Isuzu back down into second and stood up on the pegs and started up the slope, all but flying. There is a great freedom in facing death. It almost matches space flight.

"Sweeney on the phone," Jeffries called down from the flight deck.

"You take it," Kirov said. "I'm going for a walk with Bass." She already knew what Sweeney would say. Just as there was nothing left to go into the fuel tank, there was nothing left to come out of the ship. Without Bass's sacrifice, they didn't have a prayer. She and Bass walked up toward the dunes, past Glamour filming with his precious, doomed *Demogorgon* amid concentric circles of junk that had been thrown from the ship: seat cushions, Velcro mats, electronic equipment (all but one small ship-to-shore), paneling, food and water bags.

"According to my figures," said Sweeney on the flight deck screen, looking strained, "it won't work. If the engine mods do what Bass says they will, without his weight, and allowing for a nine percent margin of error, we still don't make it. We'll get into orbit six point seven kilometers *below* the *Mary Poppins*. That's too far away to reach the ship before she breaks up on Phobos. We only have . . ."

"What does he mean, we?" asked Greetings.

"He's just identifying, little sister," said Beverly Glenn from orbit.

"If we can't make it, then what's the point of, you know . . ." Fonda-Fox let his question trail off. Nobody had yet used the words *leaving Bass*.

"Quiet everyone," said Jeffries. His voice had a new and unexpected authority. In 42.3 minutes (M), right after sundown, he would be the Second, and no longer the Third, Officer. "Let Sweeney talk."

". . . one long shot," continued Sweeney, "because the six point seven miles is precisely the margin of error on the fuel computation. You know the old NASA saying 'A long shot is better than no shot at all.' I'm afraid with all six voyagers on board it's beyond the realm of possibility, but without—with five, well, maybe." He didn't want to use the words *without Bass*. "Meanwhile, you'd better start your initial checkoff because delta V is in under an hour."

"We're going to make it!" whispered Greetings determinedly. Then she sobered and added, "Without Bass."

While Jeffries started the cabin checkoff, the other voyagers looked out in silence across the Martian plain. At the base of the dunes, Kirov and Bass were walking hand in hand. Fonda-Fox had been in enough movies to know this scene well; he was only thankful (and surprised at himself that he was) that he had not been cast in the lead.

At the edge of the dunes, they walked, turned, stopped, looked up, looked down. Looked out across the high plains of Mars. Since they were communicating on earcom (with the other voyagers courtesied out), they might have had the same conversation a quarter-mile apart; but they walked side by side, as if whispering.

Her shoulders were thrown back. His were hunched forward. Her hands searched for pockets. His found a stone and winged it out, over the red sand. He was amazed at how far he could throw on Mars. The stone threw up dust like a gunshot two hundred yards down the valley they had flown up ten days ago. The too tiny sun dropped behind too big Olympus Mons, and a shadow fell over the whole world.

Clumsy in his marsuit, Bass wrapped his arm around Kirov's shoulders and turned her back toward the ship.

"Here they come," Greetings said on the flight deck.

Jeffries began to power up the gyros that would stabilize the liftoff.

"This little thing here switches speeds," said Glamour. "Forget it. This doodad adjusts the light; forget it. You won't need it. This little S thing is SEND. Don't worry about compacting image before sending it since that is macroed in. This little TD switch is TACHYON DELAY. New feature that no other camera has. It triangulates your target and simulates a shot backward, so you get an image of yourself as you would be seen from whatever you are shooting. This little switch is SAVE, this is STORE, this is REPLAY. You can watch anything through here on the finder."

"Ten minutes till liftoff," said Jeffries.

Bass nodded impatiently, his eyes drawn to the *Tsiolkovsky* across the sand. Steam boiled off the lower vents as the

LOX lines filled. Kirov was already on the flight deck and the others were at the bottom of the ladder.

Fonda-Fox gave Bass a hug and turned away quickly. Jeffries watched from the bottom of the ladder, admiring the economy with which the Movie Star captured with one move not only the single tear of the last farewell, but his stoic reluctance to let it be seen. And all, he figured, without the tear itself.

Jeffries was next. "Good luck, Bones," said Bass.

Greetings had a little speech made up, since she was the stowaway and had less right, it seemed, than . . . but Bass laid his glove across where her lips were under the mask, then patted her on the butt, NASA style; and she turned and scurried up the ladder.

Glamour filmed her and then handed Bass the *Demogorgon*. Then stood looking up, until Bass set the camera down and knelt, and the two men embraced.

Kirov hustled them all into the ship with the outer airlock light and gave Bass the thumbs-up before sealing the airlock door. Kirov had already said what she was going to say, and it wasn't, on principle, good-bye.

The launch window was short. The *Mary Poppins* had been over the western horizon for twelve minutes; if they succeeded, they would catch up with the ship before it and Phobos dropped behind the eastern mountain wall.

"I never got to say good-bye to Bass," said Beverly Glenn on the tiny flight deck comscreen; the larger screen had been left outside on the sand.

"You never met him," said Kirov. "We're counting down."

"Sweeney's running final figures," Jeffries said. "There may be a change."

"Can't wait for them. He's too far away. By the time our final weight gets to him and back, we'll be—"

"Listening to rock and roll," said Fonda-Fox. Looking for a hand to hold, Greetings found his.

"Diesel pumps cleared and up to ninety percent," said

Jeffries, who had taken the Second Officer's chair, or rather chair frame, since the cushions and rests were outside on the sand.

"He told me you had something to tell me," Kirov said.

Jeffries nodded. "That he had cancer. He was lying; that's why I didn't bother. Although in fact, my theory is that all you guys..."

"Not that. I figured he'd try that. He said you were going to tell me something about a man with a hairdo."

Jeffries nodded, fingering the little crystal pyramid in the pocket of his jumpsuit. "I'll tell you, as soon as I get a minute's peace."

"All secure back here," said Fonda-Fox.

"Ten seconds," said Kirov. "BG, you're patched into Sweeney just in case—"

"Good luck," said Beverly Glenn over the earcom.

"Good luck," said Bass over the earcom.

"Same to you," said Kirov. "Both."

Nine, seven

"Secure back there, FF?"

"I already said."

"Bass?"

Six, five

"Yeah? That you, kid?"

"Thanks."

"You got it."

"For everything. See you at the Spaceman's Ball."

"You got it."

Two one

"We have ignition," said Jeffries; and slowly at first, as if reluctant to leave their comrade behind, and then as swiftly as the F-1's full 112 percent came on, the *Tsiolkovsky* lifted off the red planet Mars.

10

WITH SOME 3.7 BILLION viewers, the Academy Awards are the preeminent ceremonial event of the planet Earth, the one that brings together more people from more parts of the globe in a single evening's entertainment than any other. The awards are the crowning achievement not only of Hollywood, but of America, of the Free World, of Western Civ; and if not, as some would have it, of vertebrate life itself, at least of that portion of it that goes to the movies. There are those who go so far as to say that the purpose of making movies is to win awards; and that the purpose of having losers is to provide the other names on the cue cards—that is, the suspense.

For the four (three, on screen) people getting out of the limousine in front of Hollywood's world-famous Cinema Cathedral, the appeal of the awards was the suspense. Fame and money they already had, and both had proven anticlimactic compared to the thrill of survival itself. What was a few million dollars (on points) compared with the lifesaving roar of the most powerful chemical rocket engine ever built, tweaked to a staggering 12.3 percent over its already staggering max? What critic's praise could match Mission Design's 29.3-minute delayed but welcome words, "You're in the slot," after the F-1 blew, its mission accomplished and its big heart broken. What avalanche of fan mail could compare with the satisfying woody clunk of the mother ship's great Russian air lock? What *Variety* listing (even #1) could equal the sight, thirteen months later, of the welcoming, blue-green, cloud-mysterious planet Earth?

Yes, they had made it home; and even though *Voyage to the Red Planet* had already, less than eighteen months into release, joined that all-time money-making pantheon of *Gone With the Wind*, *E.T.*, ("It partakes of them both," said *Newsweek*), and *Beverly Hills Cop*, its success seemed petty compared with the success of survival itself.

But the awards were another story: they brought back the suspense of the voyage, the terror and even the fun.

"How about a group shot?" called out *Variety*.

"How about just the Stars?" suggested *Christian Screen*.

"How about just Noreena?" said *Hollywood Reporter*.

First all four (three, on screen) posed together; then, while Markson looked on, just the Stars; then Fonda-Fox joined Markson, smiling at one side, as the world's first Interplanetary Composite Movie Star—Beverly Glenn and Greetings Brother Buffalo Gentry, aka Noreena Pellucidar—put her/their arms around each other and smiled while flashbulbs went off on all sides like a cloud of novas.

Live, in front of the Cinema Cathedral, they were two people; but on video, where it counted, they were seen as one image that was already familiar the world over.

"OOOoooohhhh!" said Greetings, but only to herself. She owed it to Noreena not to seem unsophisticated. The inside of the Cinema Cathedral was gorgeous (as she had expected), festooned with video cameras, microphones and lights. There were a thousand plush seats, and planted on every one was the bottom of a Movie Star! Or almost every one: seated between the stars, like the filling in a cake, were their agents, wives, lovers, managers and sometimes even friends.

It was fun walking in on the arm of Fonda-Fox, who, if he hadn't been born in a tux, had been fitted only a day or two later. It was like being home at last. If Mother and Dad could only see me now! Greetings sighed, knowing that her parents, watching from Oregon and Maine, would only see Noreena and not her.

"There they are!" said Beverly Glenn. Kirov and Sweeney

were waving from the voyagers' seats down in front. Kirov looked stunning in low-cut Mars-red coveralls with a synthetic "Phobos-ice" tiara clipped to her braid. Sweeney beside her looked suave and handsome, even with the plastic Morton-Thiokol penholder in the pocket of his tux.

"Hello, darling!"

"Hello, darling!"

—said Greetings and Beverly Glenn as they pushed through the narrow aisle. Nominees got blocks of seats, and the Mars Voyagers had three left over after they had all sat down. Greetings was excitedly hugged by the Captain she hadn't seen in six months, since the Premiere.

"Have you heard, are they coming?" Beverly Glenn whispered down the line to Kirov.

"I assume Lou at least will be here. He's been on location in Egypt, but he's up for an award, after all. Jeffries, who knows? He called the other night from the Institute in Harare to say he wasn't sure he could get away. Apparently they're right in the middle of some big experiment."

"I can't believe he left Hollywood to set up that dumb Research Institute," said Greetings. "How could anyone give up all this!"

"It's the garbage in the street, the beggars, the poverty that I hate," said Glamour, stepping out of the limo and almost into an ominous-looking substance on the sidewalk.

"You've been away, you'll get used to it again," said Sundiata Cinque Jeffries, giving a dollar each to two derelicts who had set up housekeeping near the Cathedral's entrance ramp. "After all, you *did* use to live here. Anyway, it couldn't be that much worse than Cairo."

The crowd's murmur rose to a roar as it recognized the midget, who was up for Best Director as well as Best Picture. But who was the African next to him with the pepper-and-salt dreadlocks? The roar continued as they entered the Cinema Cathedral and started down the aisle of the vast auditorium. "One of the advantages of being a midget," whispered Glamour, "is that of all the Directors in Hollywood, I'm the only one that's recognizable."

That's an advantage? wondered Jeffries. He was the only member of the crew of the *Mary Poppins* who had escaped fame. He had insisted on his privacy because he felt he owed it to the secret he had brought back from Mars. He slipped into the reserved row one hug at a time, a little surprised at how glad he was to see his fellow voyagers.

"Welcome home, uh, Sundiata," said Greetings and Fonda-Fox nervously.

"You can still call me Jeffries, if you like," he said; then seeing the seat left empty between Fonda-Fox and Kirov, he smiled. "Or even Bones!" Leaving the center seat empty, he sat on the far side of Kirov.

"How's the research going?" she leaned over to ask, whispering so the others couldn't hear. She had of course agreed that Jeffries's discovery on Mars should be kept secret from Disney-Gerber and the US government. Even the other voyagers didn't know about it; they thought Jeffries had gone to Africa to set up a medical research project.

"Slow but interesting," Jeffries said. He had taken his money from the film and from the sale of Career Spacing to set up the African Brotherhood Institute in Harare, Zimbabwe. "The government has given us university status, and I've been able to bring in several scientists from other African and socialist countries. We're making progress."

"I don't mean how's the Institute going," Kirov said. "I mean, how's the project going? Have you found out who the guy in the dreadlocks is?"

"As a matter of fact—"

"Ssshhh!" said Greetings.

Everyone around them was getting up. Kirov and Jeffries stood with them for the national anthem, led by the Academy Awards Host, an old man who had been Career Spacing's best customer for almost a decade. Jeffries hadn't seen him since before leaving for Mars and he was astonished at how bad he looked. He barely got through the anthem, and two security guards had to help him turn around and start back toward the podium.

In Harare, Jeffries had gotten a letter from his former partner saying that the Host, and a few others who had spent the past few decades more asleep than awake, were showing signs of confusion and dislocation. Jeffries had recommended discontinuing the HT; clearly when life was prolonged past a certain point, the side effects began to multiply.

Unfortunately, Career Spacing's clients had seen it (correctly) as a choice between death and decay, and had chosen decay.

While the Host still struggled toward the podium, an usher came to the end of the row and left with Greetings and Beverly Glenn. Moments later, they appeared on the stage and the Host announced: "And here to present the award for Best Tie-in Merchandising, America's newest composite Motion Picture Star, up for an award of her own, Miss Noreena Pellucidar, this year's nominee for Best Actress. In real life she's two separate people, the certified Movie Star Beverly Glenn, and the semicertifiable Miss Greetings Brother Buffalo Gentry!"

After a brief flurry of applause, they began reading the jokes from the cue cards . . .

"Greetings, Greetings . . ."

"Introducing my better half . . ."

"Almost as much fun as being stranded on Mars . . ."

"We definitely don't think the creators of the pyramid are from Mars," Jeffries whispered. "The steps I found in the canyon predate them by half a million years."

"How do you know?"

"We know because the small crystal I showed you on the ship is some kind of optical information storage device: it has layers and layers of holo displays in it. The larger pyramid that contained it is itself a display. Several holos show the stone steps on Mars, but always as ruins. Others in the same sequence show the planet millions of years ago, judging by the heavier cloud cover, but already dying. Apparently the clay was a devolutionary remnant, activated by the diesel fuel. Sort of like a corpse twitching."

"So who built the steps?"

"We may never know. Something or someone who lived and died before we were ever dreamed of. But we've learned a lot about Earth. We've made a photo survey of Atlantis from the holos, and we have an actual film of a Stegosaurus—eating its own young, unfortunately. Other holos show the Moon when it still had volcanic clouds, millions of years ago, and one shows a sector of sky as it is seen from Earth today, centering on a star called CN-861."

"Odd," said Kirov. "That's one of our navigational stars, some six light years away."

"Five point nine," said Jeffries. "But I'll come back to that. Meanwhile, the most interesting holo is of a genetic experiment that took place a little over a million years ago. An experiment that's apparently still going on—"

"Sssshhhh," said Fonda-Fox. Greetings was reading off the nominees for Best Tie-in Merchandising. All eyes were on the giant holoscreen above the stage, where the two figures were dithered, batched, bitmapped and backmixed into one, so that when the envelope was opened by Beverly Glenn onstage, it was opened on holovideo to tumultuous applause (and on TV around the world) by the star of one of the most popular movies ever made, Noreena Pellucidar.

"And the Winner is . . ."

The Winner was, of course, some nobody. It was one of the nobody awards.

"What do you mean, still going on?" whispered Kirov.

"As far as we can determine, the silver pyramid is a signal or alarm as well as a storage device, set to alert whoever planted it when we arrived. That's why it was planted on Mars instead of on Earth. Remember the movie *2001?*"

"The sentinels? Yeah, but weren't they placed on the Moon?"

"Same idea. I guess whoever planted the pyramid wasn't interested in us until we were able to achieve actual interplanetary flight."

"Us? You mean, we're part of the Experiment?"

"As far as we can tell, we're the subject."

"Sssshhhh!" said Glamour. "Maybe this is us!"

On the big overhead screen, they were showing the first clip from the nominees for Best Picture. It was from *Gone With the Wind, Part IV*, the dramatic nude triple-murder bedroom scene.

Jeffries wondered if they were shooting the Host directly with HT, since he came out after the clip looking wonderfully refreshed. "And now to present our award for Best Director—" he began.

"Nervous?" Fonda-Fox had to lean over to ask. Glamour had been standing on his seat, but now that the overhead cameras were picking out the nominees, he not only had to sit down in his seat where he couldn't see, he had to act as if it didn't matter.

"I'd like to win an Oscar," said Glamour. "Who wouldn't? But I have all the work I need. Mainly I'd like to win it for—"

He jerked his thumb toward the empty seat and Fonda-Fox nodded.

The presenting team was a nostalgia/glitz mix: the matriarchal Cher, accompanied by an unshaven young male Star in a shirtless tuxedo.

"And the Winner is . . ."

Markson tried to hide his pleasure when Glamour lost. The Winner had just contracted with Disney-Gerber (where Markson was now front office) for a new remake of *Stagecoach*, set on a desert planet (interplanetary themes were big since the success of *Voyage*) and the Oscar would help the new film get press attention. While Glamour probably deserved the award, he didn't really *need* it.

Plus, Markson rationalized, every award that *Voyage to*

the Red Planet didn't win helped their chances not only for Best Actress, but for the Big One.

"The aliens are apparently some kind of genetic engineers," Jeffries whispered. "One of the holo displays in the crystal showed a genetic engineering project, where the DNA of what we identified later as a small primate was dipped into some kind of solution that reversed eleven of its amino acids. The result, according to this holo, was the genetic coding for the language and imagization center in humans. In other words, that the primate apparently was our—"

"Omigod," said Kirov. "Adam."

"Eve, actually."

"Bass would have loved it."

"We're apparently their project. When we made it to Mars, I assume we tripped the switch or lit the light or whatever."

"And now what—we get the cheese?"

"Sssshhhh," said Beverly Glenn. There was another Best Picture nominee clip, this one a laser fight from *Welcome to High Orbit, Mr. Bond.*

"Only one left!" said Greetings. They were being left until last.

"That's what we're trying to find out. We've been all through the crystal looking for a message, but no luck. Then we started wondering about that contemporary star image, when everything else was a million years old—"

"So you did a radio telescope scan."

"Exactly. And we got a signal from CN-861, a tone series very similar to the 'music' Bass and I heard inside the pyramid."

"But that's impossible. It's too far away. They couldn't even know we've landed yet, and it'll be ten years before we get a signal back."

"Theoretically, yes," said Jeffries. "But, in fact, this signal is traveling in short bursts at a high multiple of the speed of light: 3.1416, to be almost precise. The Creators—that's what we've started calling them—apparently have developed FTL radio. Theoretically, it's possible by bouncing signals off the inner event horizon of a black hole, according to . . ."

"Cut to the chase," Kirov whispered loudly. "What's the message? What does it say?"

"We don't know yet. But we know that since they created all our languages, in a sense, we can figure it out. Last week we started running the signal through a Virtual Language Universal Grammar Syntax Decoder program worked out by a scientist from Soviet Armenia, one of the guys you recommended that I contact, in fact. When I left Harare day before yesterday, the program was only twenty-two percent run. It could take weeks. The Institute knows where I am and I'll be contacted as soon as . . ."

"Sssshhhh," said Markson. "If you two don't shut up you're going to get us all thrown out of here!"

The awards were coming at a faster pace:

Best Single Digit Sequel: "And the Winner is . . ."
Most Original Use of Flag: "And the Winner is . . ."
Best Hetero Nude Scene: "And the Winner is . . ."

Then, finally, the presenters for Best Actress came on. Jeffries looked down the row of seats, past the empty seat, and saw Beverly Glenn and Greetings holding hands nervously. Beverly Glenn looked more beautiful than ever. The golden beard that was a side effect of the HT remained, and was threatening to start a new trend among Hollywood women, judging from the crowd here at the Cathedral. Although it seemed to have chased the beards off the men.

Young Tyrone Power 5 (he preferred the Arabic numeral) read the nominees, and then silver-haired Spike Lee tore open the envelope. "And the Winner is—

Noreena Pellucidar!"

Beverly Glenn and Greetings rose as one and the crowd went wild.

There was an interlude of live music while a commercial, video only on the holoscreen above the stage, played for 3.7

billion people worldwide, the largest Oscar audience ever. Jeffries wondered what they thought of the Lean Cuisine ad in Calcutta, or in New Jersey, where food riots had closed the turnpike for three days. After the ad interlude, the Host turned with a too bright smile to the teleprompter and read:

"And now a few exciting scenes from the final nominee for Best Picture."

And there it was. Just as they had left it, as if it had been yesterday.

Mars.

At first it looked to Bass as if they weren't going to make it. With the souped-up F-1, liftoff should have been almost as easy as liftoff from the Moon. Instead, the little ship groaned, rose slightly, tipped; and since the engine wasn't gimbaled, Kirov had to bleed off precious lift through the OME slots to straighten it. "Come on!" Bass shouted, balling his fist, screaming against the roar that, even in the thin air of Mars and through his marsuit, was like a niagara.

Painfully, slowly, the *Tsiolkovsky* hitched itself straight, dragged itself into the air, blasting up a sandstorm and then clearing it; then danced on a pencil flame of fire (They've already burned too much fuel! Bass thought), then soared straight up. While Bass watched through the zoomfinder of the *Demogorgon*, the ship was gone: high on its yellow ribbon of fire, a black speck at the high end of a white trail of steam and vapor, a speck in a ruby sky that could just as easily been a trick of an old man's eye.

This was the scene the audience in the Cinema Cathedral saw, for Bass had faxed it up to the *Mary Poppins* even before he had learned that the *Tsiolkovsky* had made it into matching orbit. The next scene, the product of the *Demogorgon's* tachyon delay wizardry, was of Bass himself, holding the camera, dwindling to a speck on a desert at the edge of the dunes at the edge of a canyon on a long-dead world.

His radio receiver was patched into the *Tsiolkovsky's*, and he got the figures, raw, six minutes later. It would be fifteen minutes before Sweeney could run them through his simulator, and another fifteen before the verdict arrived back at Mars, but Bass knew as soon as he saw the numbers. He knew it in the seat of his pants. The Chrysler hemi of space had lasted just long enough.

It was over. And after rejoicing for his fellow voyagers, he sat down by the fire to mourn for himself.

The fire? Yes, they had left behind a fire.

Kirov's and Bass's final farewell came less than twenty minutes after TEI (Trans-Earth Injection). The *Mary Poppins* had avoided crashing into Phobos by the skin of her mile-long teeth, and was now safely on her way—but traveling so fast that radio communications with the landing site were already fading.

Kirov was surprised to get Bass's call since he wasn't the type for good-byes.

"One more thing, kid. Remember, Jeffries has something he wants to show you."

"He's here on the bridge with me. Everybody else is in the lounge. Is this another bullshit cancer story?"

"No, I'll let Jeffries explain it. I just didn't want him to, you know, forget. You can help him handle it. Your connections in the Soviet Union might come in handy. What he's got is pretty important, which is why he's kept it a secret."

"Kept it a secret from me, the Captain?" Kirov gave Jeffries an icy look.

"Ask him about a guy with dreadlocks. Then help him out. Treat it as my last request, okay? Now, are you alone? Before we fade out, there's one other thing I always wanted to tell you—"

Jeffries closed the bridge hatch behind him and joined the others in the Stalin lounge. Thus he never found out what the *one other thing* was; nor will we.

The clay, containing both fuel and oxidant, burned. Bass discovered this when he saw Jeffries's abandoned samples, caught in the F-1's blast circle, blazing merrily. Not wanting to leave the site where the *Tsiolkovsky* had been, he chopped up the *Faux Agnew* over the next few days and hauled it down with the ATV for "firewood." The lower the air pressure, the brighter the clay blazed, consuming its own internal heavy oxygen and released it half-burned into the air as breathable smoke. Bass found that he could sit close to the fire with his mask lifted and be almost comfortable. And a fire, he knew from long nights of hunting, is almost as good as a friend.

The next morning Bass lodged the *Demogorgon* on a pile of junk and set it on AUTO, as Glamour had shown him, so that the camera filmed him all day, and faxed its image up to the *Mary Poppins*'s data banks every night. Fax far outlasted radio, so when Glamour awoke inside the Moon's orbit (for they slept straight through on the return), he found 914,978,456K of image to work with. Most of it was of Bass sitting by the fire, but Bass had also booked image of the *Tsiolkovsky*'s takeoff and the *Mary Poppins*'s delta V.

Glamour had been able to use it all to construct the magnificent scene 3.7 billion people were now watching: the intercuts, close and then long, of Bass watching the ship ascend; the slow tracking shot of the old space warrior walking over to the fire; pulling off his mask and gloves; throwing a clay bud onto the flames; wiping a tear from one eye (brilliantly, Fonda-Fox admitted) and looking up toward the heavens he would never soar again—

Then it came, as startling on the holoscreen of the Cinema Cathedral as it had seemed to Bass from Mars: the nuclear flash of the departing *Mary Poppins* lighting Bass's features and the red dunes behind him; and then, as the music rose and swelled, the old spaceman's triumphant thumbs-up fadeout to his departing comrades.

The applause was thunderous. Greetings wept for joy, knowing there wasn't a dry eye in the house. "That'll show them," Louis Glamour thought. Kirov wiped her eyes and looked around, startled to find that everyone in the Cinema

Cathedral, including the balcony, was standing and turned toward them—facing the empty seat in their midst. In the last gesture of her command, she reached out for Jeffries's hand. He took Beverly Glenn's, who was already holding Greetings's, who took Sweeney's, while Fonda-Fox reached out to Markson and Glamour, and they all sat linked across Bass's empty seat.

"He would have hated this," Kirov whispered as the crowd sat back down for the presentation of the last award.

"For you." A hand tugged at Jeffries's sleeve and an usher in a gold-embroidered tuxedo passed him a note

"Is that what I think it is?" Kirov whispered.

Jeffries nodded. "They cracked the code. This is the message."

"Sssshhhh!" said Markson. The presenters, Loretta Spielberg-Stallone and her co-star, Woody Farrah-Close, were opening the envelope for Best Film.

Jeffries read the note and passed it to Kirov. She unfolded it and read it, and laughed. The message read: GOOD LUCK.

"Sssshhhh!" said Fonda-Fox. He had never doubted how the voyage would turn out, but this was real life, and the suspense was killing him.

"And the Winner is—"

NEW BESTSELLERS
IN THE *MAGIC OF XANTH* SERIES!

PIERS ANTHONY

75947-0/$4.95 US/$5.95 Can

75287-5/$4.95 US/$5.95 Can

75288-3/$4.95 US/$5.95 Can

75289-1/$4.95 US/$5.95 Can

PRESENTING THE ADVENTURES OF

BILL THE GALACTIC, HERO

BY HARRY HARRISON

BILL, THE GALACTIC HERO

00395-3/$3.95 US/$4.95 Can

He was just an ordinary guy named Bill, a fertilizer operator from a planet of farmers. Then a recruiting robot shanghaied him with knockout drops, and he came to in deep space, aboard the Empire warship *Christine Keeler*.

BILL, THE GALACTIC HERO: THE PLANET OF ROBOT SLAVES 75661-7/$3.95 US/$4.95 Can

BILL, THE GALACTIC HERO: ON THE PLANET OF BOTTLED BRAINS 75662-5/$3.95 US/$4.95 Can **(co-authored by Robert Sheckley)**

BILL, THE GALACTIC HERO: ON THE PLANET OF TASTELESS PLEASURE 75664-1/$3.95 US/$4.95 Can **(co-authored by David Bischoff)**

BILL, THE GALACTIC HERO: ON THE PLANET OF ZOMBIE VAMPIRES 75665-X/$3.95 US/$4.95 Can **(co-authored by Jack C. Haldeman II)**

BILL, THE GALACTIC HERO: ON THE PLANET OF TEN THOUSAND BARS 75666-8/$3.99 US/$4.99 Can **(co-authored by David Bischoff)**

ARTHUR C. CLARKE'S VENUS PRIME™

by Paul Preuss

VOLUME 1: BREAKING STRAIN   75344-8/$3.95 US/$4.95 CAN
Her code name is Sparta. Her beauty veils a mysterious past and
abilities of superhuman dimension, the product of advanced
biotechnology.

VOLUME 2: MAELSTROM   75345-6/$3.95 US/$4.95 CAN
When a team of scientists is trapped in the gaseous inferno of
Venus, Sparta must risk her life to save them.

VOLUME 3: HIDE AND SEEK   75346-4/$3.95 US/$4.95 CAN
When the theft of an alien artifact, evidence of extraterrestrial
life, leads to two murders, Sparta must risk her life and identity
to solve the case.

VOLUME 4: THE MEDUSA ENCOUNTER
                                75348-0/$3.95 US/$4.95 CAN
Sparta's recovery from her last mission is interrupted as she sets
out on an interplanetary investigation of her host, the Space
Board.

VOLUME 5: THE DIAMOND MOON
                                75349-9/$3.95 US/$4.95 CAN
Sparta's mission is to monitor the exploration of Jupiter's moon,
Amalthea, by the renowned Professor J.Q.R. Forester.

**Each volume features a special technical infopak,
including blueprints of the structures of *Venus Prime***